*Darleen's murdered husband had thrived
on adultery and sexual blackmail.
Four women were his devoted mistresses
—and Darleen's closest friends!*

DEBORAH. The upstanding councilwoman with a penchant for sex with perfect strangers.

AIDA. A rising young actress with a deadly addiction.

SAMANTHA. A beautiful Oriental karate expert with a shady past and a thirst for revenge.

JOY. One of America's most renowned newscasters, who *celebrates* the news of Mark's gruesome death.

EACH HAD A COMPELLING MOTIVE FOR THE MURDER OF MARK SAUNDERS. BUT THE POLICE BELIEVE DARLEEN HAD THE STRONGEST MOTIVE OF ALL. NOW SHE MUST FIGHT FOR HER INNOCENCE—AND UNCOVER THE MURDERER . . .

Silk and Satin

Marcia Wolfson

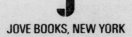

JOVE BOOKS, NEW YORK

This Jove book contains the complete
text of the original hardcover edition.
It has been completely reset in a typeface
designed for easy reading, and was printed
from new film.

SILK AND SATIN

A Jove Book/published by arrangement with
The Putnam Publishing Group

PRINTING HISTORY
Published by G.P. Putnam's Sons in 1986
Published simultaneously in Canada by
General Publishing Co. Limited, Toronto
Jove edition/March 1989

ISBN: 0-515-10079-X

Jove Books are published by The Berkley Publishing Group,
200 Madison Avenue, New York, New York 10016.
The name "JOVE" and the "J" logo
are trademarks belonging to Jove Publications, Inc.

PRINTED IN THE UNITED STATES OF AMERICA

10 9 8 7 6 5 4 3 2 1

To my great son, Alan Rechtschaffen—
light of my life

To my precious mother, Florence—
I miss you so

And thanks to my husband, Daniel; my
three brothers, Steve, Gary, and Marty;
dear Aunt Hazel; and devoted dog, Goldie

Special thanks to Archbishop William Carew
of Tokyo for guidance

It is far safer to be feared than loved.

—NICCOLÒ MACHIAVELLI

Acknowledgments

I have received a great deal of help from many people in writing this book. In particular, I want to thank my dear friends Mel Kahan, Lois Feuer-Lewin, Everett M. Lassman, Duran and Lu Weinstein, Susan, Rick and Janet Oseroff, Maura Foster, Donna Schmidt—moral support group—and my editor, Jayne Pliner. Without all of you, there couldn't be a book. With gratitude.

Silk and Satin

12/5/89

To Myra —
a lovely
woman —

Fondly,
Marcia Wolfson

PROLOGUE

Wednesday, October 30, 1985

Mark Saunders couldn't sleep. He was edgy. His eyes were wide open, as if the lids were glued back. Having wandered in the streets, he came back to the only place in the entire city where he ever felt truly secure, the corporate fortress he dominated.

Checking his Corum watch with the Krugerrand face, he strode into Saunders Tower, a unique half-corporate, half-residential pyramid soaring into the Manhattan sky. In daylight the building glittered like polished gold. But now the mirrored walls were murky with night shadows. Chilly wind whipped crackling leaves about the revolving door. A newspaper sailed down the street like a ragged kite.

A big man, he kept his shoulders hunched beneath the Burberry trench coat that he was wearing over a gray silk suit. His tie was yanked down from the throat, and the first three buttons of his white silk shirt were undone, exposing a slender gold chain.

His dark hair formed a widow's peak that was a splotch of white since birth. The face was narrow but fleshy, with no hard angles, good-looking although disintegrating around the edges from too much rich food and booze. Sensual lips, per-

manently curled at the left corner, kept his mouth in a constant
sneer. His deep-set brown eyes wavered slightly beneath
straight, thick brows.

As usual, he was a little drunk; but he wasn't used to being
alone. And on this cold night he was very much alone. And
angry. His wife had stormed out of their apartment hours ago,
after he had hit her. He imagined her in someone else's arms,
someone else's bed. Both his pace and his pulse quickened.

Bleary-eyed Tom Dunphy, a night guard who was pushing
sixty-five and had been with Minotaur Development Corporation for the last fourteen years, was on duty. His gray uniform, replete with Sam Brown belt, did little to hide his
scrawny frame. Dunphy mumbled that Saunders's wife had
been in earlier that evening. He barely looked up when his
boss signed in by the bank of elevators, as Saunders insisted
all his employees and visitors do.

Saunders reached over angrily, grabbed Dunphy by the
lapel, and shook him until his bones rattled. "Look awake,
you stupid old bastard, or I'll throw your ass out on the
street!"

He spun around and entered the one elevator with a light
on. He didn't glance back at the look of fear and hatred that
spread over the guard's face. It was the look that, as the years
went by, had come to be shared by just about everyone who
worked for the head of Minotaur Development Corporation,
one of the largest real estate developers in New York.

The mahogany-paneled elevator sped to the top floor,
opening onto a corporate vista of ficus trees, glass walls, and
two desks where secretaries worked during the day. Through
his alcoholic haze, the office struck Saunders as not quite
familiar, somehow ominous. The oiled walnut tops of the secretaries' desks had the empty smoothness of coffin lids. A
loud hum he had never noticed before seemed to fill the room.
Panicky, he looked around before finally tracking it with his
eyes to the air filter in the ceiling. He paused, warily listening
for other night sounds.

Walking across the aquamarine Aubusson carpet, Saunders
felt like an intruder. He almost ran into his office. Grateful for
the feel of the heavy teak door and its brass handle, finding

the heft reassuring, he nonetheless glanced over his shoulder before entering.

The huge door whispered open, reminding him of the oak doors at the strange villa on Long Island where he had lived as a boy. Only, this door had been designed by his father to be deceptive. Perfectly balanced so that it swung open easily, it looked so heavy that most visitors pushed too hard and stumbled into the room—to the amusement of the elder Saunders and the embarrassment of those who were fooled.

From the floor-to-ceiling office windows, the evening stars seemed close enough to touch, as if he stood atop a mountain, his city sprawled beneath his feet. He and his father, Emmanuel, had built many of the towering buildings he could see. Gleaming corporate headquarters. Fortresses for the very rich.

Saunders sat at his massive desk, which was piled high with reports on deals about properties around the city. Commercial. Residential. Worth billions of dollars.

Leaning back in his leather chair, Saunders thought, as he often did, about what it was like to be one of the most powerful men in America. To run an empire created by his father and make it even larger, greater.

Now he was verging on the biggest deal of his lifetime.

But what should have been savored as his moment of greatest triumph was tempered by the disappointments of his personal life. Again, he thought of his wife and where she might have gone. Once more, he fantasized about her in the arms of a stranger, another man's lips on hers. Her body pressed against another.

With disgust, he picked up his phone, dialing a number from memory. Unable to stop, he wondered whether it was too late to put his marriage back in order. He swallowed hard before speaking when a woman's sultry voice answered.

"I'm—in my—office," he said, the words catching in his throat. He slammed down the receiver. Hands shaking, he paused for a moment and, with a look of despair, he pressed a button by his phone.

His face flushed and glistening, Mark Saunders walked to a telescope mounted on a tripod. He had to climb three steep wooden steps to reach the telescope. Though he knew the glass was thick and strong, he felt vulnerable next to the windowed wall.

Since childhood, he had a fear of heights, and looking out that window without his feet planted firmly on the floor always terrified him. His father had insisted that the corporate headquarters be made of glass. It was another way to scare his son. Challenge him. Test him. But Mark had found in recent years that his sense of fear actually enhanced the sweetness of his business successes.

He turned and looked at the stern countenance of his father in a portrait behind his desk. The picture said much about the enormous ego of the man. He had Mark's sensual mouth, but Emmanuel's was sterner, crueler. The face was fleshier and darker-complexioned. The steely eyes were commanding. His gray hair swept straight back, Emmanuel was wearing what appeared to be a cream-colored tunic that could have been made for a Renaissance doge.

As though in a trance, Mark turned from the portrait and placed his eye against the telescope. As always, the lens was pointed at an apartment building several blocks away. While peering through, he felt a surge of satisfaction, as though *he* were controlling destiny. First, he saw a well lit but empty living room. Then a woman moved slowly into view. She appeared to be in her early twenties. She walked languorously, dispensing flashes of creamy thigh between a blue silk robe that parted with each step. The robe was tied with a golden sash.

Chestnut hair parted in the middle framed a delicate face almost stark white with makeup. Her lips were painted blood red, her black eyes mascaraed like the wings of a hawk. Pausing, she turned and stared directly at him, the tip of her tongue curling toward him. Saunders's heart beat faster, and his body stiffened as he unzipped his fly and touched himself.

Slowly, teasingly, the girl began removing her clothing. First, the sash. Then she slipped off the robe in a languid motion. Then her bra. Finally her panties. As she took off each piece, she held it up like an offering.

Now, she stood naked in her window. She never saw who was watching her, but she knew who he was. At first ambivalent about submitting to Mark's "peformances," as he called them, she had lately found herself drawn to her role. These nights excited her. She trembled, and her nipples became hard.

Wednesdays she was his. That was the bargain they had struck. Mark had told her what to do and now heat radiated from her skin as she slowly turned in profile, thrusting out her breasts. Her fingers softly stroked the pink tips of her nipples, then her left hand strayed down over her smooth belly into the silky hair between her legs. She found herself wanting to be ordered what to do.

Unable to tear his eyes away from the lens, Mark's breath came faster and faster. His gasps drowned out even the hum.

Mark didn't notice the office door had opened. Suddenly, a shadowy figure raced across the room. At the last possible moment, the intruder yelled one word. "Mark!"

Saunders whipped around. The shock of recognition crossed his face. The intruder's arms smashed into Mark's chest, pitching him backward into the wall of glass, and sending the telescope crashing from its mount. Twisting, Saunders screamed and tried to check his fall. He crashed through the window, shards of glass ripping his face and hands.

The woman stood rigid, her mouth wide open in shock and terror as she stared at the floor of the huge mirrored building where she was told to look. Part of the glass wall had just exploded as if a giant fist had bashed through from the inside. Someone was tumbling through the air, arms and legs thrashing. She placed her hands over her eyes to shut out the horror of watching someone die.

Saunders hurtled through the night wind, his eyes agape in amazement and disbelief. Then a look of comprehension exploded in his eyes. He clawed the air and frantically kicked out to place his feet on something. Anything! He screamed and screamed, his mouth wide open as the sounds became one long shriek that came from the marrow of his bones.

THURSDAY

One

Darleen awoke with a start, her head pounding. Afraid to move, she fearfully hugged a sheet under her chin and looked around, still dazed by exhaustion and something deeper than any tiredness she had ever felt before. She didn't know where she was.

The room was enormous with high windows on two sides, obviously a loft. Barren and dull, its only decorations were old Bogart and new Clint Eastwood posters on the walls. A bathroom door was open. Whoever lived here obviously lacked imagination—and certainly money.

The windows were streaked with grime, blocking whatever little morning light tried to fight its way into the room. She guessed it was about seven o'clock, a godforsaken time of day that she almost never saw.

The city had awakened long before her. The singsong scream of an ambulance siren drew near, blared directly outside, and faded into the distance. The metal-on-metal crunch of a garbage truck whined and roared, and empty trash cans banged on the sidewalk. Voices yelling in Spanish cracked the air like exploding balloons.

Her head hurt almost unbearably, and there was a puzzling

metallic taste in her mouth. Suddenly she sensed—rather than saw—that someone was in bed with her. She shivered with fear. Unable to bring herself to look, she pulled the sheet even closer around her, trembling, her eyes darting back and forth.

She felt soiled and betrayed. Never had she compromised herself, and she couldn't believe that last night she really had. Since she had first met her husband, she never considered letting another man into her life, let alone her bed. How, she wondered frantically, had this happened?

She brought both her hands to her mouth to stifle a scream. Her brow wrinkled with concentration as she desperately tried to piece together how she got here.

Peeking at the creature next to her, she almost giggled hysterically. From his snoring, she knew it was a man. Still, with his face turned away, his long black hair was like the way her mother's hair looked on mornings when Darleen was little and crept into bed with her.

Before going to sleep at night, her mother would tell her stories of how Prince Charming would take her away to a castle high on a mountain peak. The prince would be dark because she was fair. He'd shower her with riches and they'd live happily ever after.

But when the dream came true, it turned into a nightmare.

It seemed like a million years ago, when Mark Saunders—rugged, handsome, and rich—had swept her off her feet at that Christmas party in her senior year at Sarah Lawrence. He became her Prince Charming, and showered her with riches, just as her mother had predicted. For years he was loving, caring, but then, all that stopped. Her gentle husband became a monster.

When their marriage soured, she desperately hoped it would change back, that Mark would be again the way he had been. When he didn't change, she became repulsed by the glittering world she had entered. She looked on it as a trap of silk and satin.

Now the man next to her stirred, and Darleen caught her breath. Desperately, she tried to clear her mind and reconstruct what happened last night.

She and Aida had wound up at Palladium. Entering the club's vaulted interior with huge columns, where fashion models posed and people of all ages streamed back and forth, they admired the chic clothing of the SoHo designer cliques and avoided the bold eyes of punk lesbians. They danced with gorgeous gay men who moved like quicksilver and laughed when several followed them into the ladies' room, where Darleen watched in fascination as the men put on makeup.

Dear God, what had happened after that?

Dimly, more snippets of the earlier part of last night began to surface. The fight with Mark. Going out for a drink with Aida, who was always her last resort when things really got out of hand with Mark. Flamboyant, with dark, curly hair and a long, lithe, expressive body, Aida was as dark and sexy as her secrets. There wasn't a convention Aida didn't defy, a rule she didn't shatter like a champagne glass thrown into a fireplace.

Darleen knew she hadn't done any drugs herself, although Aida had taken Ecstasy because she wanted to stay up all night. She knew she hadn't drunk that much. Oh yes, there was that guy standing next to their table who'd looked like he'd messed with her drink. Aida had joked that he'd doctored it. Had he? The rest of the night was a blank.

Pressing her temples with the fingers of each hand and silently counting to three, Darleen summoned the nerve to look at the man sharing the bed with her. His body was brown and muscular—possibly Hispanic. She had no idea what color his eyes might be. Because of the angle of his head on the pillow, his mouth hung open while he slept, making him look foolish. While staring at him, Darleen suddenly felt as if she might vomit.

Oh, my God, she thought madly.

Shutting her eyes as though the act would make the man vanish, she exhaled and opened them with vague disappointment. Her eyes glistened with tears. Frantically, she tried to recall something else. Anything! But no memories returned, and she found that terrifying. Was she losing her mind? Was *she* to blame?

She knew she shouldn't have gone out with Aida. But all she wanted to do was dance and lose herself in music and motion. And the boys could dance as beautifully as Nureyev. How could she have been such a fool? What had she done?

As her eyes raced around the room, she took in an over-stuffed Leatherette chair with masking tape barely covering tears; a scratchy drop-leaf table; a cardboard box filled with dirty clothes; those awful cliché posters of movie stars.

Now only one thought played on her mind—escape. As quietly as possible, she pulled back the covers. Making fists to steel herself, she slipped out of the bed.

The room was chilly. The icy floorboards took her breath away, causing her to suck in her stomach and almost cry out. Goose pimples puckered her flesh.

Hurriedly, she gathered up her clothing, which was scattered all around the room, and darted into the bathroom, closing the door silently. Like the man and like the rest of his apartment, the bathroom was filthy and depressing. The chipped white tiles were spiderwebbed with cracks, the plastic shower curtain was soiled, and the tub was rust-stained. Hairs, toothpaste, and soap scum caked the sink. The faucet dripped. The linoleum floor was gray with grime. At least the space heater worked.

She glanced at the cracked mirror over the sink, catching sight of her reflected image. At age thirty-two, she had wavy chestnut hair that cascaded around her face in a luxurious mane. Her cheekbones were high, her lips full and sensuous. As the nausea welled up again, she felt dizzy and grabbed the sink to keep from falling. The feeling subsided, but as she looked at her pallid face in the mirror, she thought she was looking at a stranger.

Haltingly, she touched a bruise on her jaw and shuddered. She tried to push last night from her mind, but was unable. Tears streamed down her cheeks as what had happened flashed across her conscious memory.

Less than ten hours ago she had told Mark she was going to divorce him. He was standing near the sliding glass doors that opened onto their penthouse terrace, a drink in his hand. As usual on Wednesday nights, he was getting ready to go out.

Darleen had been crying, because she knew that she must tell him their marriage was over. For the past three years, she had fervently hoped that something would happen that would change Mark for the better. Instead, he got worse and worse.

He humiliated her in public, and his drinking was a constant problem. For the first time, Darleen was grateful Mark couldn't have children.

But what she really couldn't stand was his lying to himself and his blaming her for his inability to take charge of his own life. Part of that, she had come to realize, *was* her own fault. Though he wouldn't admit it, he leaned on her, and she let him, even when she knew better. At times, she thought that he had really married her only to feed on her strength because he felt so weak around his father.

Recently, she had finally accepted the fact that Mark would never become strong. She now pitied her husband, even loathed him, at times. Any marriage would disintegrate if those were the cornerstones.

"Mark," she'd said.

"What?" he snapped while staring through the doors toward Central Park in the distance.

"I'm leaving you."

A bewildered expression crept across his face as Mark turned and looked at her. When he spoke, he tried to sound amused. "Acapulco? St. Moritz?"

"I want a divorce," she said evenly.

Suddenly, Mark looked frightened. An edge of panic flickered in his eyes, and for a moment Darleen recognized the vulnerability that had once drawn her to him.

"You're kidding!" he said, but his eyes told her he knew she wasn't.

"No," Darleen said wearily. "I'm leaving tomorrow. I'll contact a lawyer and—"

Before she could finish, he strode across the room and grabbed her arm. "You can't!" he whined. "You can't!"

"Please, Mark," she said, pulling away. "You know the way you've treated me for the past three years. I won't take it anymore."

"You know why I've acted this way," he said sullenly. "You know what *you* did!"

Darleen stared at him angrily. "Don't you ever say that again! You know what I told you was true."

Mark hurled his drink against a wall. The glass shattered. "You could never live without this," he snarled, waving his arms around. "You wouldn't know what to do now without money and power."

"Don't be a fool, Mark," she said. "You know I never cared about any of that." Her shoulders sagged. "All I ever wanted was for you to be strong enough to return my love."

Mark seemed panic-stricken. He walked over to the bar and, with trembling hands, poured a scotch into a tumbler and took a long drink. "Love," he muttered. "What does anyone know about love?"

Looking at him, Darleen didn't even feel pity. She just wanted to be away from him. "If only you were man enough to stand up to your father, this wouldn't be happening," she said.

Mark turned, his face red with rage. They were standing face-to-face now. He drew back his right arm, balled his hand into a fist, and punched her. Darleen reeled back, pain exploding in her jaw. Staggering, she managed to keep her balance.

A look of horror was on Mark's face. "Oh, God, Darleen! I didn't mean it. *Please,*" he whimpered. "I'm sorry."

Darleen ran into the bedroom and locked the door. She grabbed the phone and quickly dialed. "Aida," she said haltingly. "I . . . I can't go tonight."

Briefly, she told her friend what had happened.

"You've got to get out of there," Aida said. "Meet me as planned. You can stay at my place tonight."

Not knowing what else she could do, Darleen agreed.

Shaking, Darleen turned away from the mirror. After stuffing her underwear into her bag, she wriggled into her lavender Valentino dress. Still barefoot, she crept across the bedroom as silently as a cat burglar. A sudden, harsh grunt came from the bed. Stiffening, she breathed deeply before moving again.

Her fingers white with tension, she carefully unbolted the door and gently eased it open. There was a soft scrape along a well-worn scratch on the floor. Darting one more look at the bed and seeing that the man wasn't moving, she closed her eyes and exhaled slowly while stepping through the door and pulling it shut. Her silver fox fur hung from her arm like a child's security blanket. She felt dirtier than she ever had in her life.

Once in the outside hallway, she bent over and hastily put on her shoes and coat, allowing herself a sigh of relief. As she ran down the three flights of stairs, everything was blurry. Touching her eyes with her right hand, she felt hot tears. She silently prayed that she hadn't told the man her name—especially her husband's easily recognizable surname.

Mark Saunders. One of the city's half dozen biggest real estate tycoons, or real estate *princes,* as they arrogantly called one another. Mark Saunders, who built apartments in towers in the sky. Modern glass palaces that were sliced to shards by architecture critics, bought for millions of dollars, and struck Darleen as being as empty as her marriage. As Mark himself.

Mark Saunders, handsome and vain, who had his picture in the papers more often than Mayor Koch. Mark Saunders, who was still referred to as Emmanuel's boy even though he was forty-two years old.

The man who had swept her off her feet when she was only a college student. Who radiated sexual energy and excitement. Who had seduced her with promises of glamour. Mark, who had charmed her the way he charmed people when he wanted something. Who was the first person, she had initially thought—wrongly—who didn't ask her to take care of him but wanted to take care of her. Who claimed he loved her.

He had bedazzled the poor scholarship student from Philadelphia with a different world than she had ever known existed, a world of stretch limousines and expensive restaurants and horse farms. Mark Saunders, who had opened her eyes to the universe of power and money and privilege.

The man who had fooled her because she had no yardsticks against which to measure the inhabitants of her shiny new world. The dynamic, ruthless Mark Saunders, who projected virility in bedrooms everywhere but hers.

For years he pretended she deserved the way he treated her. His never looking in her eyes. His displaying her before clients almost as if she were his whore, not his wife. Blaming her—unable, as always, to blame the right person—for what had happened. But she knew she was blameless and no longer felt guilty for what Mark had become.

She knew he would contest the divorce. Letting her go would mean challenging his father's authority, and Mark could never bring himself to do that, she thought bitterly. Despite Emmanuel's hostility toward her, he had decreed that his son could not divorce her, saying he wouldn't see the family shamed again. She didn't know whether Emmanuel was punishing her or Mark or even himself by insisting on maintaining this sham of a marriage. For years, she had been in a struggle with Emmanuel for Mark's soul.

But then, on that shameful night three years ago, she'd lost.

Once out on the busy street, Darleen forced the memory from her mind. She realized she was in SoHo, an alien part of town to her during the day. At night there was glamour and magic, restaurants and clubs like Odeon and Area, for dining, dancing, and forgetting.

But now, the harsh morning light made the grubby warehouses with huge smeared windows seem larger than life. Her heels clicking on the pavement like taps on a stage, she ducked out of the way of a forklift that, laden with crates, rumbled out of a loading dock. Clutching her coat around her, she pressed past a fat white man in a white shirt with a plastic penholder in his pocket yelling at a skinny black man who was pushing a handcart.

The day, at least, was raw and sunny, the kind of New York weather she loved. A cool breeze tousled her hair, nonchalantly achieving the effect a fashion model would die for. Her skin tingled. Her headache was ebbing. God, she hoped Mark wasn't home. She figured that after a hot bath and a few cups of coffee she might begin to get a grip on herself. Then she would leave for good and call Aida to find out what she could about last night, specifically whether someone was deliberately trying to harm her.

A taxi slowed, as taxis are wont to do when their drivers see a woman wearing an expensive fur. "Need a ride, lady?" the cabbie called out.

She nodded and got in, hugging her coat around her when she noticed the driver staring at her legs. "Seventy-second and Park," she ordered imperiously.

The driver was dark, in his late twenties, and from the look in his eyes he seemed to guess that she had nothing on under her dress. Her hem had ridden halfway up her thighs. For a moment, Darleen was angrily tempted to raise it the rest of the way just to see the look on his face. If he leered, she thought she might kill him. She flushed and realized she was shaking, she was so angry.

"Is that where the pretty lady lives?" the driver asked. The accent was slightly guttural and singsongy. Of late it seemed to be as much a requisite for driving a hack in New York as a driver's license. Deliberately, she bent forward and examined the taxi license fastened to the dashboard. The driver's picture and name, Ben Sador, were on it. Like his looks and accent, his name could have come from any of a dozen Mediterranean lands.

Meeting his eyes in the rearview mirror, Darleen said, slowly and sweetly, "Mr. Sador, I'll be pleased to tell my husband, who is on the city Taxi and Limousine Commission, how you drive without keeping your eyes on the road."

Muttering in a language she didn't understand, the driver furiously raced the car to the next red light and jammed on the brakes so that Darleen lurched forward and was forced to grab the front seat. New York madness. Sometimes the whole city struck her as being insane.

He didn't, however, attempt any more small talk.

Darleen tried to think out what she must do next. She would pack a suitcase and send for the rest of her belongings tomorrow. Although Aida had offered to take her in, it struck her that another friend, Deborah, was a better choice, because Deborah had recently gone through a divorce herself, and had confided recently to Darleen about being lonely.

Although she didn't have any money of her own, Darleen knew she could sell some of the jewelry Mark had given her during the early years of their marriage. That time now struck her as very long ago. A time when she loved her husband. A time when it seemed as if nothing could ever go wrong again.

Once the cab passed Fifty-seventh Street, a demarcation Darleen subconsciously considered the enrance to her turf, the anxiety she had been feeling eased a little. Her body went limp, making her realize how tense and tired she was. But everything was back to normal, she thought wryly. She was back in her neighborhood, Manhattan's Gold Coast, the Golden Ghetto.

"Rhodesia," as some liberal cynics called the sliver of island east of Central Park, the compound of the rich where the problems of lesser mortals were usually kept at arm's length. She was back where fate had destined her, the Silk Stocking Upper East Side where elegance was the key to life, where money could paper over sins and buy just about everything, even happiness at times, no matter what the pious liked to believe.

Stretch limousines seemed to be everywhere. Joggers in designer sweats raced by. Dog walkers had gigantic Afghans, sheepdogs, and poodles on leashes. Men with leather briefcases hailed cabs on every corner. Police on horseback moved about like Praetorian guards.

The taxi sped by the elegant Madison Avenue boutiques with the Italian and French names—Armani, Ungaro, Pierre Deux—beckoning blurs from the window. Promising elegance and bliss, they were bazaars from a modern *Arabian Nights* where genies performed magic with needle and thread. Shops where clothing and jewelry could be made or ordered for any occasion. Stores only one person in a thousand could afford.

Instinctively, she went to touch her gold horsehead pin, which was as much her trademark as her talisman, always on her coat above her heart. It was missing. *God,* she thought, *I must have lost it at that man's apartment.*

She was further dispirited when she thought Mark might be at the apartment waiting to ask her once more not to leave him. But when she thought of how he had hit her, she felt shame and anger at the same time.

Darleen resented herself for having stayed on as long as she had. She decided to erase romantic love from her heart. Forever.

Two

As the taxi pulled up to the canopied entrance to her build-ing, Jimmy Henderson, the beefy doorman, deftly opened the door. "Mornin', Mrs. S.," he said, slyly glimpsing her legs as she got out. "Are you okay?"

At first, she thought he was talking about her bloodshot eyes and she wondered what he must think, seeing her coming bedraggled at such an odd hour. But when his obsequiousness seemed even more solicitous than usual, she got a foreboding that something else was wrong.

Straightening her dress, she tightened her grip on the matching silk evening bag. No matter how gritty she was, Darleen always looked elegant, a way of making amends for the shabby clothing of her girlhood.

In a long-legged stride, she moved across the sidewalk to the front door of the massive apartment building, decorated with a shiny brass plate bearing a coat of arms with a roaring lion and a large *S*. For Saunders, of course.

The complex was part of the Saunderses' *père-et-fils* em-pire. Like much of what concerned the Saunderses, the ac-claim they received never ceased to amaze her. The gauche coat of arms was another of Emmanuel's *nouveau* marketing ideas that had somehow worked when it should have brought winces.

As always, the red-jacketed elevator operator held one just for her. Along with a table at Le Cirque, the deference was one of the perks of being Mrs. Mark Saunders. There were countless others: charge cards at Tiffany, Hermès, Bergdorf's, and wherever else she wanted them, furs from Revillon, and diamonds from Mario Buccellati, the suite at the Plaza Athenée on shopping trips to Paris or at the Quisisana hotel in Capri to relax in the sun. The boxes at Wimbledon and at the Kentucky Derby. The life-style she was about to give up.

The elevator door opened with a ping and shut with a hush. The capsule contained an original Picasso bolted to the back wall and secured under glass. The practice always struck Darleen as akin to putting plastic slipcovers on silk sofas. Still, Emmanuel's clientele loved it.

Long ago, she had figured out the reason for Emmanuel's success. It was the varying degrees of crudeness involved. He was a man without taste who thought he had it. After all, he fooled *himself,* so she could hardly blame others for being taken in, confusing glitz with quality.

His customers were all people who had made millions and now wanted to buy class. Emmanuel had somehow convinced them that he had the inside track on their dreams. Decades ago, Emmanuel Saunders had exploited people with little money by building vast tracts of cheap houses and charging all the market would bear. Later, he extended the formula by putting up cheap housing that hardly anyone could afford.

But she acknowledged there was a fairness in the arrangement. Those who shelled out their million-plus for their ridiculous living quarters were, for the most part, vulgar little men: merchants of schlock from the garment district, successful restauranteurs, discount chain store owners, record industry moguls. All the dismal robber barons of the twentieth century.

They screwed everyone else and, in a way, must expect to be exploited as well. Only, in their typically excessive style, they wanted—and got—a royal screwing. With Emmanuel Saunders and his phony Taj Mahals, they could complain about the price until the day they died and impress the hell out of their friends.

With a ping the door opened at the penthouse. Forty-seven stories above the earth, the apartment was a spacious aerie for the rich, the envy of lesser mortals—and for the past three years Darleen's prison cell. "Poor little rich girl," Aida always kidded her.

Carlotta, her Costa Rican maid in pink uniform, opened the door. Her brown face, usually wearing a polite smile, was carved into a distraught mask. Her large, dark eyes glistened with tears, and her lower lip was trembling. She looked at Darleen compassionately, then turned away sobbing.

"What's the matter?" Darleen asked, taking the woman's hand in her own.

"Señor Saunders—" Carlotta started saying, and then burst into tears again.

"Mrs. Saunders, perhaps you had better let me explain," said a man's gravelly voice from the next room.

Darleen strode into the living room. The floor-to-ceiling windows overlooked Central Park. There were potted palms, glass and brass tables, Matisses on the walls, and Lalique figurines adorning pedestals. Darleen had chosen the decorator, not letting Ernesto, the chintz artist who had designed the lobbies of Emmanuel's buildings, within ten floors of her apartment.

Rising from the mauve Roche-Bobois sectional sofa on the far side of the room was a stocky man of about forty-five. He had unruly black hair and handsome, hard looks. Ruddy complexion. Sleepy blue eyes appraising her from beneath thick brows. His nose had been broken at least once, but not badly. The mouth was full-lipped, and somehow sensitive.

His rumpled brown suit topped by a baggy raincoat and scuffed shoes said he didn't give a damn about clothes. Darleen couldn't help thinking he looked like a handsome bagman. He was the worst-dressed man who had ever been in her apartment.

"I'm Detective Sullivan. Unfortunately, I'm the bearer of some sad news," he said respectfully. "Your husband died last night or early this morning under strange circumstances. It appears he was pushed from his office window."

The blood drained from her face and Darleen took on a ghostly pallor. "Oh, my God!" she exclaimed.

Detective Brian Sullivan only half-heard her because he was ticked off. He didn't know what to think about this case and he didn't really care. He was supposed to go on vacation in three days. Until then Captain Carl "Dogface" Carter had put him on the Saunders murder.

"We can't blow this one," Carter had warned, worried that his balls were caught in a vise at City Hall over the murder of Mark "Politically Well Connected" Saunders. So he had squeezed Sullivan's balls, bringing up how he could be busted out of Homicide for threatening to punch out one of the wise-ass assistant DAs. And then doing it. "You owe me, wise guy," Carter reminded him. He'd never get the fucking vacation.

The detective crossed the beige carpet, awkwardly took Darleen's arm, and steered her toward a chair. He stood by, looking somewhat sheepish but at the same time studying her intently as Darleen covered her face with her hands and remained eerily quiet. No cries. No tears. Sitting still as a statue, her only movement consisted of deep breaths that occasionally sent tremors through her body.

At a loss for what to say, Sullivan explained some of the details of the case. The murder occurred approximately at midnight. It took a while to identify Mark. Sullivan skipped the part about why that was so. The only thing left that was recognizable as Mark Saunders was his wallet.

As he spoke, Sullivan took in Darleen's evening dress, her face—a little puffy from lack of sleep—and her weary demeanor. It was obvious she had had a rough night, and not at home. And, ten-to-one, not alone. There was a bruise on her jaw that made him wonder.

Sullivan found himself thinking how good-looking she was. Her hair shone in the morning light. He thought she was one of the rare women who woke up looking gorgeous.

"What makes you think he was murdered?" she asked unemotionally.

"Our lab technicians say there was no way he could have crashed through the glass wall if he had just slipped. That office glass is stronger than most people realize. They don't see how he could have rigged a suicide like that, either."

"No," Darleen said quietly. "Mark would never commit suicide."

Never commit suicide. The way the lady said it sounded like she wished her husband had expired that way a long time ago. He stored the impression, along with the calm way she was accepting the news of the guy's death, to pass along to whoever took over the case.

Conscious of the detective's gaze riveted on her, Darleen let her thoughts race over familiar terrain. There had been death threats over the years. Some came from Mafia-backed construction companies that Mark and his father didn't always play ball with, a few from people Mark had bested in business, still others from cranks who threatened anyone with celebrity or near-celebrity status.

Fleetingly, she even thought of a hazy conversation that came up one night at a gathering of her special group of old Sarah Lawrence friends a few months ago. In the dregs of the third or fourth martini, one of them—Deborah, she believed —had suddenly wished aloud that someone would kill Mark. Aida had said that didn't seem like such a bad idea. The other women immediately endorsed the notion. All jokingly, of course. But there was a hard edge to their talk, almost as if they meant it.

Darleen had been shocked. She knew they had all grown to dislike Mark. But what had he done to them? Though they called themselves "the sisters," they didn't tell one another everything. Instinctively, she realized he had harmed her best friends.

That night came into sharper focus. Darleen couldn't quite remember who said Mark's death shouldn't be too hard to arrange. The joke became macabre. "Get rid of the tyrant!" yelled Joy. The final solution was to push him out a window —"defenestration," a term Deborah remembered from a political science course.

The sisters murderers? It was too horrible to consider. Good Lord! How could she confuse a night of clowning with Mark's death?

Still, she couldn't shake the sense of unease. There was a strain of craziness that ran through each of them.

Sullivan excused himself to make a call and, wearily clos-

ing her eyes, Darleen collapsed on a sofa; she found herself
thinking about how "the sisters" became a group.

They were juniors in college.

There was Aida, who had been shunted from boarding
school to boarding school by rich parents who ignored her.
Even though Aida acted outrageous in class, Darleen believed
it was just that, an act; between classes, she hid in her room.

Joy was Aida's opposite. Coolly confident and self-
centered, she didn't really seem to need anyone else, except to
fill her sexual desires. Joy had stolen so many other girls'
boyfriends, she was never invited to campus parties. So she
took to bedding the junior professors, single and married.

There was Deborah, always studying or spending time in
the city working for a political cause with her sight set on
becoming the first woman president of the United States.
Deborah's roommate moved out after six weeks because Deborah insisted on studying—even when her roommate was in
bed with her boyfriend.

Finally, there was Samantha, an oriental arts expert, to
whom the gymnasium was a shrine where she worshipped
morning, noon and night, and sex was a release from her rigid
regimen.

The event that brought them all together was harrowing.
Darleen shivered when she thought about it. With an act of
will, Darleen forced thoughts of her friends from her mind,
feeling as if she had just betrayed them. At length, she looked
up, clear-eyed, as Sullivan returned to the room.

"I hope you and your men will do everything in your
power to find out who killed my husband," she said. Even as
she was saying the words, they had a taste of insincerity. Suppose? Just suppose?

"As we both know, Mark was no angel," she continued.
"Many people wanted to see him dead. When he took over as
head of his father's company, his father's enemies became his.
From what I've learned over the years, the real estate business
in New York is not for the timid." She paused wearily. "I'm
sure you'll learn that I had reason, too."

Sullivan didn't know what to make of her. He had expected
an arrogant rich bitch. But he hadn't expected her to be either
quite so exquisite or so forthcoming. Still, there was some-

thing very off here. This was no grieving widow. She struck him as a lady who couldn't make up her mind whether she was sorry or satisfied that her husband was dead. He had seen that reaction in widows before, and often enough it was typical of those who had had a helping hand, usually via arsenic, in the demise of their sadly departed.

Christ, had Darleen Saunders done in the son of a bitch?

Ruefully, Sullivan admitted to himself that something else about Darleen Saunders bothered him. In fact, made him angry. She was one of those gilded lilies who live in their goddamn ivory towers with servants catering to their every whim. They had backgrounds of boarding schools and finishing schools, never coming in contact with the gritty real world.

Still, Sullivan couldn't help thinking that Darleen Saunders might be different from the typical Upper East Side bitch who spent every other day shopping or going to a psychiatrist. She seemed smart, at least smart enough not to treat him like the hired help. There was a frankness about her that was very appealing. Catching himself, Sullivan wondered what the hell he was doing. *Yes*, he told himself, *she's different. She may have shoved her husband out of a window instead of feeding him arsenic.*

What was really bothering him, he admitted, was that she was so goddamn attractive. The women he met all seemed to be losers. Not this one. She was beautiful and had a gorgeous body. He wondered what she was like in bed.

He noticed her looking at him a little strangely, a worried glint in her eyes that seemed to have nothing to do with Saunders's death being a tragedy. It was as if she could read what was buzzing in his mind.

Nervously, he tugged at his right earlobe. Cases involving big shots always made him nervous. That went doubly for the murder of Emmanuel Saunders's son. You could step on a lot of expensive toes. Everybody on this side of town had a friend high up at City Hall, usually very high. A guy like Saunders bought and sold everyone from building inspectors to deputy mayors. The guy's company had lucked out on so many deals lately, maybe he had a couple of congressmen on the payroll. Who knows? All Sullivan knew was that he was sick over what the rich got away with.

Carlotta came in, and Darleen excused herself to Sullivan to take a call. As he watched her leave, he again appreciated what he saw. She carried herself erectly, her head held high on a long neck. Full-breasted, but not too. Slim, but not too. But he also saw her as part of a world he had gladly left behind when he divorced his wife, Paige. He had signed the papers ten years ago, finally snapping his last link to the wealthy, arrogant, selfish people whose love of money was their passion in life.

With a grimace, he looked at Darleen as she now returned to the room, and wondered how he could possibly think of her as anything but part of a murder case. He even knew a logical motive for her.

He remembered somebody remarking to him that he couldn't understand why Jackie O had married Onassis. "Don't you know the rich always want more?" Sullivan replied.

Three

After Sullivan left, Darleen remained seated, staring at the slate-gray sky visible through the living room windows. She surprised herself by thinking Sullivan seemed like a decent guy. It had been a long time since she'd met anyone really decent.

It began raining, and with a start Darleen realized that for years she hadn't really felt or seen the rain. The only times she was aware of rain was when she got wet getting out of taxis. Part of the useless life she led with Mark. She wondered if she had grown so accustomed to the life-style of the idle rich that it had deadened her soul and spirit. With the mechanical precision of a robot, she threw on furs and jewels and visited chic beauty salons such as Donsuki, where haircuts cost up to $100 and women didn't escape without manicures and pedicures—throwing away in minutes the kind of money that it had taken her mother weeks to earn. Money spent to look like a Bloomingdale's mannequin, and to have about as much feeling as one.

Her gaze fell on a photograph of her mother, and she was grateful Catherine was spared seeing her only daughter now. The photo was of an ethereal-looking woman in her mid-thirties with dark hair, standing in a park with her arm linked through her eighteen-year-old daughter's. Catherine was wearing a white blouse and dark skirt, having just come from her work as a receptionist. Darleen was wearing a navy blazer and pleated skirt and was smiling at the camera.

The photo was taken the day Darleen was leaving for her freshman year at Sarah Lawrence. When she received word that she had won a scholarship to the college, Darleen had at first decided not to go. She had never been away from home, but the reason wasn't fear of the unknown. She had been afraid to leave her mother alone because she knew how much Catherine depended upon her. But her mother made her go.

The daughter of a wealthy Main Line family, Catherine had eloped at age eighteen with a boy she had met during her freshman year at the University of Pennsylvania. Because Jim Collins was poor, or "lacking in pedigree," as her father put it, Catherine was cut off financially as well as emotionally by her parents.

At the time, Jim was working his way through school and was forced to drop out to work full time when Catherine unexpectedly became pregnant with Darleen. Then he was drafted by the Army and died in a freak accident in basic training. He was only twenty-one.

In her crisis, Catherine turned to her parents, but once again they rebuffed her. Only an elderly cousin surreptitiously gave her money whenever she could.

Trained to do nothing and lacking both a degree and self-confidence, Catherine held a series of low-paying clerical jobs while Darleen was growing up. Once after work, she immediately took to her bed, complaining of migraines. As Darleen grew older, she and her mother became more like sisters than mother and daughter, with Darleen proving to be the more capable one.

While she cooked and cleaned, her mother told her incredible stories of the sparkling parties and cotillions she had attended as a debutante, the riding to hounds, and the trips abroad. "Oh, Darleen, it was such fun. Money makes life so much easier."

Her mother would make up stories about what they would do if they were rich. The clothes they would buy, the trips they would take, the places they would live. "I know that one day you will find a man who will love you and give you everything in the world," she said frequently.

As Darleen looked at the picture, she knew that her mother had been braver than Darleen had realized at the time. Catherine was seriously ill, but she lied about it rather than see Darleen miss out on college. Darleen learned about her mother's illness only toward the end of her freshman year, when the doctor told her to rush home.

When Darleen met Mark three years later, he seemed to be the man her mother had said would enter her life and offer her everything. She was spending Christmas break with Deborah Jacobs during their senior year. As they enjoyed a continental breakfast in the bay window of the Upper East Side maisonette of Deb's Uncle Sam, Deborah was talking about whom they would meet at a party that night, punctuating her comments with facial expressions and waves of her croissant.

An intense Jewish girl, Deb was the kind of student who gave Sarah Lawrence its reputation for intellectualism. She ran the student council almost single-handedly. She studied hard and became engrossed in different projects each year, such as a paper on the kinds of women who inspired Pre-Raphaelite painters. She always wore her dark hair pulled tightly into a bun from which a few unruly wisps escaped, the only hint of how wild her hair was when she let it loose. Her lively brown eyes were set in a round face. In fact, all of her was rounded into gentle shapes with no indication of the strong bones beneath. Her caustic wit brought each man on her list down to the bare essentials.

"Oh, Jeffrey's nice, but dreary," she said, looking glum. "While Carl," she said archly, "is worldly and oh-so-weary.

"Poor Jeremy is gay, but if he ever comes out of the closet his parents will disinherit him. Then there will be a couple of guys from Harvard, and you know what that means. But mostly, it will be an older crowd. Guys already established in the business world."

Darleen had laughed at the descriptions, but she became intrigued when Deb described Mark Saunders, who was hosting the party at his father's house. "Mark is a strange one," Deborah remarked. "Very sexy. First-generation money, but

lots of it. His father is one of those self-made men who should
have been conquering rival nations hundreds of years ago.
Mark's at a point himself where he could go either way. He
could make something out of himself or wind up a ruthless
bastard like his father."

"Which way do you think he'll go?" Darleen asked.

"Frankly, I'm not sure," Deborah replied quietly. "Mark
wants to do the right thing, but he would never go against his
father."

"Why not?"

"It's very complicated. Mark has a love/hate relationship
with his father, yet he believes the old man is always right."
Deborah paused. "Can we change the subject?"

Darleen started to ask her what was wrong, but then Deborah blurted, "Wait until you see the Saunders estate. Absolutely spectacular. And strange."

"What do you mean by strange?" Darleen asked.

"I'm not quite sure how to explain it," Deborah mused.
"It's more a museum than a house."

That night they drove out to Mandragola, the offbeat Long
Island estate of the Saunderses. As the partygoers streamed
through the iron front gate, a guard made each car stop.

"I had to call days ago and tell them our license number,"
Deborah whispered as a black-uniformed guard checked the
number against those on his list.

"God, Deborah, why did you bring me? I don't belong
here."

"Don't be silly. If anyone looks like she belongs in a setting like this, it's you!"

Just then, a car honked behind them. Darleen looked
around and waved excitedly when she saw who was driving.
Turning to Deborah, she said, "Joy's here."

"So are Samantha and Aida," Deb replied.

"You mean we're all invited to this extravaganza?"

"Didn't we agree to take care of one another?" Deborah
answered.

"Go up the driveway and a valet will park your car for
you," the guard said, waving them on.

It was difficult to see much of Mandragola in the darkness.
On either side of the driveway were shimmering patches of

water, apparently ponds or streams. Every six feet, the quarter-mile-long driveway was illuminated by tall candles in glass tubing that shielded the flames from the wind.

"The Saunderses spare no expense," Deborah observed.

"Obviously," Darleen replied wryly.

As they approached, Darleen could tell the house was huge. As soon as they climbed out, a young man jumped behind the wheel and drove Deborah's car away. When the front door was opened by a butler, they entered a marble-floored entry hall. At the opposite end was a fireplace ablaze with logs that were unsplit tree trunks. Corridors and door-ways led off the entry hall, which was already crowded.

"Deborah, I'm so glad you could come," a man's voice rang out.

Darleen turned and looked up at a tall, lean man in his early thirties wearing a custom-tailored dinner jacket. His white shirt emphasized his eyes, and his full, sensual mouth looked like it had been carved on a Grecian statue. His black hair came to a snow-white widow's peak. When he smiled, he exhibited perfect white teeth. Jay Gatsby come to life.

"Mark, how are you?" Deborah replied. Turning to Darleen, she said, "Mark, this is my school chum, Darleen Collins."

Darleen shook hands and, when she looked into Mark's eyes, she felt a wave of sympathy for him. Though he was smiling, his eyes, dark and soft as velvet, were sad.

"I hope you enjoy yourself, Miss Collins," he said, holding her hand a fraction of time longer than necessary. "Excuse me while I greet my other guests." As quickly as he had appeared, he disappeared into the crowd.

"You got his Valentino look," Deborah quipped to Darleen. "But it means only that he wants to take you to bed."

Darleen laughed nervously and smoothed the one black cocktail dress she owned, hoping that its sweetheart neckline wasn't too dated. "How do you know?"

Deborah paused. "I know," she said solemnly. "There's something I should have told you about Mark before we came. . . ."

But Darleen was no longer listening. Glancing around, she was looking for the man who had swept her off her feet.

Instead, she saw Aida coming across the room, and waved to her.

Just then Samantha approached. A stunning Oriental girl with long, black hair and a butter-almond complexion, she was wearing a sleeveless white silk dress that stopped at her knees. She slipped her arms through Deborah's and Darleen's.

"Great party," she said. Pointing across the room, she added, "Hey, there's Joy."

"Who's the guy she brought?" Deborah asked.

"Not guy. Guys," Samantha groaned. "Numbers six hundred twelve and thirteen."

"I guess we should be grateful she didn't bring that little Carol from school," Deborah said in a tone of long suffering.

"You mean that little lesbo freshman?" Samantha asked.

"You got it," Deborah replied. "She's run out of professors, so she's tapping the young."

"Not like you, huh?" Aida said, nodding in the direction of Mark Saunders, who was standing in the doorway with some people.

Deborah reddened. "Oh, God," she said. "Are there no secrets?"

"You mean you and Mark . . ." Darleen said incredulously.

"Welcome to the world of grown-ups, Darleen," Aida said. "Deborah has been sleeping with the guy for six months."

"*Was* sleeping," Deborah corrected.

"You mean you dumped him?" Aida asked. "God, I'd love to get my hands on him."

"No, he dumped me," Deborah said quietly. Then she added sarcastically, "That's what I get for going with a sexy guy."

Aida looked around. "I'm so horny I could screw the butler."

Deborah looked at her strangely. "What chemical are you on, Aida?"

"'Ludes, wonderful 'ludes."

"Well, take it easy," Deborah warned as Joy came up.

A petite blonde with a pixie cut, Joy had an almost androgynous look. She was wearing an emerald satin cocktail dress and had a pearl tiara in her hair. The young men on her arms were twins, and the three of them together looked almost like triplets. They had lank blond hair and fine features. The major difference was that the boys' eyes were blue, while Joy's were green.

Joy leaned over and kissed Darleen close to her mouth. "You look great," she said.

Darleen flushed, looking embarrassed. Joy smiled at her reaction, but the others weren't amused.

"Here's Tinkerbell to round out the sisters," Aida said with a sneer.

"These delicious men are Jim and Tim Campbell," Joy gushed. She pushed them ahead of her. "You go and enjoy yourselves and I'll catch up in a little while."

"How do you do it, Joy?" Deborah asked enviously.

"Life ain't fair," Samantha added.

"Well," Joy said demurely. "I guess I just know how to give more of myself than most girls." Then she laughed, an infectious laugh that had the rest of the sisters joining her.

Darleen wondered at her friend. How could she be so uninhibited? She remembered how Joy had told her one day about being seduced when she was only thirteen by an aunt and an uncle who was a photographer.

It was during a summer vacation in Maine. The uncle had her pose nude in a field under the warm sun. Her aunt came by and watched. Before Joy quite realized what was happening, they had taken off their clothes and all were bathing nude in a nearby pond. Later, her aunt began drying her off while her uncle ran his hands through her hair and down her back, cupping her bottom in his hands. She turned to him in amazement as her aunt kissed her cheek. Then her lips. Then her breasts.

"That's when I lost my virginity," Joy had recalled. "Sort of to both of them at once. It was like taking a nice warm bath."

Darleen had been alternately appalled and enraptured by the story. She always wondered how Joy could tell it so nonchalantly.

As the party grew noisier, the sisters began mingling with others. Unable to find Mark, Darleen left the crowd and out of curiosity walked down a corridor, examining sketches on the walls. She recognized them as original works by the Renaissance masters, including Leonardo da Vinci, Sandro Botticelli, and Andrea del Verrocchio.

The doors along the thickly carpeted halls were all open, leading into large, darkened rooms. Darleen poked her head into several of them. Near the end of the hall, she came to one door that was closed. When she tried the ornate brass knob, it wouldn't turn.

"Emmanuel keeps that locked these days," a voice said from behind her.

Startled, Darleen turned and found herself looking directly into Mark Saunders's eyes. In the darkened hallway, moonlight from a window off to the right softly bathed his profile. Darleen felt a rush of warmth go through her. He looked so incredibly handsome that Darleen had to resist an impulse to reach out and touch his lips. He also looked vulnerable. There was that sadness in his eyes that made her want to hold him.

"I'm sorry," she said breathlessly.

"Not at all," Mark replied. "I was merely trying to tell you that Emmanuel keeps that door locked these days because he's working on that room."

"Emmanuel?"

"Oh, I'm sorry," he said. "Emmanuel is my father. This room is to be his Olympus."

"Olympus?" she asked in a puzzled voice, feeling foolish and ignorant.

"Like in Greece," Mark said with a laugh. "A home of the gods. My father wants one, so naturally he's having one built." Mark took her by the elbow and steered her down the corridor, showing her various sketches and paintings on the walls. His touch was gentle, but Darleen found herself shivering slightly. "Are you cold? Would you like a sweater?" he asked gently.

"No," Darleen replied, staring into his eyes again. "No, thank you."

"My father is intensely interested in Greek mythology. Greece is our country of origin. He's also a student of Machiavelli, and the Renaissance was Machiavelli's era. Hence, the artwork."

"I didn't know anyone took Machiavelli seriously today."

"Well, my father does," Mark replied with a laugh. "When

I was a boy, he read to me from Machiavelli's works, saying they contain the true secrets of success."

"What secrets?"

"How to gain power and how to use it." Clearing his throat, he said in a deeper voice that obviously was supposed to impersonate a man addressing a boy, "If you accept Machiavelli's vision of the world, you will become as powerful as an emperor!"

"Are you a student of Machiavelli, too?"

For a moment, Mark was quiet. When he spoke, there was an undertone of something she couldn't quite place. Disappointment? Regret?

"I guess I have been a captive student as long as I can remember. Am I a practitioner of those theories? No!"

"I know that Machiavelli preached ruthlessness and deceit to get what you want, but I don't know much else," Darleen said.

"There's a lot more, but essentially you are right. For a man like my father, who fought his way to the top, such a vision may make sense. But there has to be more to life."

"What do you want to do?"

"For one thing, I'd like to see our company build housing for people who can't afford it."

"That's not exactly ruthless," Darleen replied.

Mark laughed. "I know. I'm afraid I disappoint my father tremendously."

"What else do you want?"

Mark stopped and looked down at her, his mood turning serious. Leaning down, he kissed her softly, his lips barely touching hers. The kiss felt like a gentle breeze.

"What I want is a woman to love who will love me."

Darleen shivered again, and turned away feeling disconcerted and not in complete control. Mark led her back to the party, talking to her all the while.

Still, his past relationship with Deborah made her anxious. Also, there was another factor that she considered. His age. He was a good ten years older than she. Yet she felt at ease with him. Completely.

"I'd love to keep talking to you," Mark said, "but I do

have to tend to the rest of my guests. Would it be all right if I called you?"

"Of course," she blurted out.

Several minutes later, an angry voice rang above the din. "Mark! Mark, get up here!"

The partygoers' conversations subsided almost as one, and everyone watched Mark Saunders as he ran up the stairs and entered an open door.

"Christ Almighty, Mark," the voice boomed. "Tell that bunch of freeloaders down there to quiet down. I'm trying to phone Europe, and with all the goddamn racket I can't hear a thing."

A minute later, a chastened-looking Mark Saunders emerged from the room and walked down the steps. Glancing around, he could tell that everyone had heard.

"It's okay, everybody," he said uncomfortably. "But if we could be a little quieter . . ."

Mark slipped into the crowd and Darleen could no longer see him. She was angry at the man upstairs who had hurt Mark. It had to have been his father. She felt Mark's embarrassment and wished she could tell him that—well, she wasn't sure what. That she could heal his hurt?

When she returned to school the following Monday, she was both flattered and thankful when she found her dorm room flooded with red roses. The cards in the baskets were all signed, LOVE, MARK. She had been afraid she would never hear from him. What could he find appealing about a naive college girl?

The sisters kidded her, but they were impressed when on the following Saturday evening Mark Saunders, wearing a navy Italian suit, arrived at Sarah Lawrence in a chauffeur-driven Rolls-Royce Silver Cloud. After they dated several weeks, going to a restaurant near school, Mark invited her to dine in the city one evening.

That evening, Darleen was wearing a simple, straight, copper silk long-sleeved dress with a scooped back. She had borrowed diamond earrings from Deborah.

Mark had the chauffeur drive to Manhattan, where they went to Windows on the World, the restaurant atop one of the World Trade Center towers.

She found herself the total focus of his attention and, to her surprise, she wasn't as uncomfortable as she had expected to be.

"I could get used to this," she joked when the headwaiter left presenting a dessert wine list, after a glorious meal of pâté, squab, and champagne.

"I was hoping you'd say that," he said.

The evening sky was right outside their window, and Darleen looked out dreamily. "Everything is at our feet," Mark said. "The city is ours. The world is ours."

The words echoed what her mother had said about someday meeting a man who would offer her the world. "My mother would have loved this," she said.

"Perhaps mine would have as well," he said.

"What do you mean by perhaps?"

"I never knew my mother. I don't even know whether she's alive. You see, she left my father right after I was born."

Once again, Darleen felt incredibly sorry for him. He was such a nice person to have experienced such pain. She wanted him to know how much she felt for him, but wasn't certain how to bring that about, so she tried to let him know that he had made her happy. "Thank you for bringing me here," she said. "This is what the gods must have felt like on Olympus," she said. Indeed, Darleen felt breathless yet strangely powerful looking out.

She also felt a little light-headed from the champagne, but pleasantly so. When she looked at Mark, he was smiling at her, and she felt a rush of pleasure when he reached across the table and held her hand.

"I'm afraid you've enchanted me," he said.

Darleen met his eyes. Once again she thought how beautiful and pained they appeared. She rested her other hand on top of his. "That's what I thought you had done to me."

Mark signaled the waiter for the check. "I'd like to show you my apartment," he said.

She looked at him and realized that he loved her.

"All right," she said.

On the ride to his place, Mark pulled down a shade on the window, separating them from the chauffeur. "You are a lovely, lovely girl," he said softly, his hand caressing her hair and then her cheeks and throat.

Darleen leaned over and kissed him passionately. When he responded, she broke off and pulled away. There was a look of amazement on her face but she was smiling. "God, I never felt this way before," she said shyly.

Mark smiled. "I was about to say the same thing."

He paused. "Darleen, you make me feel like—well—like I can do just about anything."

"But you can. Look at how successful you are."

"My father is the successful one. I'm not so sure I'd be all that much if he weren't behind me."

Darleen reached out and brushed his lips with her hand. "Don't say that, Mark. You—you're wonderful!"

Mark laughed again and leaned back. "How did I ever find you?" he muttered.

When they entered his penthouse, Darleen looked around at the massive living room and then went from room to room, finally turning to him. "You live here all by yourself?"

"Yes," he laughed.

"Now I'm going to ask another stupid question."

"What's that?" Mark said.

"Why do you have two kitchens?"

He laughed again. "I do a lot of entertaining. Caterers often need both kitchens." Then he leaned down and kissed her. "No more questions," he said.

Trembling, Darleen responded to the kiss. When he began undressing her, she let him, and she was surprised when he appeared almost as shy as she was when he led her into the bedroom.

Six weeks later, Darleen and Mark were walking across the Sarah Lawrence campus on a golden Saturday afternoon. Mark was very quiet, which she had learned meant that he was mulling something over. Slipping her arm through his, she asked, "Tell me, Mark, what's the problem?"

"No problem—well, yes—it *is* a problem."

"What are you talking about?" she asked with a laugh. "You sound like the sphinx giving a riddle."

Mark didn't laugh. He seemed to be in agony. "I realize we haven't known each other terribly long," he began, and then he faltered, and spun her around so they were face-to-face. "Oh, damn it."

Darleen looked at him, suddenly frightened, but she couldn't say why. "Please, tell me what's wrong."

Mark turned away. "I want you to marry me."

Darleen touched his cheek. "I'll marry you," she said softly. "I love you."

Mark looked at her and his face brightened for the first time all day. He took her hand and kissed it.

"I love you and I always will," he said.

When she told the sisters that night, Deb, Samantha, and Aida reacted with the unbound enthusiasm she had hoped they would.

"That's terrific," Deb said. "Just wish it had been me."

"Wonderful," echoed Samantha.

"Great," said Aida.

But Joy seemed angered by the news. "He's not good enough for you!"

"Joy, what are you talking about?"

"I'm talking about you, throwing yourself away on some-one like him."

Joy took her books and hurriedly left the room, slamming the door behind her. Darleen started running after her, but Samantha grabbed her arm.

"Don't bother. She'll get over it."

"Get over what?" Darleen asked.

Samantha looked at her skeptically, then took her hand from Darleen's shoulder. "You really don't know, do you?"

"Know what?" Darleen asked irritably, her mind else-where, finding herself tired of the ambiguities.

"Forget it," Samantha said. "Tell us, have you set the date?"

Four

Darleen's engagement officially introduced her to the world of silk and satin. Mark's Rolls-Royce brought her in from school one day to Bergdorf's for a fashion show he said he wanted her to see. The prospect excited her. Darleen had never been to this store, let alone to a fashion show.

When she entered Bergdorf's, she hesitantly approached a saleswoman to ask her where to go. "You mean the show for Miss Collins?" the woman asked.

"Yes, why—I guess it is," Darleen said, not knowing until then that the show was Mark's doing. For the first time she had an idea of the dimensions of Mark's wealth.

"Fifth floor," the saleswoman said.

Darleen took an elevator and stepped off into a reception room of plush carpeting, leather sofas, and glass-topped tables. A moment later, she was greeted by a beautiful woman about thirty years old with frosted hair and impeccable makeup who smiled. "Miss Collins?"

"Yes."

"My name is Marion. Will you please follow me."

As she trailed behind the woman, Darleen couldn't help admiring Marion's silk dress with a maroon silk sash. Tall and sleek, the woman looked like she had stepped out of the pages of *Vogue*.

They proceeded down a short hallway, then the woman pulled aside a curtain revealing a room with a runway. Mark was sitting on a gray leather sofa. Smiling, he got up and came over and kissed her.

"Hello, lovely."

"Hello, yourself," she said.

"Marion, you can begin now."

"Of course, Mr. Saunders."

Mark took Darleen's hand and walked over to the couch. Moments after they sat down, a waiter wearing a spotless white jacket, red cummerbund, black pants, and bow tie brought in an ice bucket. He took out a bottle of Dom Perignon and popped the cork. Smiling, he handed them glasses of champagne.

The moment the waiter disappeared, a tall, beautiful black model wearing green silk lounging pajamas walked down the aisle, pausing in front of them and turning around.

"This is the newest Dior, Miss Collins," Marion said.

The girl again turned around in front of them before moving on. She was followed by an elegant girl with a long red braid, who was wearing a black silk cocktail dress with a deep-cut vee back. Coming down the runway, like the preceding model she stopped before them, turning around carefully before moving on.

"That is the Givenchy," Marion said.

Darleen sat enraptured. "I can't believe we are the only ones here," she whispered to Mark.

"For me, you are the only one here," he said.

The next model was an aristocratic-looking blond girl wearing a silver brocade top over matching pants. Her tanned midriff was bare.

So it went for an hour. Model after model came out, and Darleen was struck by the beauty and elegance of both the women and the clothes. What she was wearing suddenly seemed very shabby in comparison. When she felt that way, she flushed, almost as though she were ashamed of her background.

"Oh, Mark. These models are beautiful."

"They can't hold a candle to you," he replied.

Darleen couldn't recall ever having been so happy.

At the end of the show, Mark turned to Marion. "Please take Darleen and get her measurements."

"Will you please come with me, Darleen?"

Moments later, Darleen was in a spacious fitting room, standing on a carpeted platform. Several women helped strip off her clothes, and the most thorough measurements of her life were taken. She flushed as parts of her body that she never knew anyone ever measured were duly recorded.

When she came out, Marion turned to Mark. "Have you decided on anything, Mr. Saunders?"

He looked at Darleen, pretending he wore a monocle. "Yesss," he said slowly in a mock German accent. "Ve vill give ze young lady one of everyzing."

"No! You can't!" Darleen exclaimed.

"This is your trousseau," Mark said. He knew there was no one else to buy it for her.

Darleen looked at him lovingly. "Thank you," she said simply.

From Bergdorf's he took her to Cartier, where they were shown into a private room. A suave-looking man with gray hair and wearing a three-piece blue suit came up to Mark. "Ah, Mr. Saunders, how very nice to see you again."

"Philippe, this is Miss Collins, my fiancée."

The man beamed an ingratiating smile on Darleen. *"Enchanté, Mademoiselle."* Turning again to Mark, he said, "Is there anything in particular you wish to see?"

"Some silver and gold necklaces and bracelets to start, I think," Mark said thoughtfully.

Darleen sat in wonder as velvet-covered trays of gold, diamonds, and jewels were placed before them. Mark occasionally held pieces up to her throat, her wrists, her ears. "You are fine-boned," he said, "so you should wear delicate jewelry."

When they left the store, her head was spinning, and she was wearing a slender gold chain with a tear-shaped ruby. Mark had ordered rings, bracelets, other necklaces, earrings, and pendants. The one she prized the most was an antique gold horseshoe pin with diamonds, because Mark had told her she reminded him of a spirited horse.

Five

The following weekend, Mark waited until they were in the back of the limousine before telling her where they were going. "It's time to visit my father," he announced as she settled into the soft leather seat.

Darleen looked at him with a wave of concern. Since they first dated, Mark had been reticent about discussing his father. In fact, he hardly talked about him at all. When he did, she caught the tension in his voice, as though he were torn between intense emotions: love and hate, just as Deborah had said.

"My father can be very difficult," Mark said. "I told you when I first met you that we don't see eye-to-eye on much. He sees me as gullible and, well, somewhat less than the son he wanted to leave his business to one day."

It was twilight when they drove up the enormous driveway to the magnificent stone and stucco manor house. With its turrets and arches, the estate looked as if it were a transplanted Italian villa.

"Why it is called Mandragola?"

"It is the title of Emmanuel's favorite comedy by Machiavelli. The idea that Machiavelli wrote comedies appeals to his sense of irony."

When Emmanuel strode into the foyer to greet them, he was more impressive than his surroundings. Mark had told Darleen his father was a dynamic man, a quality she found very sexy in Mark himself. Still, she wasn't prepared for this.

Emmanuel Saunders radiated energy—and tension. He was shorter than his son, but more powerfully built. His head was leonine, disproportionately large even for his sturdy torso, his face craggy and deeply tanned. His gray eyes were almost as steely as his hair, piercing in their directness, and revealing the arrogance of a man accustomed to getting what he wanted, or to taking what he was denied. There was no doubt he was master of his universe.

He wore cream-colored slacks and a turtleneck, giving him the appearance of a fencing master. But most striking to Darleen was his effect on his son. Mark shrank in his father's presence.

"So this is the girl you want to marry," Emmanuel said gruffly.

He coolly appraised her from head to toe, lingering on the curve of her breasts and buttocks. He reached out and too familiarly pushed a strand of hair behind her right ear. His touch sent a shock through her body. "Beautiful," he muttered.

Emmanuel placed his hand familiarly on the small of Darleen's back and she found herself trembling as he inched his hand lower. With an act of will, she pushed his hand away, walked away from him and stood next to Mark, who sheepishly listened to his father, all the vitality drained from his expression.

"You didn't tell me your father was a lecher, Mark," Darleen said, staring defiantly at Emmanuel.

Ignoring her, Emmanuel turned to his son and asked severely, "Did you get that property on Third Avenue?"

"No, the Whitmans bought it."

Emmanuel looked at Mark with disdain. "You goddamn fool! Can't you do anything right?"

Darleen was horrified. She had found Mark spoke to her easily about the real estate business, and she found his stories fascinating. Now, tongue-tied, Mark cowered in his father's presence.

"Don't speak to him that way," she found herself blurting out, yet not knowing where the words came from.

Emmanuel stared at her as if she were some strange creature from another planet.

"Mark told me about that deal on the way over here," she continued. "It was a good thing you didn't get that property. Isn't that right, Mark?"

Mark looked hesitantly from Darleen to his father and back again, gaining courage from her strength. "Uh, that's right, Father. I checked out the deed and it would be impossible to build there for at least six years."

"Why didn't you tell me?" Emmanuel snapped.

"You never gave him a chance to," Darleen said, angrily.

Emmanuel looked at her carefully, as though assessing a formidable opponent. "Miss Collins, I expect I shall see you again," he said, bowing graciously and kissing her hand. "Now, if you will excuse me, I have work to do."

Though his parting words and actions were courtly, Darleen was worried by what she detected in Emmanuel's eyes. He looked like a panther, circling his prey nonchalantly while waiting for the proper moment to strike.

Relieved that Emmanuel was gone, Darleen took Mark's hand in hers, shuddering as she remembered the way Emmanuel had appraised her—as if she were a horse, or worse, a prostitute. That and the verbal sparring had left her exhausted.

Mark flushed. Turning to her, he read the expression of revulsion on her face.

"Don't judge him too harshly," he said. "He has gone through a lot. Since my mother left him he considers all women whores who betray the men who love them. I was brainwashed with that message when I was growing up, because I reminded Emmanuel of my mother. Also, he blames me for Stephen's death."

"You've never talked about Stephen before," Darleen said gently. "Who was he?"

Mark drew her to a brocaded couch and, haltingly, began to tell her about his older brother. "Emmanuel had expected Stephen to inherit his business empire one day.

"Stephen was ten years older than me, and he just seemed so far beyond me that it wasn't like having a brother at all. He was . . . it was like he could do everything. He wasn't afraid of anything. I was afraid of everything."

He paused. She sensed his pain and stroked his forehead tenderly.

"When I was little," Mark continued, "my father would say, be like Stephen. In high school and college, Stephen was captain of everything. Swimming, wrestling, lacrosse. Even the debating and chess clubs.

"During summers in college, Stephen worked for Emmanuel. Even though he was younger than the other men, he bullied them to get work done. Just the way my father did."

Suddenly, Mark's face became ashen, and his hands trembled. He forced himself to go on, wanting her to know all. "One summer, Stephen was overseeing a big project. He took me out one morning and had me ride up the elevator to the top of a building under construction. I hate heights, and I didn't want to go. But Stephen forced me, taunting that I was a baby.

"When we got up there, we were all alone. Stephen went out on one of the girders and began clowning around. He slipped and clung to a girder, begging me to help him. But I couldn't move, I was so scared. Then he fell to his death."

"Oh, Mark," Darleen said, gently.

"Father actually called me a murderer," he said sadly, and they both cried.

Sitting now in her penthouse, Darleen wept again as she thought about how much the story paralleled Mark's own horrible death. Then she thought about how Mark had changed during the years of their marriage. How the man who was kind and generous had become like his bullying brother as he turned into the son his father wanted—and lost all the good qualities he had. A terrible Jekyll-and-Hyde metamorphosis that had left her black and blue for the last time.

Now, Mark was dead. She had to find the strength to tell Emmanuel that the last of his sons was gone.

She picked up the phone, and dread gripped her as she

dialed the number for Mandragola. After two rings, a servant answered.

"Mr. Saunders, please. Tell him it's his daughter-in-law."

A minute later, she heard Emmanuel's voice for the first time in three years. "You must want something," he said curtly. "Make it fast."

"It's about Mark," she said softly. "Mark is dead. The police believe he was murdered."

There was a long silence on the other end of the line. Finally, Emmanuel spoke, his voice filled with venom. "You killed him, didn't you, you bitch? You began killing him slowly three years ago, and now you've finally finished the job."

"Stop it! Stop it!" she said quietly, determinedly. "If anyone harmed Mark it was you. If this were any other time, I would tell you exactly what I think of you!"

Shaking, she hung up. Tears ran down her face and she felt sick. She had to talk to someone. Picking up the phone again, she began calling the sisters. She needed them now more than ever before.

Six

Joy Livingston was lying on a mat in the living room of her apartment, luxuriating in the shiatsu massage when the call from Darleen came. She had turned on the answering machine so that her morning calisthenics and massage session wouldn't be disturbed. She listened while Darleen left a message.

"Please call as quickly as you can," Darleen told the tape. There was an unusual urgency in her voice. "It's very important!"

As Martha Hendrick's supple fingers worked themselves over her naked back, Joy decided that nothing could be important enough to interrupt this. She was in a frisky, playful mood. Reaching out, she patted Martha on the thigh nearest her right hand.

"Mmmmmmmmmm, this is wonderful," Joy said, raising her blond head. "*You're* wonderful."

A pretty, athletic woman of twenty with short reddish hair, Martha was wearing a gray sweatshirt, blue shorts, and sneakers. With a spray of freckles across her nose, she looked innocent and vulnerable. Her face reddened at Joy's words and she instinctively withdrew her knee. Joy laughed teasingly.

Three mornings a week, Martha put Joy through a vigorous physical workout in Joy's apartment. They had met a month ago at the Big Apple Health Club, where Martha was an instructress, a job she had taken to spend a year "experiencing" New York City before going back to college in Ohio. Since she needed the extra money, she had leaped at Joy's proposal that she give her private sessions. A lot of rich people preferred saving time by hiring someone to put them through their paces at home.

Also, she was flattered because it was Joy Livingston, anchor of the most popular local evening news program in town.

Joy was indeed an experience. Charming and nice, but a little strange, something that Martha couldn't quite place. Uninhibited, but more than that. *It must have to do with a woman with a high-powered career and life-style,* Martha thought.

Martha tapped a bare shoulder with an air of finality. "All done," she said.

Joy stood and let the white towel draped across her buttocks fall to the floor. She was small and slim and surprisingly full-breasted, richly tanned from head to toe. Her short, blond hair framed a delicate, heart-shaped face with green, feline eyes. Joy Livingston was acknowledged to be one of the most beautiful women on television.

Unself-consciously, Joy walked across a living room decorated in severe Swedish modern that set off her collection of African masks on the walls. She turned on the television, dialing to the *Today* show. "The workday begins," she groaned.

Martha found her eyes lingering on the woman standing before her. Once again, she wasn't sure what to think. She had never met a woman who made her so aware of her body.

Martha liked her, and she was pleased that Joy treated her like a friend, not adopting the patronizing manner of most rich women at the club. But at times Joy got a little too familiar, asking questions about Martha's sex life that embarrassed her. Martha had told her about her boyfriend, Tommy, but not any details.

Did all sophisticated women act like Joy? She was still in awe of wealthy women who lived in luxurious skyscrapers and rode about in limousines and even hired women who bought clothes for them. That awe went doubly for one who made her living in the glamorous world of television—Martha found it exciting that the lovely woman she touched was the same beautiful person on the TV screen in the evening.

But there was still that other factor in their relationship, the times when Joy complimented her on the way she looked and on the shape of her body. On such occasions, Martha felt strangely embarrassed and didn't know how to respond.

No woman had ever talked to her that way. Not many men had. Was this part of that sophistication she lacked?

"Well," Martha said, turning away as she pulled on sweatpants and a nylon jacket. "See you on Friday."

Suddenly, her way was blocked by Joy. They were almost the same height, and Martha found herself staring directly into the TV star's eyes.

"I need a favor," said Joy, folding her arms under her own breasts. "I'm about to take several days off and go to my beach house on Fire Island. I don't want to give up my workouts, and I was wondering if you'd join me?"

Martha hesitated.

"Of course, I'll pay you for your time. Say two hundred dollars a day? C'mon, it's very pretty out there. You'll like it, especially this time of year, after the crowds."

Martha flushed. She was flattered, overwhelmed by the amount of money, and nervous at the same time. She didn't know what to say.

"I'm not sure, Miss Livingston . . . Joy," she stammered. "I'll have to see. I could use the money. Uh, I'll let you know Friday, if that's okay."

"That will be fine," said Joy, with an amused smile.

Moments after Martha left, Joy lowered the volume on the television set, then picked up the telephone and dialed Darleen's number.

As the phone rang, she wondered whether the pretty little jock would take her up on the Fire Island offer. She hoped so. The child had an exquisite body along with marvelous hands.

If she came, should she tell Jacques not to? Or would he simply make the holiday more interesting? A Jacques and a jock. The alliteration pleased her. As did the potential combinations.

Her reverie was interrupted by a voice on the other end of the line. "Saunders residence."

"Mrs. Saunders, please. Tell her it's Joy."

While waiting for Darleen, she decided to keep Martha to herself, at least the first day. Jacques could come next. Handsome, worldly Jacques, who took her idiosyncrasies for granted. The trouble with most men was they were intolerant, too inflexible in their sexual attitudes and appetites.

Joy knew herself to be fortunate. Her amorphous sexuality came across the TV tube and was a major reason why her ratings were so high. Both men and women loved her. At the same time, she was discreet about her private life. Very discreet.

Finally, Darleen came on the line, calmly telling her that Mark Saunders was dead. Murdered.

"The police were here when I got home this morning," Darleen said. She paused. "Joy, I know this sounds terrible, but I don't feel anything."

"Oh, Darleen, he never was any good. Wasn't I the only sister who told you not to marry him?"

Joy always wondered at her beautiful Darleen's magnificent control. A lot of it, she believed, came from that repressive childhood her friend had had. Always the little adult patiently putting up with everyone's problems.

Joy ruefully recalled the first time she had called on Darleen to help her through a rough time. She had been sleeping with a female student who'd had a nervous breakdown. After classes one day, Joy returned to her room and found the girl had smeared lipstick all over her walls.

Joy went across the hall to Darleen's room. She was afraid of what would happen to her if the nature of her relationship with the girl got out. "What the hell do I do?" she asked.

"Stop thinking about yourself a minute, Joy," Darleen said. "Think of that poor girl. Tell the administration. You don't have to tell what was going on between you. Just say you are a friend and that she needs help."

"You're right," Joy said.

She followed the advice and the girl did receive treatment and got better. Afterward, she remembered thinking there was a depth to Darleen that other girls at school didn't have.

Joy snapped back to the present. "What do you want me to do, Darleen? You know I'll do anything for you."

"Could you tell the rest of the sisters for me? I tried Aida this morning, but she was out. Still! We started off the evening together, and—"

"God, I guess she'll never grow up."

"Don't forget, I was with her," Darleen replied as if she were exhaling stale air.

"Please tell the others and arrange that we all get together soon. I'm in need of moral support. I know it's terrible, but I don't know whether to cry or cheer."

Joy was silent for a moment, thinking only Darleen could experience such a dilemma. She considered telling Darleen she would bring the champagne but thought better of it. "Of course. Do you want me to stop over after work tonight?"

"Just see if all the sisters can come tomorrow night."

"Okay," Joy said. After a pause, she added, "Darleen, this isn't exactly tactful, but do any news organizations have the story on Mark's death yet?"

"I don't believe so."

"You don't want to talk to the press. Have the public relations people at Mark's company handle all media."

"You're right, Joy. Always thinking ahead. Thanks."

Joy cradled the receiver and picked it up a moment later. She dialed and asked for Hank Thompson.

"Hank, it's Joy. If we don't have an obit on Mark Saunders, work one up. His body was found this morning. He was murdered!

"How did I find out! Sources, my boy. *My* sources."

Business being taken care of, she began calling the others, reaching Deborah's maid and leaving word on an answering machine for Aida and with Samantha's latest guy.

She left the message, "The wicked witch is dead."

Among themselves, they sometimes referred to Mark as the wicked witch who kept the beautiful Darleen locked away in an ivory tower. Naturally, it was a gross exaggeration, but like all whimsical descriptions, it contained hints of truth.

While leaving the messages, Joy wore a smile of satisfaction. She critically examined her body in the floor-to-ceiling mirror on her living room wall. What she saw pleased her.

She ran the palm of her right hand lightly across her nipples and over the patch of blond hair between her legs. She was horny as hell.

But then, wasn't she always?

Joy had turned out to look just like her mother, Karen, a Midwestern farmer's wife. Karen married at sixteen, had Joy a year later, and ran off two years after that.

Joy's father drank when he was angry, and he was always angry. Angry at the land because it got worse and worse. Angry at Joy because she reminded him of his wife. When Joy was twelve, the farm was lost, and her father was a useless drunk. She began making a circuit of living for a few months, sometimes a year, with one relative or another. She came to realize the only person she could trust was herself.

When she reached puberty, Joy became fearful. As the new girl with no one to stick up for her, she was often the victim of boys who tried to feel her and taunt her sexually. Finally, if it were to end, she knew she had to end it.

One afternoon, when she was living with an aunt outside Des Moines, Bobby Hastings, one of the boys who was always grabbing at her, blocked her path as he usually did when he wanted to taunt her. He was sixteen years old and one of the boys other girls talked about as if he were a god. "How's about it, Joy? Why don't you give me what I want."

"What could that be?" she asked coquettishly.

The boy was a little taken aback, because Joy had always cowered before. "Come over to that barn and I'll show you," he said.

"Think you're man enough?" she asked tauntingly.

"I'll show you," he said, and grabbed her arm.

She pulled away from him. "Save your strength," she said.

Once they were in the hayloft, Joy took all her clothes off and stood naked before the boy who was staring at her, his eyes bulging. "Now you," she said.

When he was naked, too, she said, "Now lie down."

The boy flopped down on the hay, giving a little laugh, but he seemed unsure of himself. "C'm'ere, bitch," he said. He didn't notice Joy slip her hand into her school bag as she crawled toward him. When she was next to him, she suddenly placed the point of a hunting knife at his throat. Bobby Hastings was terrified when he looked in her eyes.

"I could kill you," Joy said, her face a mask of rage. "I could kill you, or I could cut your balls off." She slid the knife down his chest, toward his groin. Tommy was afraid to move for fear of what she would do.

"I'm sorry," he said, beginning to cry. "I'll never say anything about you again."

"You bet you won't."

Joy got up and put her clothes on and left. She enjoyed the power she felt over the boy. After Bobby told other students the story of what had happened to him, the jeers and taunts stopped, replaced by looks of fear. But some girls continued making awful comments about her behind her back.

Thus, after the summer in Maine with her aunt and uncle, Joy, quite calculatingly, began seducing the boyfriends of girls who had treated her cruelly. For her, sex became a source of both enjoyment and revenge. Never did she view what she did as wrong. Never did she fall in love, and never did she see her partners as other than people who fulfilled her own needs.

It was a more mature Joy who, three years later, moved in with relatives in Phoenix. She had become discreet in her sexual life. By the time she was a senior in high school, she was sleeping with the teacher who was the advisor for the school newspaper. His status as a teacher coupled with the fact that he was married meant that he would never tell anyone about their liaison.

"You are an unusual young woman," he told Joy one day. "I know you will become a reporter, and a good one, but don't go to journalism school."

"Why not?" she asked.

"You will learn more in your first few weeks on the job than you will taking all the journalism courses a school can offer," he replied. "Your best bet is a liberal arts background. Preferably at an Eastern college."

"Why the East?"

"I think the schools are generally better. And your chances for a scholarship are probably better, too, because you come from here, and they like to diversify their student body."

"Do you have a place in mind?"

"Sarah Lawrence," he said. "It has a reputation for being broad-minded, and you, my dear Joy, are someone who can shock as many people as get to know you. Once you are out of school, work hard for what you want."

Her response to work had become second nature to Joy. She was good at her job and worked hard at her craft long before she arrived in New York to reap the golden rewards of the media capital of the world.

For all her sexual liaisons, Joy never mixed business and pleasure. She could have moved her career along at certain points by sleeping with a ranking executive, and there were plenty who offered her such assistance. But she made up her mind when she entered the business that if she succeeded it would be through her skills on the job, not in bed.

Now, Joy thought of Fire Island. She wished it were Saturday and little Martha was at her beck and call. After all, Mark's death called for a real celebration.

Seven

Maurice Devane, a nervous little man with thinning, mousy hair, was in a suit. Wearing Calvin Klein jeans and a pink polo sweater tied loosely around his neck, he paced back and forth across the drafty Broadway stage, shaking the script angrily first at Paula, and then at Jack. The others in the cast looked on wearily. They had seen it all before.

"No! No! No!" he bellowed to the degree that his falsetto voice allowed.

"For God's sake, we're supposed to be *professionals*! Take it again from where Tony enters and starts his lines. And, if anyone happens to see Aida—We all remember Aida, don't we?—tell her if she misses another rehearsal, I'm going to stick this script up her ass!"

Maurice hadn't seen Aida come up behind him, and he leaped two feet off the floor when she goosed him and yelled, "For Christ's sake, Maurice, I'd let you do it if I thought you could!"

Several members of the cast who witnessed what had happened put their hands to their faces to keep from laughing, and started telling others. Soon, everybody was watching Aida and Maurice.

"Where have you been?" he demanded, snapping out, "Take five, everyone."

She fell into the role of a chastised child, looking down at the floor in shame. A very elegant child, wearing a red Escada jumpsuit with the scarf strung through the epaulet, and low-heeled red pumps from Susan Bennis/Warren Edwards. Her only jewelry was a pair of David Webb earrings.

Maurice was still livid, so she switched to the role of a terrified woman. Reaching out and grasping his hand, she uttered her lines with heart-wrenching earnestness, much like two years ago when she played Stella in *A Streetcar Named Desire*.

"Maurice! Maurice! If you only knew the terrible danger I was in last night. You would eat your anger and talk sweetly to me."

"What happened? What's wrong, my dear?" he asked, suddenly solicitous.

Tony snickered. Then the whole cast laughed aloud.

Maurice's anger relit. "How dare you mock me after walking in late?" He spun around and stormed out.

Aida rolled her eyes. Looking at the rest of the cast, she shrugged and trailed behind him, realizing it would take a while to coax him back into good humor. She needed this play, and the play needed Maurice Devane, one of the best directors in this business, even if he was an ass.

Truth was, she had overslept after being up all night. She remembered leaving Darleen at Palladium with that little sleazebag, probably a queer, who seemed intent on proving he could make it with a woman if he sniffed enough amyl nitrate.

Invariably, Aida blamed her relationship with the sisters when she messed up, and today was no exception. They always, she told herself, expected erratic, irresponsible behavior from her. She argued to herself she just lived down to their expectations. Aida-the-wild-one. Still, it was a role she was tiring of. She would soon be thirty-three. She often felt a hundred three.

But the sisters weren't the real problem. The real problem was Aida's lack of self-esteem. Her childhood had much to do with that. From the moment of conception, Aida was an unwanted child.

Aida had been born in London to a British aristocrat and his strong-willed American wife for whom lovemaking was a passionless chore. Until the age of eight, Aida was permitted to see her mother once a day—at the dinner table. Even then, the rule was that children be seen and not heard. So Aida sat quietly while her father invariably underwent a nightly inquisition by her mother about why he hadn't gotten the promotion, hadn't been invited to the Queen's garden parties, or, most frequently, why he pretended to be lord of the manor when it was her mother's money that supported their grand life-style.

At eight, Aida was sent off to the first of what became a series of boarding schools. For a while, she bloomed. She met a friend, Diane, and they became as close as twin sisters. One afternoon, they went to see the movie *Pollyanna*. "That's me! That's me!" Aida shouted, as Hayley Mills, after being stifled in Jane Wyman's staid, loveless home, got out and won the hearts of people in town—and finally her aunt's heart, too.

After the movie, Aida spoke very seriously to Diane. "Someday, my mother is going to start loving me, just like you love me now."

But that summer, while Aida was at camp, Diane died in a horse-riding accident. No one told Aida until she returned to school. After that, she hid in her room for more than a week. Her parents were called, but they never came. They told the headmistress to handle it. But she couldn't. No one was really able to handle Aida after that.

She bounced from school to school, attending just enough classes to get passing grades. Most often she was alone in her room, playing with dolls or putting on puppet shows—for Diane. The only school activities in which she became involved were school plays; she found she could be somebody else, *any*body else, and pretend Aida didn't exist at all.

When she was fifteen, Aida found another way to forget about herself. Another girl gave her an amphetamine, enough to send Aida over the rainbow to a world without cares, a place where she wanted to stay.

At sixteen, Aida played her first real-life role. The dealer who sold drugs to the kids at her school got busted. A group of students who used drugs sat around in one student's room trying to figure out how they could get a new supply. Several of them knew of another dealer, a South American who was holed up in a hotel near the airport.

"Who's going to make the buy?" a girl asked.

The other students looked uneasily at one another. "I don't know," one of the boys replied. "And after the other dealer got nailed for selling to students, this one won't deal with us directly."

"I'll go," Aida said, looking defiantly around the room. To date, she had never really spoken much to anyone. Her outburst was strange, but the other kids knew how Aida loved drugs.

"You?" asked the boy whose room they were in.

"Oh, Aida," said another girl. "It's crazy for *anyone* to go."

Aida went to her room, and put on a tight sweater and jeans. Stuffing her hair under a bandanna, she put on false eyelashes and heavy makeup accentuating her cheekbones—and making her look ten years older. Twenty minutes later, she returned to the room where the kids were still talking about where they might find drugs.

"Hey," she yelled in a hoarse voice. "You kids know Aida?"

They looked up. "She was here a little while ago. I guess she's in her room."

"Where's that?" Aida asked.

"The next floor up, down at the end of the corridor," another girl said. "Do you want to call her?" a boy asked, pointing to the phone on a table by the door.

"I don't have to," Aida said in her own voice.

"Aida?" asked one of the girls incredulously.

"Yes," she said, taking the bandanna from her head.

"That's great!" a boy said. "You fooled everybody."

"Just the way I'll fool the dealer," she replied. "Now give me the money."

When she arrived at the airport hotel that evening, Aida was already stoned. The dealer took her to his room and let her sample his wares. She was so zonked that, when he fucked her, she didn't even know what was happening—nor did she care. The dealer gave her more drugs than she bought, telling her the rest were for what she had done in bed.

Later that night, she returned to the campus and dispensed drugs to all the kids who had given her money. There was a look of admiration in the eyes of the others that she couldn't fail to notice. That was the first time in years Aida had classmates respond to her, and she began acting crazy. She didn't always get the response she wanted, but anything was better than nothing.

So, when acting—whether on or off the stage—Aida found she could be someone else; she decided to make acting her career. She also found that she could use her body to get drugs and to get men. Several years later, one guy she came on to knocked her up while she was at Sarah Lawrence, and that, of course, led to the formation of her sisters, her only real friends since Diane, years and years ago.

Aida remembered all too well how she met the sisters. Sick and terrified, she had banged on Darleen's door in the dormitory.

When Darleen opened the door, she found Aida collapsed on the floor. Her nightgown was covered with blood. Kneeling down fearfully, Darleen felt Aida's forehead. She was burning up.

"Help!" she screamed.

Several more doors opened and girls—Joy, Deborah, and Samantha, girls Aida saw every day but hardly knew—rushed out of their rooms.

"I think she may be dying," Darleen said. "We have to get her to a hospital."

"Call an ambulance," Joy said.

"No, we've got to take her ourselves," Darleen said. "These local volunteers take forever. She'd be dead by the time they got here."

"But it's after curfew," Deborah said.

"We need a car," Samantha said.

"Who has one?" Joy demanded.

"I do," Deborah said, "but there must be someone we can call."

Darleen looked at her sharply. *"There is no time*. This girl is *dying*!"

"Okay!" Deborah said, her face flushing as she ran into her room and returned with car keys in her hand.

Aida remembered being carried to the car. The sisters reconstructed the rest for her. The race to the hospital went by in a blur. At the emergency room, a young intern took one look at her and rushed her into the operating room.

A nurse asked the others questions about their classmate, and the girls were embarrassed to realize how little they knew about Aida. They couldn't even tell the nurse where Aida was from or if her parents were alive. As they looked at one another, the fact that each of them could be in the same awful position one day dawned on them.

They huddled together in the waiting room. All of them wore worried expressions. They didn't talk, except to make occasional comments that they were sure Aida would pull through.

About an hour later, the doctor came through the large swinging doors leading to the operating room. "Thank God you got your friend here," he said. "Another hour and she wouldn't have made it." Watching their morbid expressions melt away, he smiled and added, "I must be good. I managed to save the baby even though he was only six months along."

"Baby?" Deborah blurted.

Bewildered, the girls looked at one another. Nobody had even noticed that Aida had recently taken to wearing looser clothing. "Don't say anything," Joy whispered.

"When can we see her?" Darleen asked.

"She's still sedated," the doctor replied. "Why don't you come back tomorrow morning?"

"How long will she be here?" Samantha asked.

The doctor looked at them. "She's been through a lot. We'll have to keep her for about two weeks."

After they returned to the dorm, they found they couldn't stop talking about the experience they had shared. Unconsciously, they clung together and stayed up the whole night talking in Darleen's room.

As morning light came through the window in the room, Samantha brought up the likelihood that Aida would have to leave school. "Finals are coming up next week," she said. "Once the administration finds out why she's in the hospital they'll never let her take them."

"I'd hate to see her lose everything," Darleen said. "There must be something we can do."

"There is," Joy said, smiling mysteriously.

"What?" Deborah asked.

"We all have classes with her," Joy said. "We could take her exams. Who would know? They're all take-home exams."

"But it's not right," Deborah said, looking around at the others.

Samantha's eyes locked on Deborah's. Her expression was serious. "What's right isn't always something you can neatly put into categories. Your duty to others may mean doing what society believes is wrong."

"Besides," Joy said, "it'll be fun."

During the following week, each of them took one of Aida's exams. They got together each afternoon and secretly went to the hospital to visit their convalescing classmate. When Aida told them tearfully that she had already signed the papers to give the baby up, each of the girls reacted differently. Joy left the room almost as though she were pretending the baby wasn't real. Samantha accepted the decision with little emotion, simply saying she didn't think Aida had any other choice. Darleen and Deborah both cried and told Aida how sorry they were.

Thirteen days later, the day after Aida was released from the hospital, the girls sat in Aida's room with a bottle of champagne.

To this day, Aida recalled crying the moment she held up her glass and looked around. "This is the first time in my life anyone has helped me. You acted like the sisters I never had. I will do anything for you, anything."

"To the sisters!" cried Deborah.

"Besides," Aida said, starting to smile through her tears, "this is the first time I ever made the dean's list."

As they clicked glasses again, the girls felt closer to each other than they ever had to anyone else. They felt bound by an experience they knew they could never share with outsiders. They had sworn to Aida that they would never tell anyone what had happened. And when she gave up her baby in the hospital, they all felt like they had given up a part of themselves.

As she followed Maurice Devane into his office, Aida vowed to get straight. No more drugs. No more wild times. Work would be her life, and she would try to find true love. She recalled that the sisters had begged her to take such a vow several years ago, when they'd all gone back to Sarah Lawrence for a weekend of nostalgia.

What a weekend. They had stayed at an inn not far from campus, all of them in two connecting rooms, joking and remembering.

During the day, the sisters visited the campus. With its parklike grounds and gracious old stone buildings, Sarah Lawrence looked like an English village. Red and golden leaves blew around them as the women pointed to the top of Westlands Hall, where they all lived when they first met.

"It seems like yesterday," Deborah said.

When they returned to the inn, they began reminiscing. "Remember the time Joy sneaked back into the dorm without a stitch on?" Deborah said. "The dorm counselor saw her creeping bare-assed down the corridor!"

"Thank God, she didn't catch up to me," Joy said in a Mae West voice. "This guy and I were making it on a golf course when some wiseass kids grabbed our clothes and ran off. Thank the Lord he'd left the keys in the car."

Aida leaned back and took a drag on the joint Samantha was passing around. There were several opened bottles of wine on the table, as well as Aida's cocaine. Periodically Aida picked up a straw and inhaled some of the white powder.

"Hey, go easy on the stuff, partner," Deborah said to her.

Looking up bright-eyed, Aida began rattling. "Remember the time Samantha won the bet by going topless to her economics class? That poor teacher almost died of embarrassment!"

"Yeah, he couldn't take his eyes off my boobs," Samantha said.

"What I liked best was that you told him your oriental religion forbids wearing anything above the waist that day," Joy said, howling.

"What about the time we all—with the exception of Darleen, of course—rode around town mooning the locals," Deborah said. "I didn't think I had it in me. God, Darleen, how did you ever put up with us rowdies?"

"I was just amazed that you could bring yourselves to do what you did," Darleen replied. "I was too inhibited to do anything."

Suddenly, Joy shouted. "Whoever had great sex in the past week, stand up!"

They looked at one another. All remained seated. "Just as I suspected," Joy said. "My work schedule is horrendous. What's everybody else's excuse?"

"Well, we all know the plight of our married sisters," Aida said. "Deborah's husband doesn't know how to do it, and

Darleen's coping with that bastard Mark. Me? I just haven't met anybody."

"Same here," Samantha moaned.

"Stop moping! Let's enjoy ourselves like the old days," Joy said. "I know. We'll go to a disco."

"Great idea," Darleen said. "I haven't danced in ages."

The bar they chose was dark, with flashing strobe lights over the dance floor. "These places never change," Deborah said as they sat down and ordered drinks.

Joy pointed across the room at a guy wearing jeans and an open neck shirt. "That's the one I want," she said. "A little cowboy."

"Joy never changes, either," Samantha said, sighing wearily.

"He can't be more than eighteen," Darleen said in disbelief.

"But he has the body of a twelve-year-old," Joy said, with a growl that sent them into spasms of laughter.

A minute later, Aida disappeared into the bathroom. "Two-to-one she's snorting coke in there," Deborah said.

"Different strokes," Joy said, shrugging. "You only live once."

"Is that living?" Darleen asked, but nobody answered her.

For half an hour they danced with one another, except for Joy, who had picked up the cowboy. Suddenly, an hysterical scream rose above the din of the music. Some let out screaming whoops in response.

The sisters looked around and there was Aida. In the dizzying, distorting, flashing lights, she looked like one of the witches from *Macbeth*. Her hair was disheveled and her blouse was ragged and torn. But what was frightening was her face, twisted into a mask that was ferocious and cunning. People on the dance floor backed away as she picked up a beer bottle and smashed it into a strobe light mounted on the wall. She looked like she could kill someone.

"Jesus H. Christ," muttered Joy.

"Grab her. Get her to the car," Darleen said. "I'll pay for the damage."

Twenty minutes later, the subdued group put Aida to bed. The other women went into the next room and shut the door.

"This has gone too far," Deborah said. "We've got to do something, or she'll destroy herself."

Suddenly, they heard piercing screams. "Oh my God," Darleen said, and she ran to open the connecting door. "She's gone!"

They began searching for her. On the ground floor of the inn, Darleen thought she heard muffled sobs. She opened a door leading to the basement, and carefully walked down the darkened stairs. There she found Aida curled up behind the furnace, crying hysterically.

Darleen took Aida in her arms and rocked her like a baby. "It will be all right," she said, softly yet firmly.

Darleen got the others to help Aida back to the bedroom. After putting her to bed, they stayed in the room with her.

"What are we going to do?" Samantha said.

"I'm calling Mark," Darleen said.

Mark arrived less than an hour later. He'd brought a doctor with him, and the doctor called for an ambulance that took Aida to a sanatorium where she went at Mark's expense.

That was the first time any of the sisters really worried about Aida and her drugs. Until then, drugs were considered only as a recreation. A little LSD or Ecstasy to go to a disco. A little grass. A little coke. A little problem, if that. And they were all grateful to Mark Saunders.

Aida remained at the sanitorium for a month. When she checked out, her body was free of drugs, and she hadn't felt so good in years. But ugly reality quickly drove her back into the other world, the one where she wasn't responsible for what she did.

Still, whatever else she was, Aida was a good actress. When she stepped into the office where Maurice was letting off steam, she played the repentant angel.

"Maurice, I don't know how I could have done this to you or the cast. I realize how difficult your job is. You don't need me to give you grief. It won't happen again. Ever."

As she said the words, she realized she wasn't acting. She tried to see where her life was going, and what little she saw scared her to death. She was not only worried about the drugs, but also nearly broke. While other actresses and actors lived in near squalor as they learned their craft, Aida had lived oblivious to money. Now her mother's inheritance was virtually gone. She still had the apartment on East Seventy-fourth Street, but not a great deal more. When she thought about being penniless her breath quickened, and there seemed to be a weight crushing her chest. The weight became suffocating when she thought of Derek Summers, the rising young director who had fallen in love with her. Forever-and-ever love. He'd left her three weeks ago, leaving a void in her life that was an aching loss. He hadn't left her for anyone else, but rather because of the things in her own life that she wouldn't give up. What he said she couldn't give up.

Maurice asked, "Aida, Aida. You have so much promise. Why fuck yourself up like this?"

"Sheer stupidity," she said; finally an answer that made sense.

Maurice eventually let her off the hook with a mere warning.

When Aida returned home, she listened to the message Joy had left on her answering machine. She knew who the "wicked witch" was right away. In fact, she didn't seem surprised. She just shuddered at the thought thàt she had been with Darleen only last night, and what a terrible night that had turned into.

When she called Darleen, however, her voice carried convincing strains of shock. Given her gifts as an actress, it was difficult to tell whether she was sincere.

After the brief phone conversation, Aida paced her apartment fretfully, wishing she had some place to go to take her mind off what was bothering her. She decided to visit Darleen, figuring she owed her sister that much—but dreading seeing her at the same time.

As she stepped from the door of her apartment building, the blast of cold air convinced her to take a cab the few blocks to Darleen's. Climbing into a taxi that had stopped for a red light, she said, "Saunders Tower."

The ride went by in a blur; bad thoughts were whipping about in her mind.

"Holy mackerel," the driver said, interrupting her despair.

"What is it?"

She peered out the window. They were at the great, glittering Saunders Tower. People thronged the entrance, and television crews were everywhere.

"Sure you want out here, lady?"

"No, not really," she said. She paid the fare and got out.

The icy air stung Aida's face as she pushed through the crowd blocking the entrance to the building. At the front door, she was dismayed. The lobby was so jammed with bodies and TV equipment, it looked as if she would never get through.

"Can I help you?" the doorman asked curtly.

"I'm Mrs. Saunders's sister, and I'm trying to get to her apartment."

The message had a magical effect. He became deferential and sidled up to another doorman wearing a similar brown uniform that made them look like they were in the Soviet Army. "I'll be back in a moment, Miss," he said.

As soon as the doorman walked away, a man who had been eavesdropping approached Aida. He was small, thin, and sallow-complexioned. His brown suit seemed several sizes too large, and he had a notebook in his hand. "So you're Mrs. Saunders's sister," he said loudly.

Aida stared straight ahead, stone-faced.

"My name's Rod Wilson," he persisted. "I'm a reporter with the *News*. Tell me, what do you think of the murder?"

Aida's face became ashen. She tried to push past the reporter, but he blocked her way. He was asking her questions and she couldn't focus on what he was saying, as if he were jabbering in a foreign language. Tears filled her eyes and she looked around frantically for a way to escape.

Then other newspeople flocked around her like ants to jam. "Who do you think killed him?" one shouted.

"I heard your sister and Saunders hated each other," a young woman needled.

"Was your sister screwing around?"

"Did she kill him?"

Aida put her hands to her ears and tried to burrow through them. Suddenly, the big doorman firmly took her arm and pushed through the crowd, knocking the reporters aside until she was safely inside one of the elevators.

"Sorry, Miss," he said. "From here on, I'll keep those vultures away from you."

Riding up to Darleen's apartment, Aida felt hot tears streaming down her face. Feeling utterly alone, she began weeping for herself.

Getting off at the penthouse, Aida started walking past a New York policeman, who immediately rose from his seat.

He was big and meaty, and his face expressionless. The

door to the apartment was ajar. "Nobody goes in," he said.

"I'm Mrs. Saunders's sister," she said loudly.

From inside, Darleen called out. "Is that you, Aida?"

"Yes!"

Darleen came to the door. "Let her in, please."

The cop shrugged and backed off. His bored expression said it all. "Whatever you say, Mrs. Saunders," he mumbled.

As soon as Aida entered, she momentarily forgot her own problems. Poor Darleen had circles under her eyes, which were red from weeping. Aida embraced her, but Darleen's arms hung listlessly by her sides.

Suddenly, Darleen's face took on a serious look and she wandered over to the windowed wall and looked out silently. Aida could see that Darleen was struggling to bring up something that she didn't want to face. Aida was certain what it would be and she felt ashamed and panicky. As soon as Darleen spoke, Aida's fears were confirmed.

"Aida, do you know what happened last night?" Darleen asked, barely controlling her emotions. "What happened to *me*?"

Aida let out a soft sigh. There was no way she could say anything that made any sense. That would only screw up her own life even more. That appointment she'd had to keep. The *job* she had. There was no way she could tell Darleen without fucking things up for her, too.

"For Christ's sake, we're all adults, Darleen," she replied irritably. "I don't know what happened. I'm not your guardian angel."

Darleen flushed. "I'm not suggesting you should be. But I can't remember anything from the time you left me until I woke up this morning."

"All I know is, I left Palladium about eleven thirty and you were dancing with those gay guys we met," Aida said.

Frustrated, Darleen held her hands to her temples. "That's the last thing I remember, too." She looked sick as she continued in an anguished voice, "I woke up this morning in SoHo with a man. I have no idea who he was. Or how long I was with him. Or what I did . . ."

Aida put her arms around Darleen. "Maybe I wasn't much of a friend leaving you there alone. But don't ever feel guilty for being unfaithful to Mark. He got exactly what he deserved!"

Aida said hotly, her face contorted into a mask of hatred.

Darleen looked at her in shock. "My God, did . . . did *you* kill him?" she asked Aida.

Aida caught herself and calmed down. "Are you crazy? Of course not," she answered. "Did you?"

"I just told you, I don't remember a lot about last night." Suddenly she looked shocked. "I . . . I suppose I could have."

Aida put her hand on Darleen's shoulder. "Look, I'm sorry I said what I did, but this has me unnerved, too. But for God's sake, don't tell the police that you are drawing a complete blank on last night." She started buttoning her coat and added, "I've got to run, but Joy said something about you having the sisters over tomorrow? Do you think you're up to it?"

"Yes, I want everybody here."

"Okay," Aida said, bending over and kissing Darleen's cheek. She stopped and looked curiously at her friend. "After the way he treated you, why were you faithful to him?"

Darleen shrugged. "Look, I know as well as anyone what Mark was like. It's just that, as long as I remained married to him, I didn't take the institution lightly. Even though my marriage was a sham, marriage to me means you behave certain ways."

When Aida left the elevator, the crowd of journalists in the lobby had thinned, but as she made for the front door she ran smack into superanchor and fellow sister Joy. Both were taken by surprise. They hugged without much feeling.

"I didn't expect to find you here with the riffraff," Aida said. "I didn't think you ever left the studio."

"Oh, sure I do," Joy groaned. "On this story, I'm, uh, close to the news."

Aida looked at the beautiful little blonde and shook her head cynically. "Anything for a story, eh, Brenda Starr?"

"Oh, cut the crap," Joy said. "Actually, I'm surprised you're here."

Aida glanced around nervously. "Why?"

"When I heard that Mark was murdered, I said to myself, Aida finally did it."

"You're nuts," Aida hissed.

"Well, you did hate him," Joy said tauntingly.

"I hated him," Aida said tearfully. "But I always thought

you hated him more than I did. Did you kill him?"

Joy stared at Aida as if she were out of her mind. Turning, she motioned to her sound man. "Charlie, let's pack it in. I already have an interview with the grieving widow. I'm not going to wait in this lousy lobby all day just to catch her if she runs out."

"Don't evade me, Joy," Aida said, softly but persistently. "You hated Mark as much as I did, but for a very different reason."

"And what would that be?" Joy said icily.

"Because he got *Darleen*."

Joy flushed slightly and started walking away. "You don't know what you're saying."

Aida laughed. "C'mon, Joy. You've been in love with Darleen since school. We all saw how you reacted when Mark came into her life. Now tell me. Did *you* kill him?"

Joy spun around; she glanced from side to side to see that no one overheard them. The chilling look of menace on her face was so intense that Aida actually took a step backward. "Don't fuck with me, Aida, if you know what's good for you," she said quietly.

Eight

Diego "Cookie" Garcìa propped the satin pillows behind his head. Feeling like he wasn't there even as her tongue licked him, he remembered a friend who had been a Marine in Vietnam and had told Cookie about a prostitute eating a bowl of rice while he was screwing her. Cookie now knew how the girl could eat dinner while fucking and enjoy the meal more.

Cookie had business cards that said he was a dog walker. He joked that he was really a dog fucker. In the past year and a half, he'd screwed so many of these human pooches that he couldn't remember what they were like, let alone their names. And not all of them were dogs.

The one going down on him now, for instance, was some looker.

He looked around the large ornate bedroom from the canopied George IV poster bed; the room was decorated in yellow and lavender. There was a gilt Louis XVI desk, a velvet Victorian love seat, a silk oriental rug, and a Monet hanging on the wall.

The sharp scrape of teeth interrupted Cookie's mental wanderings. "Hey, take it easy, bitch!" he ordered.

Deborah Bartley, summa cum laude, Sarah Lawrence class

of '75, city councilwoman representing the Upper East Side Silk Stocking district, looked up, breathing hard, beads of sweat on her brows and breasts. Her eyes narrowed.

"Don't *ever* call me that!"

Cookie's first impulse was to slap her, let her know who was boss. But this one was worth coddling a little. She reminded him of Wonder Woman. She appeared short and gawky with her glasses, bangs, black hair pulled back in a bun, and boxy suits. But when she let her hair and clothes down, she was something else. And all he had to do was touch her tits or ass or pussy and she'd melt like hot wax.

Deborah could feel his contempt and flinched. Why did she let a tough little kid like Cookie call her a bitch? Why did she fantasize about making love to guys like this on trains and planes? Never knowing who they were, not even their names. Just wanting them to touch her. To lie with her. To bring her to the edge of ecstasy.

She didn't like to probe why. When she did she was ashamed. But even the shame was thrilling. Stimulating. Sometimes, at city council meetings, her mind wandered over such boys—and she felt herself moisten between her legs.

For Deborah Bartley, Cookie was a one-hour-a-week diversion and necessity. Not him, really, but anyone like him. Straightforward sex for money. No chance of love. No chance of involvement.

Except for her psychiatrist, she didn't tell anybody about her liaisons. Not even the sisters. This was nobody's business but her own.

Cookie reached up and gently twisted her around, pulling her under him. "Hey," he said softly. "You were hurting my money machine, you know?"

Deborah half-listened to the little shit. Her body trembled as she choked back a sob. She was so hot now he could call her anything and she wouldn't care. She slid up his body, her tongue licking his sweaty skin, her teeth biting his nipples, her nails digging into his buttocks.

This boy was good. Sometimes she could get him to go on and on and on until she was in ecstasy, the real world obliterated from her mind.

She had found his name in the Yellow Pages. Someone to

walk Stephen's Afghan, which in turn was later part of the divorce settlement.

But the first time Cookie walked into her apartment, swinging his hips in those tight jeans like he'd just stepped out of a porn flick, Deborah spotted the kid for what he was. She also intuitively knew he spelled danger, and she made a feeble attempt not to succumb to her lust.

"You," a psychiatrist had once told her, "worked so hard, yet you don't feel you deserve your success. Your flirtation with sexual danger is a way of threatening your career, assuaging your guilt. Your father told you women should never have a career, and part of you still believes that, and seeks punishment."

The psychiatrist made her work through why she submitted to personal humiliation. She had a strong religious background that went haywire. Her father, Saul, was a rabbi who was harsh on himself and his family. It was unnatural the way he spent so many hours praying on his knees with tefillin wrapped around his arms, cutting into his flesh. It was equally unnatural the way he punished her—whipped her, in fact—if she even looked at a boy.

Deborah thought of her father and felt waves of anger and humiliation. Always talking of women and their bodies, he called all women vile. Each Saturday, she had to stand behind a screen in the back of the synagogue while her father went through the rituals of prayer. At home, he went into rages, beating her and calling her, "Slut! Whore!"

She resented her mother, who stood by her husband no matter how strange his rantings, never shielding Deborah from the old man's wrath. Sex was always on his mind—and soon it was always on Deborah's. And sex became associated with degradation.

Deborah escaped her household through her Uncle Sammy, who made a fortune in the fur trade. As a young man, Sammy went to the other extreme from his brother, Saul, and renounced his religion. Tall, heavyset and self-assured, Uncle Sammy yelled at Saul for the way he treated his daughter. Whenever he could, Sammy had Deborah to his house and bought her stylish clothes, not the pathetic clothing that she was forced to wear at home that hid her arms and legs.

He also took her to political meetings, where she got to know powerful people and accepted the compromises political figures always lived with. Unbeknownst to her parents, she was a volunteer in various city political campaigns. She fell in love with politics and set her ambitions on making it her life.

Her uncle also articulated a philosophy that made sense to her after what she had been through. A cynical man, Sammy told her one day, "Your father is an example of how religion creates madmen. All religions are barbaric and crazy."

He told her he was a Zionist, but that didn't mean he had to be religious. "I'm a Zionist out of self-preservation," he said. "I look like a Jew, and because of this there are people who would like to kill me. Because of this craziness, which is just another religious craziness, I must protect myself. Zionism is one way to do that, because it means Jews can live without fear."

Besides the introductions to power brokers, Sammy explained the roles of the political leaders, the shadow men who supported them, and the pawns they used. "Politics is life with all its goodness, compromises, and evils," Sammy said. "It *is* life—only more so."

Sammy paid for Deborah's tuition at Sarah Lawrence. Once at school, she never returned home, feeling she had escaped her father forever. "I will have a career," she shouted at her father when she left. "I'm going to be President of the United States, and not you or anyone will dare stop me!"

After law school she married, and then came to feel that she hadn't escaped her father at all. His mark on her seemed indelible.

In retrospect, she thought she had married Stephen Bartley because he fit in nicely with her career. He was wealthy and preoccupied with his work, which gave her the wherewithal to spend both the kind of money and time she needed to move ahead in the realm of New York politics.

With Stephen, there was no chance of love, no involvement. He was a decent sort, but he knew next to nothing about women. All he knew how to do was make money. Deborah called him an "idiot savant of stocks." A powerful man on Wall Street, he was head partner of the brokerage house of Bartley Wade & Stephens. He was courted by foreign ministers, and by sheiks, and by an adviser to the White House, but then his reputation on the street wasn't indicative of the rest of his life—or even of the way he looked.

Mr. Average. Average height. Average looks. Average intelligence. Horn-rimmed glasses. Blue-striped suits and boring as hell. But nice. And Deborah cared about him.

Early in their marriage she'd had several affairs, but they had been disastrous. Emotions. Jealousies. Petty garbage that she couldn't stand. Besides, their circle was relatively small—and very indiscreet. If she had continued in such a fashion, Stephen would inevitably have found out. She didn't want to hurt him.

One day she was talking to her uncle about how unsatisfactory her sex life was. Sam was the most tolerant man she knew, and his advice had always proved sound. But this time, she thought he was going too far.

"Look," he said. "There's no sense in being frustrated just because your husband's no good in the sack. Go out and buy a guy."

Deborah laughed. But her uncle simply looked at her and shrugged. "Look, Deb. You wouldn't be the first Upper East Side lady to come up with that solution." He paused. "But if you decide on that," he resumed, "be *very* discreet. Never do anything that would blow your political career."

As usual, Sammy was right. The only sexual satisfaction she found was in tawdry encounters with young men for hire, such as "Fast Eddie" Tremaine, the out-of-work actor who passed himself off as a foot masseur and mostly worked the chic hotels and apartment buildings along Central Park South. Handsome Eddie with the golden hair did your feet for thirty-five dollars, and the rest of you for a bigger tip.

The first time Deborah bought a boy was in Palm Beach. One of the more ironic sides of the venture was that it was set up by Veronica Houghton, née Veronica Bartley, Stephen's sister. Deborah and Veronica had become good friends and had taken a vacation together.

Tall and willowy, her black hair cut in a page boy, Veronica was a model of decorum. No bikini for her; she wore a maillot that demurely covered her body. She sat in the sun with Deborah, talking and reading magazines and coolly ignoring the advances of men who occasionally tried to stop and chat.

At dinner the first night, Veronica stunned Deborah when she said, "Listen, Deb, I know Stephen isn't exactly Valentino."

"And how do you know that?" parried Deborah.

"He dated my roommate at Wellesley for the better part of a year," she replied. "A nice boy who doesn't know why God gave him a penis is the somewhat crude way she expressed her sentiments."

Deborah burst out laughing. "Well, I have to admit there's something to that."

"Frank is something of the same sort," Veronica said, referring to her husband, Francis John Houghton, a partner at Stephen's firm. "Perhaps it has something to do with the business. All the bulls and bears running out of steam on the Street instead of in their bedrooms."

"Okay," admitted Deborah. "Our sex life leaves a lot to be desired. But what can we do?"

"Well, there is a way to enjoy yourself—ourselves—and nobody has to be the wiser," Veronica said.

Looking down at Deborah's stricken face she laughed. "For God's sake, Sweetie, I'm not suggesting lesbianism, if that's what it sounded like. Have you noticed some of the beautiful boys around the pool and the beach—"

"Have I ever!" Deborah said. "They're gorgeous."

"They're also available . . . for a price. Follow me."

When they returned to their suite, Veronica made a quick and surreptitious phone call from the living room, and a few minutes later there was a soft rap at the door. Veronica opened it and led in two of the handsomest boys Deborah had ever seen. Copper-colored, muscular, with gleaming teeth, thick black hair, and dark eyes.

Veronica simply took one by the hand and led him into her bedroom. The other led a stunned but delighted Deborah into hers. Within minutes he had stripped off her clothes and was naked beside her in bed.

The rest of the night was largely a blur of the best sex Deborah had ever had. The only thing she remembered was a naked Veronica walking into her room and taking her boy away, but her momentary disappointment evaporated when the other boy walked through the door as a replacement.

When she awoke the next morning, the whole experience seemed like a wildly erotic dream. Only when Veronica called her for breakfast, which room service had delivered, did she believe it was real. There was Veronica, sitting at the table smiling like the Cheshire Cat and, when she looked in the mirror, Deborah realized she was, as well.

There had been other trips to Palm Beach, and she wasn't frustrated at home. Veronica gave her the phone numbers of several youths, including Fast Eddie. Deborah kept her liaisons to Thursday afternoons when the maid was off, and tried to be discreet.

There was always the potential for danger in such trysts, and twice she had been afraid. The first bad encounter was in Palm Beach, where a boy turned on her and beat her with his fists until she gave him a thousand dollars. The second occasion, she believed, was even worse.

His name was Tim, and he was one of the youths Veronica passed along. The trouble arose when he recognized her from her picture on a campaign poster from two years ago. After they'd had sex he had gotten out of bed, and the next thing she knew, he was standing at the foot of the bed snapping photographs of her sprawled there.

"What are you doing?" she demanded.

"Just taking pictures of one of the ladies running for city council," he said laughing.

When she tried to grab the camera away from him, he shoved her away. "I'll let you buy them off me," he said. "If you don't want them, I'm sure these photos will be worth a lot of dough to somebody else. Maybe *Penthouse*."

Deborah knew that she was between a rock and a hard place. "How much?" she asked dully.

"Five thousand," he said.

"I need a few days," she muttered. "Now get your ass out of here."

After the boy left Deborah started to panic but caught herself. She was as sure that this boy would continue to bleed her as she knew that her husband was impotent. Calculatingly, she thought of someone who could help. When she was still a child, her good old Uncle Sammy had introduced her to a man who, she later learned, could fix anything. He was always around City Hall, quietly talking to deputy mayors and council members. Ostensibly a go-between for the construction unions, Nicky D'Angelo, she knew, was an ambassador for the Mafia.

Deborah didn't trust the phones. The next morning she saw him in the ground floor hallway of City Hall Annex. Catching up with him, she touched his arm. "Do you have a minute, Mr. D'Angelo?" she asked.

An enormously fat man, he had slit eyes and was bald as a baby's ass; his looks had earned him the apt nickname Dago Buddha. He assumed a slight air of surprise when he saw who she was. "Ah, Deborah. How is Sammy? Does he want to see me?"

"Uncle Sammy is fine," she said. "*I'm* the one who wants to talk to you."

Deborah nervously told him she had a problem that she would like to take to the police, but unfortunately there were too many complications, so she could not. She didn't explain the nature of the problem, but she gave just enough information for him to draw his own conclusions.

D'Angelo's face was impassive. "You sure you want this?"

Deborah steeled herself, although she felt the perspiration running in rivulets between her breasts. She wasn't going to let anyone stand in the way of her career. *No one,* she told herself. "Absolutely," she heard herself reply coolly.

The would-be extortionist subsequently disappeared without a trace, and Deborah knew that, sooner or later, Nicky D'Angelo would want the debt repaid. And although Deborah realized what a close call she'd had, she returned to boys for hire after she assumed office. She paid the hustlers well to keep their mouths shut. Nevertheless, when Stephen had heard the rumors last year from Mark Saunders, he had left her. He was shocked and too much of a gentleman to say anything about her in public.

She wished she could have said the same about Mark, whose threat had been hanging over her like a guillotine.

Deborah got out of bed and pulled on a robe. She knew Cookie could be dangerous. The doorman had seen him coming in too often and was smirking. She didn't need any more

rouble. She went to a wall safe and opened it. Taking out two
ne-hundred-dollar bills, she placed them on the bed.

"Cookie, I can't see you anymore, but it has been lovely."

Just then, the telephone rang. By the time she got to it,
here was a message on her answering machine. She, too,
new who the "wicked witch" was, and she couldn't have
een happier knowing he was dead. Once again, she had
lodged another head-on collision. . . .

Nine

While Deborah was on the phone, Cookie crammed the money into his jeans pocket and prepared to leave. He was pissed off. Now he had to drum up a new client. He hated the real old ones. *Man, who wants to get into bed with a sack of bones, even if they pay more?*

He also hated being tossed out like a used rubber. *These rich bitches want and get everything,* he thought bitterly.

He noticed that the wall safe was still open. He reached in and grabbed the rest of the money and a manila envelope which he shoved under his shirt.

Safely back on the street, Cookie reflected on how crazy his life had gotten. He'd started out as a dog walker, dealing a little dope on the side. But then he'd found that a lot of ladies were more interested in what he could do for them than for their animals.

That was okay with him. He hated the fucking dogs. Instead of walking them, he used to go to an arcade on Lexington Avenue and tie them outside while he played the video games. Once, when he had six real expensive dogs out at the same time, he thought about selling them, making a quick buck, and splitting for Puerto Rico and looking up his old man. That was after a cop hassled him for not picking up dog shit. Fuck them.

Then, one day, this woman started coming on to him when he brought her dog back. Not bad, either. About thirty. Tall and thin, like Jackie O. She was wearing a red silk robe and he could tell from the way her nipples pointed through it that she was naked underneath. She offered him a drink and he gave her a little weed. The next minute they were in the sack. And he was fifty dollars richer.

Sex was never a big deal with him. Money was. He'd first gotten laid when he was thirteen. There was nothing special about it. He'd been drunk or stoned or both; he couldn't remember the girl.

What he liked about what he did now was being able to buy whatever he wanted. And the gifts. Man, some women gave him clothes, watches, gold necklaces. One old bag wanted to take him to Europe. But what the hell would he want to go over there for?

Some of the broads were stoned crazy. He slapped some of them around and they asked for more. One woman had him beat her ass with a hair brush. No sex. Just that. Weird.

He got off on the power trip as much as on the money. As a kid, he would see his mother coming home exhausted after cleaning, cooking, and washing for bitches like these. He thought he was paying them back. He didn't realize he was just another part of the service industry working for tips.

Even so, he knew he was fucking over their old men. Their husbands were the kinds of guys who saw him as Puerto Rican lowlife. He wished the jerk-offs could see their wives balling a Spic they wouldn't let in their fuckin' offices except to empty the wastebasket. And paying their hard-earned money for it.

Whenever he could, he stole the business cards of the men whose wives he screwed. Someday he'd send each of the cocksuckers a letter.

Dear Mr. So-and-So,

Because of inflation and rising business costs, my fee for fucking your wife has gone up.

Sincerely,
Cookie the Spic

Someday he was going to score big off these rich shits. He'd already sold stolen keys to some of their apartments to Fernando Rivera and his gang of burglars. But that was bull- shit. No. One day, he'd hit the big time.

Ten

Six men, dressed in black, uttered the same bloodcurdling yell as they tore across the room, feet and arms flying, intent on destroying the seemingly frail woman cowering in front of them.

Cowering? Looks can be deceiving. Samantha Kwan, ninth-degree karate black belt, was coiled, ready to explode. Like a heat-seeking missile, she attacked, finding chins, throats, and groins of her adversaries. The men fell to the floor like logs felled from a tree.

It was over in an instant, but the onlooker, an elderly Chinese man, had seen more than enough. All this had been staged for his benefit.

The tattered attackers were his foot soldiers.

Untouched, Samantha Kwan bowed respectfully before her elder.

Looking at her intently, the man said, "You are ready. Did you realize what would have happened to you if you had failed the test?"

"I would not be allowed to complete my mission. My life would have been lived in vain," she replied, her serious countenance unchanging, her black eyes unblinking as she stared back.

"You will succeed," the old man said, his tone, not his face, betraying the confidence he felt.

"You are most kind, Uncle."

She lowered her head, but he immediately placed a finger under her chin and raised her head. "These years have been hard on you," he said. "For the honor of your house, you have sacrificed much of the kind of life a woman should lead."

As she shook her head in protest he raised a hand to silence her. "The coming years will be harder yet. In this country, they do not understand us. They view us as criminals, but they don't understand the harmony of nature. There cannot be good without bad. Order without disorder. Justice without injustice. The yin and the yang. We are all those things and more."

Samantha knew well how the Triads were perceived in America. In college, she once did a term paper on them for a political science course. Her research included a State Department dossier entitled "The Criminal Triads" that examined the powerful tongs in Hong Kong and, by focusing on one of the major families, the Kai-chungs, unintentionally shed some light on her background. Her family's fall from power had occurred about twenty years ago:

The Kai-chung Triad dates back about 1,000 years. For centuries, this Triad was one of the most powerful in China. The armies fielded by this house rose to power during the Ming dynasty (1368–1644) and were instrumental in expelling the Mongol Yuan dynasty and unifying all of China proper. When Western influences made themselves known at the Ming court, the Kai-chungs prospered through controlling the entry of foreign goods into China. Through the centuries, that has been their primary occupation. Clandestinely, they forced payment of all foreign companies trading in China. Those that tried to avoid such payment were victimized by pirates controlled by the Kai-chungs. They were also involved in the opium trade and prostitution. Twenty-two years ago, the three brothers who were the heads of the Triad were assassinated by the Chan

Triad. The rest of the immediate family was also murdered, including children. Only a daughter escaped. Her whereabouts are unknown.

The cold facts of the paper made Samantha vividly recall that night, dwelling often on the details so that she could never forget. It was known among the remaining Kai-chungs as "the night of terror." Her parents had awakened her in their palatial home in Hong Kong, and brought her to a room in a seedy hotel near a wharf, where they sat waiting. Though sleepy, she understood bits and pieces of their hushed conversations. Most of her aunts, uncles, and cousins were dead. It was a tong war. They must flee or die.

Her father arranged passage on a ship leaving within hours. "We must stay here until it is time to go," he said.

Suddenly, the door of their room crashed in. A man dressed in black head-to-toe rushed at her father with a knife. Her father kicked him in the stomach and smashed him across his skull. There was the pounding of feet racing up the stairwell.

"Hide her," her father yelled at her mother.

Her mother hastily put a jade ring on Samantha's finger, kissed her, and led her to a hole in the wall. "Get in," she ordered, and shoved Samantha through the dark hole. On the other side, Samantha found herself in another dilapidated room. She stayed crouched in the dark, staring through the hole. Other men dressed in black rushed in. Three of them grabbed her father. One pulled a black hood over his face. Two held him, while the third took a knife and slashed his throat. Then they seized her mother and dragged her from the room. Samantha's memory after that was a blank, and she thought that she must have fainted.

That was Samantha's introduction to the Chans. Later, she learned that her mother had been forced to become a concubine of one of the Chans, and finally she had killed herself. Samantha herself had been found by her uncle, who secretly trained her body and mind in the martial arts, telling her she must prepare for the day when she would become head of the Kai-chungs and make the family powerful again.

Looking up at her uncle now, Samantha felt the weight of history on her shoulders.

"Now that you are about to become the leader of the Kai-chung Triad," he said, "you will never have the opportunity to live like other women."

"There is no other way, Uncle," she replied.

"Yes, and now we must act quickly in light of what you told us about the real estate venture the Chans entered in conjunction with Saunders. It would make them perhaps too powerful to stop later."

"That deal will never come about," Samantha said decisively.

"Will Saunders pose a problem?"

"No," she replied grimly. "Mark Saunders will not be a problem."

Samantha Kwan, née Sung Ling Kai-chung, had been something of a mystery at Sarah Lawrence. Her name was changed when she came to the United States as a student, and none of the girls knew her real name—or even that she had another name. The only memento she had of her childhood was a jade ring chiseled in the shape of a dragon.

A face like a porcelain figurine, she had appeared one day in the middle of sophomore year as though she had been born that day. Other girls quickly learned that the past was taboo with her. She talked vaguely of a home in Hong Kong—but never of a family.

She was brilliant, but she seemed to deliberately refrain from displaying her intelligence, almost as a way of not calling attention to herself. Occasionally, a Rolls-Royce appeared that carried an Oriental man, sometimes two, and she disappeared with them for hours before she returned, and the men sped away to where they'd come from. She called them uncles, but never with the slightest hint of affection.

There were two reasons why the other students were in awe of her. All the students knew about the first: her martial arts expertise. Few, if any, of the girls had ever seen a woman who had mastery of such skills. The second reason, known only by the sisters and by her lovers, was Samantha's remarkable sex-

ual appetite. That was why Joy came to know her before the
rest of the sisters.

Unbeknownst to each other, Joy and Samantha were both
sleeping with a young English professor who had a reputation
as a stallion in the sack, which Joy took full advantage of.
One day, he told Joy he had to stop seeing her because another
girl had totally exhausted him. Intrigued, Joy wormed it out of
him that it was the beautiful Oriental student who was ex-
hausting him. "She's even more phenomenal than you, Joy,"
he said with a laugh.

Coming home from the martial arts trial, Samantha was
surprised to find Aida waiting for her on the front steps of the
grimy former factory that contained her SoHo loft. She wondered if anything was wrong. She hadn't seen her for weeks,
although they talked on the phone, no matter how briefly, just
about every few days.

Indeed, Samantha realized at that moment that she hadn't
seen any of the sisters for quite a while.

The two women hugged warmly.

"Thank God you're here," Aida said.

"Is anything wrong?"

"Mark Saunders is dead. Killed!"

Outwardly, Samantha accepted the news calmly. But her
stoicism was only a mask. In death as in life, Mark Saunders
produced a strong emotion in Samantha.

"How's Darleen taking it?" she asked Aida. "Have you
talked with her?"

"God, yes. She's taking it well—and weirdly. I went over
to her apartment before coming here."

"What do you mean by weirdly?"

Aida's face burned with shame, but she finally exhaled a
deep breath. "Look, I know she's been through a lot with him,
but—but he put everyone else through a lot, including me.
But still . . ."

Samantha didn't press the issue. She touched Aida's arm
sympathetically. The small gesture had a soothing effect.

"I'm afraid to go to my apartment tonight," Aida said
softly. "There was this guy who came over and he was a
creep. . . ."

Aida started shaking when she thought of Mad Manny.
He came two nights ago shortly after she'd called him.
Black and skinny, he wore tight black pants and a ruffled
black shirt and gold chains. His sloped face and flat nose
gave him a snake-like appearance. He was called Mad
Manny because he would burst into crazy, hysterical giggles
for no apparent reason.

A girl was with him. Spanish and in her early twenties, she
had a fine bone structure, and her black hair was streaked with
blond. She could have been beautiful, except for the deadness
of her eyes, the puffiness of her face, and a dusty complexion
—sure signs of a junkie. She was introduced as Marie; her
voice was soft and refined. She wore short white boots, a red
leather miniskirt, and a white silk blouse open to the navel
beneath a raccoon coat.

"Marie'll do anything for ol' Manny. Won't you, Marie?"
Manny said.

The girl nodded slowly.

Manny opened a leather briefcase and took out a vial of
cocaine. He made three lines on the glass top of a coffee table
in Aida's living room. Aida took a gold straw and quickly did
one of the lines. Then she did another.

"Shall I let you have one?" Manny asked the girl.

"Yes," Marie replied.

"Then you be good to me," he said.

Manny unzipped his fly. The girl took off her coat and, as
Aida watched with a mixture of horror and fascination, she
took off her blouse. Her breasts were full and pointed slightly
toward the outer sides. She yanked up her miniskirt and knelt
before Manny, her head going between his legs while her
body was turned toward Aida.

After the lines, Aida saw what was happening with a
heightened awareness, but she pretended not to care. Now
awake and talkative, she found herself chattering, telling
Manny about the new play while he stared at her contemp-
tuously.

She left them in the living room and went to take a shower,
hoping hot water would somehow cleanse her of what she'd
witnessed. As the water soothed her, the drug wore off, and
she resolved to change her life before it was too late. She

didn't hear the bathroom door open, or the shower curtain being pulled back. Suddenly, Mad Manny, naked, stepped into the shower with her. His hands were rough and bony as he grabbed her and shoved fingers between her legs.

Aida began screaming. "No! Go away!"

She twisted away from him and ran to her bedroom. As he pounded on the locked door, she picked up the telephone and dialed the police emergency number. Manny picked up the extension in the living room while the police were asking for her name and address. "You gonna come to me one day," he hissed into the receiver. "You gonna come to me and I'll deal with you then." Then he laughed crazily.

The door slammed a moment later. About ten minutes passed before the police arrived. Ten minutes during which Aida tried to be lucid. Hide the cocaine. Think of a story.

The police were sympathetic, so her story went smoothly. She told them she had noticed a man on the elevator but thought he was delivering something. No, she didn't see him get off on her floor. Yes, it was possible that she had left her apartment door unlocked.

Now Aida looked at Samantha.

"Darleen actually asked me if *I'd* killed Mark."

Samantha looked at her so cooly, Aida almost cried. "Sam! Not you, too?"

"One thing I've learned, Aida, is all of us are capable of doing just about anything."

"Including murder?"

"Perhaps."

"And you think I had a good motive," Aida said angrily.

"Perhaps we all did."

An hour later, Samantha used the key John Ming had given her to his apartment in the West Village. A thirty-five-year-old fashion photographer, Ming had met Samantha at *Chanèle* magazine, where she worked as an illustrator. She had liked him immediately. He was neither the typical swaggering macho asshole photographer, who saw his camera as an extension of his cock, nor a fluttering fag who thought he was artistic and wanted to turn women into mannequins. Only later did she find out he was a member of the Kai-chungs.

John had listened intently when she explained what she wanted, asked knowledgeable questions, and made a few suggestions that could make the shoot better. He had treated Samantha like an equal, which in the fashion world was as rare as finding someone who wasn't into kinky sex. He had that on his side, too.

John was asleep in the bedroom when Samantha poked her head in. A sheet covered him from the waist down, but his stone-etched torso was exposed. That was another factor that attracted her. He was in terrific shape.

She went into the kitchen and made tea, bringing it back into the bedroom. She sipped from her cup while swaying slightly in a rocking chair near the bed and staring at the man lying there. Samantha had only been in love once. Or thought she had been. As she got older, she didn't want to make that mistake again. The pain was too great. But she cared for Ming more than any man she had ever known. Not out of love. A large part of her feeling was based on their strong sexual attraction, and looking at him made her grow horny.

Often, after karate workouts, she felt a surging sexual desire. And today's, of course, had been more than just a workout. So much had depended on how well she did. She needed a release from the morning's tension.

Walking over to the bed, she gently lifted the sheet off the sleeping man. With her jade ring, she delicately scraped his flaccid penis, which immediately responded to her touch.

"I didn't hear you come in," he said groggily.

She moved closer to him. "Take off my clothes," she whispered. It wasn't a request but a command.

Suddenly he was awake, his fingers swiftly slipping over her clothing. Her silk blouse drifted down over her shoulders revealing small, firm breasts. Her pants slid lower, showing her small waist and slim, powerful thighs.

He led her onto the bed and high on his chest, his tongue darting between her thighs. She felt herself go wobbly. The hunger surged through her—consuming her as it always did.

"Enough," she groaned.

She inched down his body, climbing on top of his cock and surrounding it. At once, their bodies began pulsating as one.

Stretching every muscle, Samantha looked like a series of artist's sketches for a sculpture. As always, all else was obliterated. The old men, their money, the dark memories from long ago, the heat of the hatred and revenge—Mark Saunders.

Ming always wondered where she went in her sexual ecstasy. He never asked, and he never would.

Eleven

Tony Dragonetti thought he was losing his fucking mind. As the executive vice president of Minotaur Development Corporation, he needed time to think, and he didn't have it. And, he was afraid he'd never get it.

He sat in his forty-sixth-floor office with a Dow Jones ticker to one side of his walnut desk, an eight-foot-high American flag on the other. He stared out the window looking as if King Kong were about to grab him from outside, then he glanced at his telephone, which was blinking like cop-car red lights. The goddamn calls were pouring in like bums to free booze.

Ever since the word had gotten out that somebody had used his boss to demonstrate what a mess gravity can make, Dragonetti had been in his office answering the phone. Contractors demanded reassurance that their projects were still on. Real estate agents swore Saunders had given them handshake deals on property that, overnight, had mysteriously proceeded to quadruple in value. A couple of shits who were buying apartment buildings that were almost completed wanted a cheaper price.

"Life's a motherfucker and then you die," he muttered.

A compact man of forty-seven, Tony Dragonetti took life seriously. And he took Mark Saunders's death fucking seriously. He wished to God he knew what was going to happen next. His sallow face, big, sad eyes and pencil-thin mustache gave him the look of an overworked French waiter.

Dragonetti was dressed corporate Common Market: conservative blue suit, Countess Mara tie, Bally loafers. He had blow-dried hair, a diamond pinky ring, an ex-wife, four ex-children, and a stomach that paid him back for every rotten thing he'd ever done. The bottle of Maalox in his desk drawer was as big as a camp-size mayonnaise jar.

"No more calls, Betty!" he screamed out to a twenty-year-old girl sitting at a desk outside his office. She was dressed in a black blouse and skirt and stockings with black flowers running up the side. Her lipstick was black, her mascara blue, and orange streaked her black hair. But her face shone through with the prettiness of a young Elizabeth Taylor.

Dragonetti hadn't hired her for her brains, and now he wished he had a secretary who knew what the fuck a secretary was supposed to do. She was funneling every goddamn call to him if they mentioned his name. And a lot, he was sure, who didn't. "I don't care if it's the fucking President. Except for Fitzgerald, no more calls!" he bellowed.

Fitzgerald was the shrewdest real estate lawyer in town, and Dragonetti wanted to hear from him. Fitzgerald would have a feel for the fallout from Mark's death—especially with regard to the other real estate princes who, as far as Dragonetti was concerned, owned New York—lock, stock, and judges. With Mark now dead and Emmanuel incapacitated, would this handful of sharks devour Minotaur Development?

Plucking a Valium from the ashtray on his desk, he gulped it down with water from a stainless carafe.

"Hey!" Betty shouted. "You can't go in there."

The office door flew open and Sullivan and Mays strode in, flashing their badges. "I'm Detective Sullivan and this is Detective Mays." Mays was wearing a dark brown Armani leather jacket, blue satin shirt, cream-colored slacks, and cowboy boots.

Dragonetti couldn't take his eyes off him. A spade as big as a nightmare, and twice as ugly. "Didn't mean to upset you, man," Mays said sarcastically, "but we thought you might have ideas as to why somebody turned your boss into ragout, and who that somebody would be."

Closing his eyes, Dragonetti wondered what the fuck he could tell them. Mark was a crook, but everybody who makes over half a million a year in New York is a crook. Mark was a genius—the *New York Post* said so. Who wanted to kill him? Who the fuck *didn't*? Unconsciously, he reached for another Valium.

"Sorry," Dragonetti said, looking from one cop to the other. "But, as you can see, this isn't a good time. In three minutes, I won't know who the hell I am."

"We'll only take two," Mays said. "Did Saunders get any threats lately?"

"Nothing serious . . . I remember Sol Feinstein said he was going to kick Mark's ass after we took a deal at Fifty-fifth and Third away from him. But he certainly didn't say he'd kill Mark."

"You mean Feinstein who operates Duo Realty?" Mays asked.

"The same, Officer."

Sullivan made notes in a spiral notebook.

"How about anybody at the company here? Did the man fuck over anybody lately?" Mays asked.

"Naw. Mark wasn't the world's most likeable boss, but nobody around here would have thrown him out the fucking window . . . at least, I don't think so."

"The guard on duty in the lobby last night says Mrs. Saunders stopped by for a second but nobody came up here after Saunders did," Sullivan said. "Is there another way in?"

"Just the boardroom off Mark's office," Dragonetti answered.

"Don't you have to take the lobby elevator to get there?" Sullivan asked.

"No," Dragonetti explained. "That glass tube running up the northeast corner of the building has an elevator that goes directly to the boardroom."

"Who has access to it?" Mays asked.

"Just the directors."

"How'd they get along with Saunders?" Sullivan asked.

Dragonetti shrugged. "Depends on who you're talking about."

"Give us their names and how to reach them," Mays said.

"Okay. But I'll bet you find none of them killed Mark. And I can personally vouch for one."

"Who?" Mays asked dryly.

"Yours truly. I'm one of the inside directors. That means I work for the company and also sit on its board."

"Who are the others?" Mays asked.

"Emmanuel, of course. And Mark was, after he took over as chief executive. I guess Mrs. Saunders is one, too, now. No doubt you know she inherits Mark's fifty-percent share of the company."

"No, we didn't know," said Mays.

"How long had Mark Saunders been head of the company?" Sullivan asked.

"Two years. Since Emmanuel's accident."

"What accident?" Sullivan asked.

"You see, Mark took over after Emmanuel had a real bad car accident. Lucky he wasn't killed. It surprised Emmanuel how Mark stepped in and kept the business booming.

"Before that, Emmanuel kept a pretty tight rein on him. He gave Mark a vice presidency title when he was a kid and a lot of dough, but for years Emmanuel treated him like an office boy."

Dragonetti paused. "You know what Emmanuel said when he gave Mark the company?" he asked rhetorically. "He said, 'Son, destiny stepped in to make a man out of you.'"

Sullivan and Mays looked at one another. "I guess that's one way to do it," Sullivan said.

"Yeah, but Mark had already started getting a lot tougher. I guess the old man just didn't see it."

Sullivan got to his feet. "We'd like to examine any pending agreements the company has for projects, plus work completed on all others for the past two years."

Dragonetti debated for a moment. Should he give them the stuff he had already collected from Mark's office? There was a second set of books and Mark's personal notebooks, papers, and videotapes. Mark videotaped people the way other paranoid chief executives bugged their telephones, Dragonetti

thought. He couldn't keep up with all the goddamn hidde
cameras.

He knew his boss was into a lot of weird stuff, both on an
off the job, but he refrained from going through Mark'
things. The less he knew, the better off he was.

Still, he didn't want the cops going through Mark's papers
either. God only knows what illegal shit he'd gotten Minotau
into. As bad as his job was, he needed it—and Minotaur—t
pay the bills.

"Fine, officers. I'll have my secretary show you what yo
want," he said, leading them away from his office safe, wher
he had stashed Mark's stuff.

He pressed a buzzer on his desk. Nothing happened.

"Betty!" he finally yelled. "Get in here!"

Betty Perkins, who gave the best head Tony Dragonetti ha
ever had, strolled leisurely into the office.

"Why didn't you answer the goddamn buzzer?"

"I didn't know it was for me," she replied with a perplexe
look.

"Would you please show these officers to Mr. Saunders'
office."

"Of course." She looked at the detectives expectantly an
led the way out.

Sullivan and Mays became keenly aware of why Dragon
etti kept the punk Vampira around. Betty Perkins's walk coul
have been choreographed by Madonna.

The cops gone, Dragonetti made the mistake of answerin
his phone. Murray Schuman's whiney voice sounded fright
ened. "Tony, I've got to meet you."

"What is it, Murray?" he snapped.

"I can't tell you over the phone."

Dragonetti checked his watch. "All right. I'll see you a
Harry's Bar about noon."

Harry's, off Hanover Square, was where they met whe
Murray had one of his emergencies. The firm Murray worke
for, Atlantic Real Estate Appraisals, was on Nassau Street
not far from City Hall. Harry's was far enough away so Mur
ray wouldn't be seen with Dragonetti, yet popular enough s

that he could lie and say they had just bumped into one another if anybody did see them together.

When Dragonetti entered Harry's a couple of minutes past noon, the bar was already packed with Wall Street types drinking to celebrate or to curse their rotten luck. Scanning the bar, Dragonetti spotted a fat little man with a round pink face and wire-rimmed glasses. He wore a rumpled gray suit and was sandwiched between two beefy men.

"Hello, Murray," Dragonetti said, walking up to the man with his hand out.

Murray glanced up from his drink. With a startled gesture, he grabbed Dragonetti's hand and shook it.

"Maybe you shouldn't call me by my name," he whispered.

Dragonetti was already tired of the little fuck. His stomach had bothered him all the way down on the subway. With the murder, he knew he'd be working past midnight. He didn't need fucking Murray's problems.

Yet, Murray was too important to ignore. Companies like Minotaur needed the Murrays of the world. The guys who highballed their appraisals of properties so real estate developers could borrow more against them than they were worth. Done for a pathetic amount of cash to stretch their pathetic salaries until next payday.

"How's the wife?" Dragonetti asked inanely.

Murray didn't hear him. His face was glistening with sweat, and he kept glancing around as if he expected FBI agents to cuff him any second. "I got a table in the side dining room," he said conspiratorially.

As soon as they sat down he blurted, "They're on to us."

Dragonetti looked at him, his patience wearing thinner by the minute. "Now don't go off the deep end, Murray. Who's on to us?"

"Your bank, Metropolis, sent two examiners to see me," he said, draining the last of his drink and holding it to the waiter for another. "They want the files on appraisals I've done for Minotaur over the last eighteen months," he continued. "And they also want the properties in that waterfront deal."

Dragonetti sat back. "What waterfront deal?"

"You know, the one Mark Saunders put under a different company name."

"Oh, yeah, that." Dragonetti sidestepped because in reality he knew nothing. "So?"

"So? *So?* Is that all you have to say? They're talking about fraud and shit like that, and all you can say is, So?"

"Calm the fuck down!" Dragonetti said harshly. "When did this happen?"

"This morning. Just before I called."

"Do they have the files yet?"

"No. They're supposed to come back in tomorrow."

Murray gulped his new drink and looked at Dragonetti, his eyes watering and begging for help. His lips were trembling.

"My boss is asking what's going on. Everything's coming undone. I could go to prison, Tony. For Christ's sake, I've got three kids. What's going to happen to them? What the hell's my mother going to say?"

"Just sit tight and don't give them any reports. I'll handle it."

Neither of them felt like eating. After Murray had a third scotch and went back to work, Dragonetti placed a phone call to Phillip Randolph, senior vice president of Metropolis Guaranty Trust, and made an appointment to see him in an hour.

Dragonetti was bothered by Randolph, and he wasn't sure why. He knew Mark had soured on the guy after initially making it sound like he had signed up the Messiah when he appointed Randolph to Minotaur Development's board of directors. Also, Dragonetti's antennae picked up that Emmanuel had little use for him.

An hour later, when ushered by a secretary into Randolph's spacious wood-paneled office at Metropolis's Park Avenue headquarters, Dragonetti wasn't sure what kind of reception he would receive. He had never said much to Randolph at board meetings. A smart businessman who kept his own counsel, Randolph was cold and calculating.

Randolph's office was all muted grays and browns. Nothing jarring, but nothing arresting. Dragonetti found it boring. Bankers and their goddamn offices. "The biggest bandits around, but they pretend to be gentlemen," he muttered.

Randolph rose from his desk when Dragonetti entered. His face, hair, and suit were matching shades of gray. Though

Randolph's face gave nothing away, Dragonetti had an inkling the banker knew why he was there.

"Tony, how are you?" Randolph asked with the kind of familiarity Dragonetti only got from guys he grew up with, in the Gowanus section of Brooklyn.

"Not so good, uh, Phil," he said, "because of your bank."

Randolph looked concerned, solicitous, and he motioned Dragonetti to a chair. "I hope it's something I can help with," he said.

"Damn right. Call your examiners off Atlantic Real Estate Appraisals."

Randolph sat behind his desk, took off his metal-framed glasses, and wiped them. A frown creased his brow.

"Uh, real estate doesn't fall under my immediate jurisdiction," he said. "Tell me what the problem is."

Briefly, Dragonetti outlined the situation. By the time he was done, he hadn't said that Minotaur Development, Atlantic Real Estate, or Murray Schuman had done anything unethical, let alone illegal. Yet there was no doubt that was the case.

"I see," Randolph said. He looked hard at Dragonetti. "I will see that the examiners find something else to do with their time . . . this once."

"I was hoping you would," Dragonetti said, his stomach feeling a little better for the first time all day. For Christ's sake, the guy was on Minotaur's board. This is what he was supposed to do. Still, Dragonetti wondered what the "this once" crap meant. Guys like this never did anybody any favors unless they had ulterior motives.

Randolph got up and walked to the window, feigning a casual stance as he looked down on Park Avenue. "Now there's something you can do for *me*," he said quietly.

Dragonetti looked up. Once again, he caught something in the banker's voice. A hint of a threat.

"Tell Emmanuel Saunders that I helped you out," Randolph said. "And tell him the next time there might be worse trouble and perhaps I won't be able to help."

Dragonetti left the office feeling more ill at ease than when he'd entered. The next time? Dragonetti sensed he was caught in some kind of cross fire between Randolph and old Emmanuel, but for the life of him he couldn't figure out why.

And then there was this waterfront project. What the hell was that?

"God, what a fucker of a day," Dragonetti muttered to himself as the elevator doors closed.

FRIDAY

FRIDAY

Twelve

Edward Fitzgerald sat in his office glaring at the young attorney who stood uncomfortably in front of his desk. Since Saunders's death, Fitzgerald had been nervous and irritable. And worried. The last thing he wanted to hear was some sniveling little bastard raising issues of propriety and ethics.

"You see, Mr. Fitzgerald, using this dummy corporation as the owner of those properties may not be legal, and it really is unfair to the people getting the eviction notices," said John Cummins, an attorney with the firm of Fitzgerald, Meehan & Golden.

Black hair and horn-rimmed glasses and a navy pin-striped suit, Cummins had a face that was bland but bore an earnest expression. He was two years out of Yale Law School. Shifting slightly from foot to foot, he telegraphed his uncertainty about being in this office and addressing this particular issue.

"Mr. Cummins," Fitzgerald said angrily, "since when are you paid to debate the merits of a transaction that I personally set up?"

"I, uh, I'm not, sir. It's just that, uh—"

"You know what I am going to do, Mr. Cummins?" Fitzgerald interrupted. "I am going to have you personally negotiate the eviction notices."

The young attorney looked up, startled. "I couldn't possibly do that, sir. Why, that would make me part of—"

Again, Fitzgerald interrupted icily. "You can, and you *will*. Do you know why? Because you want to keep your job with one of the most powerful law firms in the country. That's why. Your degree from Yale brought you a tryout in the big time, not a sinecure. There are hundreds of ambitious little shits like you out there begging for the chance you have."

Cummins's face flushed, and he looked like he might burst into tears. His right hand was shaking as he automatically took off his glasses and wiped them. "Yes, sir," he said shakily, and quietly he left the office.

Considering the situation for a moment, Fitzgerald now wondered if he should ask the boy to dinner. Cummins wasn't bad-looking, and he was young and looked muscular. Right now, he was particularly vulnerable. Power had its rewards, and Fitzgerald found out long ago that many young and ambitious lawyers would do anything to get ahead, or to hang on to their jobs when they felt threatened.

He pressed the intercom button on his desk. "Miss Devers, will you invite Mr. Cummins to have dinner with me Sunday night. Eight o'clock. Yes, at the Center City Club. Oh, and will you reserve me a room at the club. I'll stay in the city that night."

Fitzgerald agitatedly turned back to the list in front of him. Charlie Gorman at New York Guaranty Bank was in. So was Vic Sterba at Mackenzie Brothers, and Cal Girard at First Connecticut. Could he pull it off without Mark Saunders? And, if he did, how would the big syndicate people react? What would the Italians do to the Chinese? What would Emmanuel do? What could he *possibly* do?

More than once in the past two years, Fitzgerald had offered a prayer of thanks that Emmanuel Saunders was out of Minotaur. Nothing would have worked so far if he hadn't had to turn the company over to Mark.

The thought of Mark Saunders crashing through his office window suddenly made Fitzgerald shiver. Unconsciously, he looked at the windows in his office. Thank God, they were chest-high and there was no danger of being pushed out. The thought of plunging twenty-nine stories to the sidewalk made him want to throw up.

"Sir," his secretary said over the intercom. "There's a Mr. D'Angelo here to see you."

"Show him in," he said nervously, glancing back at his windows.

Nicky D'Angelo was enjoying himself immensely when he entered the office, but you could never tell it by looking at him. But then, his expression never changed, whether he was talking about buying a cop or about the time he accidentally smothered a prostitute to death while making it with her.

D'Angelo's enormous bulk was covered in a black silk suit, pale blue silk shirt, and black knit tie, all made for him by a tailor down on Mulberry Street. He stuffed himself into a tub chair facing the desk.

As the former head of the Cement Workers Union, D'Angelo was the unofficial link between City Hall and the legions of construction unions in New York. Nicknamed "the Buddha," D'Angelo looked as out of place in the law offices as Fitzgerald would have at a boccie club. The law office decor was tasteful and expensive. Walnut paneled walls were lined with bookcases and hunting scenes. There was a red leather couch, and Tiffany lamps on the tables.

The Buddha looked at a wall covered with photographs. There was Fitzgerald with every president from Eisenhower through Reagan, as well as congressmen and senators, including a large one of Senator Joe McCarthy, for whom Fitzgerald had worked during the height of the McCarthy Communist witch-hunts. There was a photo of Edward Fitzgerald, Sr., his deceased father, who had been a congressman. The largest photo was of his mother, Carol, an imposing, stern-looking woman who had her son wear dresses until he was eight years old and whose husband had feared her more than any political boss he knew.

The wall also displayed a degree from Harvard Law School, from which Fitzgerald had graduated when he was only twenty. There were also pictures of several good-looking young men, who looked like they might be actors.

"Maybe there should be a picture of you and me together," D'Angelo said with a mirthless laugh.

For years, the two had had a tacit understanding that D'Angelo wouldn't come to the office. But Saunders's murder had changed a lot of deals that had gone down around the city. After eyeballing Fitzgerald for a minute, the Buddha tossed a copy of the *New York Post* that landed faceup under the lawyer's nose. The headline: MIDAS MURDERED!

"Mr. Fitzgerald, my people are worried." The words rumbled from his lips like from the inside of a barrel.

The lawyer walked around the desk and stood by the fat man's chair. "Why should they be worried?"

"Please, Mr. Fitzgerald. Neither of us is stupid. Minotaur pays millions to the construction workers of this city. To the campaign funds of politicians. To the upkeep of nice offices such as this one. And to me. Now we want to know *why* that handsome Mr. Saunders was killed."

Fitzgerald dabbed at his brow. He hated this fat pig for barging into his offices, embarrassing him, making demands on him. But there was little that could be done about that right now.

"Be assured that the mayor will personally expedite the investigation." Fitzgerald paused. "You may also be assured that I am as interested as you in knowing if there were, uh, business or political motives for this murder."

"That makes me happy," the Buddha said sarcastically.

While talking, D'Angelo increasingly took a professional interest in the lawyer. He tried to figure the amount of pressure it would take to snap his scrawny neck. The first guy he had killed—more than forty years ago, when he was only sixteen—was a neck job. He had been amazed at how easy it was. And he had loved it. He bet himself he could do Fitzgerald in twenty seconds.

D'Angelo couldn't figure Fitzgerald out. He knew his coming here would bug the son of a bitch, but Fitzgerald was so rattled that something else had to be gnawing at him, and the Buddha wanted to know what it was. "So, are the rest of the princes going to move on Minotaur?" he asked, tossing out a line and hoping he had the right bait.

Fitzgerald looked at him sharply, momentarily debating

whether to answer. "I had the distinct impression they already were."

"You mean *they* killed him?" D'Angelo asked skeptically. That didn't add up, he thought. Men as rich and powerful as the princes might have somebody killed, but not one of their own—unless they all agreed to it. It was an unwritten law among them, one they all honored—or they would all be dead by now. No, if they wanted to harm another prince, they would most likely kill him slowly through business deals, strip him of everything until there was nothing left.

Fitzgerald's answer stunned D'Angelo, its openness indicating the lawyer was indeed rattled.

"No, but I know they thought Mark had fucked them over on a big deal." Fitzgerald remembered Mark telling him about it right here in his office two days ago.

Young Saunders had burst into Fitzgerald's office unannounced. "Ed, I've got to talk to you," he had said. Next, Mark had flung himself on the couch. "Goddamn," he'd said, letting out a sigh. "I just came from a special meeting of the princes. It was a fucking nightmare."

"Jesus. What happened?"

"Gimme a drink first. Scotch."

Fitzgerald could tell Saunders had already been drinking, and he thought how stupid it was for anyone to imbibe so early in the day. "Ice?"

"No."

Grabbing the drink, Saunders took a swallow. "They know about the Waterfront Project. I swore up and down I wasn't part of any deal that would go behind their backs, but they didn't believe me."

Fitzgerald suddenly looked very worried. "Do they know about me?" he demanded.

"No," Saunders said. "For Christ's sake, I told them I didn't have anything to do with it. Do you think I'm going to tell them *you* did?"

"Do you want to back out?" Fitzgerald asked.

Saunders glared at him. "Fuck, no! This is my shot at Emmanuel. One that will outdo *everything* he's ever done."

Saunders paused. "Think of something, Ed. Get them off my ass. Fast!"

Saunders stood and paced. "Jesus, Ed, they could ruin me! Fuck it. They might kill me!" Then he looked straight at Fitzgerald. "Us, I should say."

Mark finished his drink. "Just get them off me. I don't care what it costs." Slamming the door, he left without looking back.

Fitzgerald snapped out of his reverie when D'Angelo spoke.

"What did you say?"

"Emmanuel wants revenge," the Buddha repeated, slowly rising to his feet and letting himself out the door. "He told me he and Mark had gotten real close. If I was the killer, I'd take my chances with the cops before Emmanuel got me."

Thirteen

Samantha climbed out of the taxi at Mott and Canal Street, in the heart of Chinatown. She had taken the day off from work. It was almost eleven o'clock and the morning was cold. The sidewalks were thronged. Shops and restaurants were crowded. The teeming mass of Chinese was everywhere.

It was easy to see why Chinatown was growing so fast. For years now, immigrants had poured into the ghetto. Legal. Illegal. From Hong Kong, Taiwan, and even the mainland. Chinatown was spilling north into Little Italy, worrying both the police and the Mafiosi because of the increase in regulated and unregulated crime. Neither the cops nor the Italians knew which was worse: the random violence of the Chinese youth gangs or the controlled corruption of the Triads.

Samantha walked south on Mott, pushing through the crowds, feeling exhilarated. She loved being part of the surging sea of people who were like her. The feeling of anonymity. Since coming to the United States in her late teens, she always had the feeling of being an outsider, except here.

Halfway down the block, she entered a small shop with odd designs on the window. There was no one in the front

room. The walls were covered with intricate pictures. Birds.
Serpents. Flowers. Hundreds of them.

A curtain parted in the rear of the shop and a small, wiz-
ened Chinaman emerged. He spoke to her in Chinese and she
replied in kind.

"What is it? Why are you here?"

"I have heard of your mastery from many, many people,"
Samantha replied.

"You wish art?"

"Yes," she replied. "This!"

Samantha pulled a long cardboard cylinder from her bag,
twisted off one end, and extracted a paper from it. Unrolling
the paper, she showed the old man the design.

"Ah," he said. "I have longed for this for many, many
years."

"I know you are one of us."

"It will be very painful."

"I know."

"When do you wish to start?"

"Now."

The man looked at her for a moment. "It is possible," he
said. Turning to the back, he said, "This way."

Samantha followed him behind the curtain into the tattoo
parlor. She was shedding one life and beginning another.

"You know of my technique, so that you can better with-
stand the pain?"

"I do."

"You may leave your clothes over there," he said, pointing
to a small room.

When Samantha returned she was nude. A young man,
also naked, was lying on his back on a mat on the floor. He
looked at Samantha impassively.

"Please stretch out on top of him," the old man directed.

Samantha placed herself on the boy, the heat of his flesh
against her from head to toe. He placed his hands on her
buttocks and she could feel him beginning to swell.

Suddenly pain shot through her back as the tattooer began
his work. Her body jerked against the boy's, and she could
feel him enter her. Soon she was lost between pleasure and
pain, flinching in turn from each.

Fourteen

The beige 1983 Dodge sedan barreled along the Long Island Expressway, turning off at Exit 70 for the Hamptons. The morning was unusually bright and clear. A pungent scent of ocean filled the cool air. Sullivan was in shirtsleeves, his tie down several notches, and his collar unbuttoned. Mays wore a red satin shirt with wide red stripes, the buttons open to mid-chest, the sleeves pushed up to his elbow. They were glad to be escaping the city for a little while.

"Mays, you look like a dago candy man in that getup."

Mays laughed. "Your mama, Sullivan."

Suddenly, the big detective's mood turned serious.

"I know this is a bucket of political horseshit we're stepping into," Mays said. "I feel it in my bones."

Although he didn't work that often with Mays, Sullivan appreciated the big man's instincts. He, too, worried about walking into a political shooting gallery on this one. Saunders was a very powerful man with a murdered son. Calling on Emmanuel Saunders at his estate in Southampton could be tantamount to putting their heads in a buzz saw.

"I checked Emmanuel Saunders out with a City Hall type," Sullivan said. "He's real big. One of those real estate princes the politicians went to hat in hand when the city was on the verge of bankruptcy and asked them not to pull up stakes. They didn't, and City Hall has been, shall we say, grateful ever since."

"Get any dirt on him?" Mays asked.

"Some mob ties, but not provable."

"A record?"

"No," Sullivan said. "But three years ago, he was arrested for almost beating a crane operator to death on a construction site. Seems the guy was pissed off at Saunders's son, so he dropped a wrecking ball on Emmanuel's car."

"Three years ago? I thought this jack was an old man?"

"Pushing seventy."

"A tough old dude," Mays said. "How'd he beat it?"

"Nicky D'Angelo made the guy drop the charges."

"I should have realized Saunders used that fat fuck-fixer."

"The word is, somebody at headquarters helped them out."

"Figures," Mays said.

"I talked to Mike Roche at FBI. They investigated Saunders for some big federal contracts," Sullivan said.

"So?"

"Interesting guy. A Greek immigrant. To be real Americans, his parents changed the name from something that sounded like a mouthful of marbles to Saunders. One story is, young Emmanuel worked for some Italian contractor, stole a big contract from him out here on the Island."

"Just another three-piece thug," Mays said disgustedly.

"Not quite. The guy's an architect, self-trained. He's created designs that are models for developers all over the country."

"Anything else?"

"Yeah. Roche says the guy's eccentric."

"What the hell's that mean?"

"That's what I asked. Roche just laughed and said we'd find out for ourselves."

"I'll tell you this," Mays said. "People I talked to at Minotaur called both him and his son bastards in the same breath. They may have loved each other, but nobody else did."

Passing the concrete tepees on Hill Street, and the signs on cute little boutiques, like BUTTERFLY PEOPLE, they entered Southampton. Mays swung the Dodge around a corner and about two miles on Dune Road he turned right into a driveway.

The car came to a halt in front of a twenty-foot high, elaborate wrought iron gate that looked like it had once barred the entrance to a Florentine palace. Spanning two huge granite columns, the gate was both beautiful and menacing. Designs of delicate flowers and vines wove between spikes and spears, and in two-foot-high Gothic letters was the word MANDRAGOLA.

Barely visible through the latticework was a stone guardhouse with glass windows facing the driveway. Inside, a guard wearing mirrored sunglasses spoke into a microphone.

"Identify yourselves," the guard commanded.

"Detectives Mays and Sullivan. New York Police. We've got an appointment with Mr. Saunders," Mays said into a microphone atop a metal post near the driver's window.

The massive gate slowly swung open. The driveway beyond stretched into the horizon.

"Park your car on the left," came the same metallic voice.

Mays turned left into the parking lot as big as a baseball diamond. They got out, and shivering in the cold breeze off of the ocean, Sullivan reached back and grabbed their suit coats, tossing one to Mays.

Big, blond, and built like a bull, the guard stepped from the booth. He was clad from head to toe in black leather: jacket, pants, boots. A black leather holster was strapped to his right thigh, the cover unbuttoned. A Remington 870 SWAT shotgun was cradled in his arms.

"Would you look at that," said Mays, whistling low as he took in the guard. "He'd give Hitler a hard-on."

The guard raised a dog whistle to his lips, and moments later two Dobermans streaked into view. The dogs stopped on a dime, flanking the detectives.

Then a small black vehicle similar to a golf cart with a back seat silently appeared. The driver, dressed in the same black uniform, beckoned for the detectives to get in. Sullivan and Mays looked at each other, shrugged, and climbed aboard.

"Eccentric? Fuckin' weird," said Mays.

The vehicle sped off, the dogs running along behind. As they wound up the driveway, the view was spectacular. On either side were brooks and ponds and formal gardens with marble Grecian statues, plus flower beds that looked like impressionist paintings come to life.

"Flowers this time of year?" said Mays.

"He must have his own hothouse and an army of gardeners," Sullivan observed.

"That right?" Mays shouted to the driver.

The man turned, his face impassive, his mirrored sunglasses reflecting the bright daylight. "Right," he said, with the trace of an accent.

Sullivan found himself entranced by the view, wondering how it reflected the man who created it. How ironic, he thought, that a man such as Saunders could acquire his money through ruthlessness, then use it to shape a Garden of Eden. *Crime still pays.*

"Goddamn! Look at that!" Mays shouted.

The house had come into view. It combined both Renaissance and modern elements—a contemporary Florentine villa. There were arches and cylinders, leaded windows and solar panels, all blended into a mansion that was at once graceful and rugged. Formidable, yet enticing.

"He really is an architectural genius," Sullivan found himself saying.

"Oh, that's right. You know about all this stuff, don't you, with your fancy college degree," Mays said sarcastically.

"Not fancy," Sullivan said. "Just a double in architecture and fine arts."

Mays shook his head. "Christ, man, if I had that background, the last thing I'd be doing is sitting here with me looking up some weirdo whose son bought it. Me? I grew up in the streets. You don't have an excuse."

"I did it for my father," Sullivan said quietly. "He was a cop."

"I thought Carter said you came from dough, man," Mays said.

"My stepfather has money," Sullivan said, ruefully. "I hardly knew my father."

Sullivan painfully recalled just how little he did know about Joe Sullivan, the Boston cop, and how his father, in a very real sense, had changed his own life. When he was a struggling young architect worried about his wife's extravagance, the junior Sullivan received a call from a woman identifying herself as Peggy Sullivan, his father's sister.

"I was wondering," she said hesitantly, "if you would come to Boston for your father's funeral."

When he arrived at Aunt Peggy's small row house, she greeted him warmly and told him something of his background. His father's family had emigrated to America at the turn of the century. Joe was the eldest of seven children.

"Joe was so bright," she recalled. "He went to the Boston Latin School and won a scholarship to college, but our father died and so he couldn't go. Joe went to work to take care of the rest of us."

Aunt Peggy's voice turned bitter. "He met your mother, Theresa McGheehan, about ten years later, after the rest of us were grown. He felt sorry for her, and he fell in love. She was only seventeen and she came from a very poor family.

"I don't think Terry—that's what everybody called her before she became such a grand lady—ever loved Joe. She married him to escape her family. When World War II broke out, Joe joined the army and Terry started working at the shipyards, where she worked for that bum she married after she divorced Joe."

Peggy looked at her nephew. "Your father loved you very much," she said. "Why, he even drove down to Yale several times just to watch you walk across the campus."

"But why didn't he ever contact me?"

"He promised your mother he wouldn't after she told him you were getting everything he could never afford to give you."

When going through his father's personal effects, Sullivan found a diary. Leafing through the pages, Brian realized how loving and caring about people his father had been. Entry after entry referred to bag ladies he helped find housing, kids without fathers he helped find jobs or took to parks on weekends, and how proud he was of his son at Yale. "My greatest lament," his father wrote, "is that there is no room in Brian's world for me."

Sullivan had cried when he'd read those words. Suddenly, he realized that he wanted to get as far as possible from the world his mother craved. When he returned to New York, he took down his architect's shingle and entered the police academy, enjoying the irony of seeing his life come full circle with that of his father's. His mother was mortified, and Paige, in outrage, walked out on him.

Now the memories fled as the cart pulled up to Mandragola's front door, a portal that would have done justice to Westminster Abbey. The dogs stayed within striking distance. The detectives alit as the door opened and a woman emerged. She wore a stiffly starched maid's uniform and beckoned for them to enter.

"My name is Marga," she said pleasantly. Though her English was good, she spoke with a strong Greek accent. "Mr. Saunders will see you in a few minutes. He asked me to show you to his Olympus."

"His what?" Mays asked.

"Olympus," Marga repeated. "It will be easier to let you see it for yourselves."

The detectives followed her down a marble-floored hallway. Mounted on a pedestal in the corridor was a model, apparently cast in gold, of Saunders Tower.

When they arrived at the open doorway, the maid stepped aside so the officers could enter. "This is Olympus," she said.

Sunlight filtered through the glass-domed ceiling into the large, oval room. Hibiscus and ficus trees grew randomly. Water streamed down a rock wall into a pond. The rest of the floor was grass with a flagstone walkway leading past a half dozen marble statues mounted on pedestals.

"Okay, my man," Mays said. "What am I looking at?"

"A re-creation of a Greek garden," Sullivan answered.

"Who are the statues?"

"Greek gods."

Sullivan approached a statue of a bearded man with an eagle at his feet. "This is Zeus."

"What's that in his hand? A cucumber?"

Sullivan laughed. "It's thunderbolts. You are looking at the king of earth and air. The top dog. A warlord with a celestial artillery."

"You mean a Greek power broker."

"You got it."

"And who's that?" Mays pointed at a dashing boyish figure.

"Apollo. The most beautiful and beloved of the Olympians. Kind of a sun god. But he could hurt as well as heal men's souls."

"And that?" He pointed at a winged boy.

"Even you ought to know Eros," Sullivan said in mock disdain. "The Greek Cupid."

"Man, do I know Cupid. He's been kicking my heartaround since I was old enough to look at girls."

The maid interrupted. "Mr. Saunders will see you now," she said. "Will you please follow me?"

The room the maid led them into was long and rectangular, and as big as a tennis court. Polished mahogany and oak were everywhere, including an eighteenth-century grandfather's clock with painted moon face and London-style case. A ponderous refectory table stretched along the wall at the far end of the room.

"Mr. Saunders will be right in," Marga said. Looking down, she added, "Watch your step."

Even as he did look down, Mays tripped over the edge of a paper thin carpet. "Damn," he muttered. "Rug's so thin I could crumple it with my fingers."

"Nirvan," Sullivan said.

"Come again?"

"A kind of Persian carpet. The thinner they are, the more expensive. The finest crumple like that."

"Hell. This one's old, so it can't be worth much."

"Exactly one hundred and twelve years old," the maid said.

"Which makes it worth, say, a hundred and fifty thousand dollars," Sullivan estimated.

"Quite right, Detective," the maid said approvingly.

She disappeared, and they wandered around the room looking into a glass case. Sullivan exclaimed, "My God. These sketches could be by Alberti. In the fifteenth century he adapted classical forms to Renaissance architecture. Nobody'd ever done that."

"Sullivan," Mays called out. "Look at this."

Mays was standing on the opposite side of the room, staring up at a picture above a huge marble fireplace. "Who's this guy with the long beak? His armor looks like the inside of a cuckoo clock."

Before Sullivan could answer, another voice did. "Detective, you prove that art is in the eye of the beholder."

Both policemen turned. The doorway was blocked by stern-looking Emmanuel Saunders. He held his head high and his powerful torso erect.

"That's a painting of Niccolò Machiavelli, a man who

weighed his words judicially—offering offense only if he could gain from it."

"Tell it to Sullivan," Mays replied. "He's the one who knows about this stuff."

Saunders stared hard at Sullivan. He moved slowly into the room. "So you know something of Machiavelli?"

"More than Mays here, I guess," Sullivan replied. "He was a Florentine diplomat whose writings advocated the use of cruelty, deception, and cunning."

"Ah, but what most people don't understand is that cruelty, deception, and cunning have their place," Saunders said. "Machiavelli knew they were tools to achieve great purpose. His was the greatest mind this world has ever known. A genius of politics the way Leonardo and Michelangelo were of art."

Saunders's voice became more animated as he continued. "Machiavelli's lasting achievement was giving us a blueprint for achieving power. Indulge me for a minute."

Reaching onto a table on his right, he picked up a thin, leather-bound book. Opening brittle, obviously much worn pages, he started to read.

"A prince should therefore have no other aim or thought, nor take up any other thing for his study, but war and its organization and discipline, for that is the only art that is necessary to one who commands."

With a satisfied air, he closed the book. "Today, Detectives, businessmen are princes, and the way business is conducted is war. To command, to succeed, requires ruthlessness, cunning, and—"

"Cruelty?" Sullivan interjected.

Saunders looked at him dispassionately. "Yes, Mr. Sullivan. Sometimes cruelty."

Mays rolled his eyes. "Hey listen. This dude's theories are interesting, but we've got a job to do."

Saunders didn't appear offended. "You, Mr. Mays, if I judge by your directness, are an instinctive follower of what Machiavelli believed. Yes, on to business. Gentlemen, we are talking about the murder of my son. My heir. The crown prince of the Saunders empire. I loved him, gentlemen. His murderer must be found."

Saunders headed back to the door. He called over his shoulder, "Please follow me."

"In a second," Sullivan called after him. He was looking at a picture of a handsome, blond young man who, despite his youth, had a commanding presence. "Whose portrait is this opposite Machiavelli?"

Saunders slowly faced them. For the first time, his expression was one of vulnerability. His eyes were pained.

"He was the bravest and the best. My elder son Stephen. Dead now."

"What happened?" Mays asked.

"A construction accident. Stephen was a god, gentlemen. A god!"

Abruptly, Saunders walked across the hallway to another room, leaving the detectives little option except to follow him.

The detectives almost gasped at the diametric contrast between this room and Olympus. With its floor-to-ceiling bookcases and tabletops with architectural plans pinned to them, banks of telephones, Dow Jones ticker, state-of-the-art computer terminals and television monitors suspended from the ceiling, the room was obviously Saunders's office. Somehow the high-tech office equipment blended harmoniously with the oiled walnut paneling and the stained-glass windows.

Dominating the room was a massive platform with a huge diorama of Manhattan. The Empire State Building stood about three feet high. The rest of the buildings, streets, and parks were in scale.

"Sit down, gentlemen," Saunders said. "Let us discuss who may have killed my son."

With heightened interest, Sullivan and Mays eased themselves into leather chairs in front of Saunders's desk. Suddenly, a red light flashed on a control panel to the right of Saunders. The old man pressed a button and one of the TV monitors flashed on. The screen showed a portion of the fence encircling the estate. Visible was a black uniformed guard accompanied by a Doberman. The guard spoke into his walkie-talkie.

"All clear, sir," he said. "Thought we might have an intruder, but it was just a wild dog."

Saunders turned off the monitor. "Mark was enamored with video and sound equipment," he said. "After my accident, he had the entire estate wired so that it would make it easier for the guards to protect me—and easier for me to see and hear what was going on."

"You mean you can see and hear what's going on any place out there?" Mays asked.

"Inside, too."

"Do you have any idea who killed your son?" Sullivan asked abruptly.

Saunders paused thoughtfully before speaking. "Yes, I have a pretty good one."

"Who?"

"Either his wife or one of her friends." Saunders reached into a desk drawer and extracted two videotape cassettes and two letters, and pushed them across his desk toward Sullivan.

"My son had a private safe here. When I was told of his death I opened it. I don't know the nature of the material on each of these tapes or in the envelopes, nor do I want to. All my son ever told me is that they pertain to his wife's closest friends and, if anything ever happened to him, the clues found here would lead the police to his killer."

"But you said his wife wanted to kill him."

Saunders stared through a large window that overlooked a formal garden. When he finally spoke, his voice was thoughtful. "My son changed dramatically within the past several years. He used to be tentative, weak. But he became strong. Part of that strength came from distancing himself from his wife. She had hurt him terribly, gentlemen."

"What do you mean?" Mays asked.

"I'm afraid she was unfaithful to Mark."

Suddenly he turned around. "Now, if you will excuse me, I am tired. You may call me if you have any further questions. Oh, and gentlemen, one other thing. *She is the one I think did it!*"

Fifteen

When Sullivan and Mays returned to headquarters at One Police Plaza, they were told Captain Carter wanted to see them.

"Ten-to-one Carter's already talked to Saunders," Sullivan said sarcastically.

As they approached Carter's office, Mays nudged Sullivan with his elbow. "Look at Dogface," he muttered.

Through the glass door, they watched the captain slick back his gray hair weave while admiring his reflection.

"Why do I always think of the Fonz at age fifty when I look at the fool?" Mays asked.

Carter was wearing a brown tweed suit from Paul Stewart and Bally loafers, part of his dress-for-success wardrobe, as he unabashedly called it. Still, he hadn't shaken his old nickname, Dogface, acquired after he was caught in the storeroom riding one of the dispatchers doggie style while yelling, "Woof! Woof!"

"Get in here," Carter growled when he caught sight of them. He began rubbing his hands together like a fucking Shylock. "This Saunders case is just about wrapped up. Right?"

"Hell, no," Sullivan said. "Whoever takes my place when I go on vacation's going to have his work cut out."

"Vacation's off," Carter said, refusing to look at Sullivan.

"Wrong," Sullivan said grimly.

He couldn't help thinking that everything about Carter was wrong. He used a word like "guy" to be one of the boys, but it came out sounding like an insult. He spent his dough on clothes and cocktail parties for politicians, and more time schmoozing at City Hall than Mayor Koch. He knew approximately as much about police work as a rookie. His making captain was a fucking disgrace.

"Don't wrong me!" Carter said. "You can't go on vacation. Emmanuel Saunders is too important."

"Look, Captain, I've had this fishing trip set up for months," Sullivan said wearily.

"I don't care if you've had it set up for ten years," Carter said, his voice a high-pitched whine. "I've had heat put on me from everywhere in this city to get this case cleared up and, as much as I hate to admit it, I need you on it. For Christ's sake, Sullivan, put your damned rich boy Ivy League background to some use. Who else am I going to use?" Turning to Mays, Carter said, "Look around the squad room and tell me. I need somebody who knows that world.

"Besides," he said, turning back to Sullivan. "I can break you for what you did to that assistant DA."

Sullivan smoldered but backed off. He had lost his temper a couple of weeks ago and punched out a wiseass assistant district attorney, and this wasn't the first time Carter brought it up. Now he felt like he was on the verge of doing the same thing—to Carter.

"Come on, guys," Carter said more cheerfully. "It shouldn't take long to wrap this thing up. Emmanuel put you on the right trail."

"Suppose somebody else did it?" Mays asked nonchalantly.

Carter's face screwed up into a crafty look. "Frankly, Emmanuel and I—oh, did I tell you? Emmanuel and I serve together on the board of the Police Athletic League—anyway, Emmanuel and I think the daughter-in-law is the killer. She hated Mark."

"Shall I call her and ask her to come down and confess?" Mays said, trying not to conceal his smirk.

"Don't act like a goddamn simpleton, Mays," Carter said.

He turned to Sullivan. "And you, buddy, are going to find out."

"Oh, really? How?"

"Darleen Saunders is part of that artsy-fartsy world that you know so well. Just come on to her. Tell her you want to help her."

"I'm through with that world," Sullivan said angrily. "You know that."

"Look," Carter said heatedly. "My ass is on the line."

"Then call Dial-A-Date."

"The alternative is to go back to pounding a beat. I'm serious, Sullivan. Whatever you feel personally, your job is to catch killers. Then you can fish for any damn thing you want."

Feeling trapped, Sullivan said, "What makes you think Darleen Saunders will even look at me?"

Carter smiled teasingly. "Emmanuel said she's a slut, didn't he?"

Before Sullivan could respond, Carter ducked out of the office and was halfway across the squad room.

"Asshole!" Mays said in Carter's wake.

Sullivan glanced disgustedly at his partner. "Might as well see what Carter's good friend gave us this morning."

They went to an interrogation room and opened the first envelope.

"This is bad stuff," Mays said.

The first envelope contained a letter written by a woman. The lady made no bones wanting to see Saunders dead.

Mark:

    Because of your lies and deceit, my marriage is in ruins, and my political career is in jeopardy. I don't know what cruelty drove you to hurt me, but I swear, come near me again, and I will kill you!

The note was unsigned, but there was another letter written by the same person. This one was signed: Deborah Bartley.

The second of the envelopes contained affidavits from

members of the cast of a play, *The Magnificent Gentleman*. The statements said that Aida Miller had publicly threatened to kill Mark Saunders. There was also a typewritten note saying Aida Miller was an actress.

Next, they watched two videotapes. Each was pornographic. The first was of an Oriental girl in an S&M encounter; the cassette had a label marked SAMANTHA KWAN, presumably the girl's name. The next was a menage á trois, with the label bearing the name JOY LIVINGSTON.

"The blonde looks familiar," Sullivan said as he was watching Joy.

"She should," Mays said with a chuckle. "Joy Livingston's the hottest anchorwoman in town."

"I'll say she's hot," Sullivan muttered.

"Looks like Saunders was blackmailing these women."

"Maybe, and maybe that's why Darleen Saunders hated her husband."

"Yeah, that fits," Mays said. "He blackmails her friends. She finds out and, in a fit of rage, kills him."

"Could be," said Sullivan. "I'd better pay her another visit." He paused. "Damn that Carter. I hate not playing straight with people."

"Take this with you," Mays said. He handed Sullivan a black metal object about the size of a half dollar and about a quarter inch thick. "With this little transmitter, I'll be able to pick you up from a quarter-mile away."

Sixteen

As Sullivan entered Saunders Tower, the evening sky was eerily reflected in the mirrored walls of the building. Until yesterday, he had never been in the damned place in his life, and now he had trepidations about returning. He had always prided himself on being a square shooter, and now he was on an assignment to trick someone.

The desk clerk recognized him and nodded. Sullivan found himself thinking that the poor bastard worked as long a day as a detective. "Call Mrs. Saunders's apartment and tell her I'm coming up, will you?"

Crossing the lobby, he entered an empty elevator and pressed the button for the penthouse. He checked his watch; it was a few minutes to seven.

When the elevator stopped, Darleen Saunders's maid was waiting by the open apartment door. "Hello, Detective," she said politely. "Mrs. Saunders is out, but she is expected back shortly. Won't you come in?"

As on his first visit, he was led into a living room. Alone in the room, he found himself resenting the people who could afford to hang artistic masterpieces in their homes. That, he decided, was what separated real money from the upper mid-

dle class. Then, remembering why he had come, he attached
the transistor to the bottom of a Van Gogh.

He thought again about Carter's sneer about Darleen being
a slut. She hadn't struck him at all like that, but then he'd
never been a good judge of rich women. His ex-wife, Paige,
was a constant reminder of that. Paige refused to have children, and slept with her boss at the record company where she
was a producer. Sullivan had tried to change her mind about
the former, and called her on the latter. The bad memories
made him angry all over again.

Maybe Carter is right, he thought bitterly. *The rich, bitch
widow did it.*

He jumped to his feet when he heard someone enter.

"Hello," a woman said.

Sullivan found himself staring at a beautiful blonde whom
he recognized as Joy Livingston.

"I'm waiting for Mrs. Saunders," he said.

Joy's eyes lingered on him appreciatively. She liked his
wide-set eyes and strong chin, but smiled at the rumpled
clothes and scuffed loafers. "I'm a friend, Joy Livingston.
Darleen ran out for a few minutes. She obviously didn't know
you were coming, Mr.—"

"Sullivan. Detective Sullivan."

"Really?" She took out a notepad and pen. "What can you
tell me about the investigation?"

"Actually, Miss Livingston, I was hoping you could help
me. In fact, I was going to call you later."

"But we just met," she replied teasingly.

Sullivan smiled in spite of himself. "Well, then, what can
you tell me about Darleen Saunders?"

"Plenty! We're old school friends," Joy said approvingly.
"Darleen was not only the most beautiful, but the *best* of us.
She waited on tables to pay her way through college."

Joy was about to continue when Darleen entered, looking
elegantly disheveled and carrying a bag of groceries. When
she looked up she spotted Sullivan.

"Why, hello," she said, and smiled. "Do all policemen
work 'round the clock?"

Sullivan caught his breath. She was even more beautiful
than he remembered. Her smile dazzled him.

"Do all rich women carry their own groceries?" he parried.

She smiled again and handed the bag to Carlotta. "Keeps me honest," she said.

At that moment, Sullivan hated his job. "Mrs. Saunders—"

"Darleen," she interrupted.

"Can we talk privately?"

"Toodle-oo," Joy said. She walked out of the room, but poked her head around the corner. "Don't worry, Darleen. I didn't tell him that you think he looks like a young Robert Mitchum. Bye-bye."

Darleen blushed. "Joy is still something of a schoolgirl."

Sullivan turned professional. "I've been to see your father-in-law."

Darleen looked stricken. She sat down on the sofa, quietly crossing her legs and clasping her hands around her right knee. "Emmanuel," she said disdainfully. Getting up again, she walked toward the glass wall, her mood now matching the gray afternoon sky. She turned and faced Sullivan.

"Just what did he tell you?"

Sullivan told her Saunders suspected her of killing his son and had given the police information implicating her best friends. He didn't specify what the materials were.

"Who are these others?" she inquired.

"Deborah Bartley, Aida Miller, Joy Livingston, and Samantha Kwan."

As he pronounced each name, Darleen managed to keep her face impassive, but she had a sinking feeling in her stomach. Once again, the night when the sisters joked about pushing Mark out a window flashed through her mind.

"Would you mind telling me where you were when your husband was killed?"

Darleen clenched her hands into fists, and a look of fierce concentration on her face was followed by an expression of utter frustration. "Please, I am totally exhausted, and can't even think. Would you mind if I gave you a statement later?"

Sullivan was disappointed. Part of him—a big part, he realized—wanted her to come up with an airtight alibi that he could check out; then he'd start digging into the other women. Innocent people immediately rattled off where they were and

what they were doing. *So much for letting my hormones inter-
fere with my judgment,* he thought disgustedly. "All right,
Mrs. Saunders. I'll take your statement later. Good night."

Riding down the elevator, he knew tomorrow he'd duti-
fully take down an alibi, one she made up, or maybe one she
was able to buy. *Never underestimate the power of money, my
boy,* he told himself.

Outside, Sullivan climbed into the Dodge next to Mays.

"You were coming in loud and clear," Mays said. "We'll
know a lot more tonight. She got a phone call right after you
left. There's a little meeting of her friends in her apartment."

Sullivan and Mays had barely finished setting up their tape
recorder in a van outside Saunders Tower when Darleen called
the meeting to order. "She's coming in loud and clear, my
man," Mays said, pulling back one of his earphones as he
spoke. "Now let's see what these chicks have cooked up."

"Goddamn," Sullivan muttered as Mays turned on the igni-
tion. "You don't suppose they did him in *together*?"

Seventeen

Darleen was dressing while Carlotta admitted the sisters and got drinks for them. Deborah was the first to arrive. Coming directly from the office, she was wearing a gray silk blouse under a two-piece blue pin-striped business suit. She kept her briefcase at her feet when she sat on the sofa, and she took out a file to read while waiting.

Joy came next. She handed Carlotta her raccoon coat without looking at the maid and sat down next to Deborah. "Isn't it wonderful that somebody finally got the prick," she said gaily.

Deborah looked at her and couldn't help smiling. "That's what I like about you, Joy. You get right to the point."

Aida arrived a moment later, and looked hesitantly at the others as she threw her mink over the back of a chair and sat down without talking.

"Aida's playing the role of a Trappist monk," Joy said sarcastically.

"Shut up," Aida muttered.

"Why, she just broke her vow," Joy said.

Samantha entered the room and handed Carlotta her fitch. She obviously had stopped at home before coming, because she was wearing a black silk tunic over jeans. "Hi, every-body," she said.

Deborah spoke up. "Look, we've got to do what we can for Darleen. Okay, so Mark wasn't our favorite person, but he was her husband. And he wasn't always a bastard."

"Christ, he changed so much that I think he must have dropped too much acid," Joy said. "What do you say, Aida?"

"What?" Aida asked irritably.

"Is that what happens to people who take too much acid?" Joy asked sweetly. "Or is it some other drug? I'm sure you know."

Samantha shook her head and spoke over her. "Deborah's right. Darleen's always been there for us. It's time we helped her."

"Helped me with what?" Darleen said, entering the room.

"Whatever you need," Deborah said.

"I appreciate the sentiment," Darleen said. "But after what I'm about to tell you, you may think you need help just as much as I do."

The sisters looked at one another. It wasn't like Darleen to be enigmatic.

"I assume you will tell us what the hell you meant by that," Joy said.

In her gray silk Halston lounging suit, Darleen walked to the center of her living room. Though the strain of recent events was reflected in the deep circles under her eyes and in her nervous hand gestures, Darleen nonetheless had a look of strength and purpose.

"I originally invited everyone because I was feeling very low. Now, there's another reason. The police were here ear-lier. They say we're all suspects in Mark's murder."

A strange stillness settled over the group. The telling fra-grance of Ferré in the air suddenly struck Darleen as being stronger, and she realized that all her senses were razor-sharp. Joy and Deborah were seated on the couch. To Joy's right, Samantha sat in a leather recliner. Always a little apart from everyone else, Aida was in a similar chair on the other side of the room, fiddling with her Chanel chains.

"That's crazy," Aida said, finally breaking the silence. She looked around and added, "Right?"

Each of the sisters stared at one another, a look of distrust on each of their faces. Each seemed to be taking the measure of the others for the first time in a long while.

"Well, well, well," Joy said with wry amusement. She was sitting on the sofa with her shoes off and her legs curled up, looking like a college girl in her camel slacks and camel and black cashmere sweater. Darleen looked at her and almost shuddered; Joy didn't seem to have changed at all over the years. Darleen couldn't help thinking of Dorian Gray.

"So we all knew Mark was a prick, but did one of us kill him?" Joy continued. "Now, which of us could have done such a naughty thing?"

"Shut up, Joy," Aida said.

Unperturbed, Joy stared at Deborah and said, "Deb, who blamed him for breaking up her marriage?"

Turning to Samantha, she said, "And Sam, who has been trained to kill?

"Maybe Aida, who is crazy enough these days to do anything for a fix."

"What about you, you bitch?" said Aida.

"Of course. There's always me. I know! I did it because I'm jealous of Mark for marrying Darleen!"

Darleen looked troubled, but she didn't respond. Suddenly, the sisters struck her as strangers.

"Come to think of it," Joy continued, "you could have killed him yourself. You've told us all what a living hell he put you through the past three years. Maybe you got a little nerve up and—"

"Joy, stop!" Deborah said. "It's bad enough we're all suspects without turning it into a theater of the absurd."

Joy settled back, a teasing smile on her lips. "But why would anyone," she said mockingly, "ever want to kill Mark in the first place?"

"Knock it off, Joy," Samantha said. "We know how you were always whispering things about Mark to Darleen."

Joy's voice became harsher. "You know, Sam, there were *some* things I never *whispered* to Darleen."

"What's this all about?" Darleen demanded.

"I'll tell you," Samantha said, staring at Darleen. She exhaled slowly and began. "You told us what a mess your marriage was. How you and Mark hadn't slept together in recent years."

Darleen looked pained. "I . . . but what does that have to do with what Joy was getting at?"

A long look passed between Samantha and Joy. Finally, Samantha exhaled slowly. "About eight months ago, he was sleeping with me," she began. "I think Joy was concerned enough about our friendship at the time that she didn't tell you . . . or that I was betrayed." For a moment, Samantha studied the drink in her hands, furrowing her brows as she thought about her intense love relationship with Mark. She wondered how much to tell the women.

"When I first met Mark, I wasn't attracted to him," she began. "I never liked men who felt sorry for themselves, and Mark traded on self-pity, using the rotten relationship with his father and his not having had a mother when he was growing up. God, I never thought I'd fall for someone like him. As he became more powerful, more dominant in his business, I found myself drawn to him."

The first time she'd felt the attraction was at a party *Chanèle* gave when Minotaur Development was awarded the contract to construct the publishing company's new world headquarters.

Mark had stood in the center of the large gathering, next to *Chanèle*'s owner and founder, Lionel Blake, a flamboyant gay given to wearing lavender ascots. "The spirit of Lionel Blake is what makes America what it is!" Mark proclaimed. "He's a man of vision and exquisite taste."

A few minutes later, Mark came up behind Samantha and whispered, "I had to give his lover ten thousand dollars to convince the faggot not to color the building lavender."

The next day, he invited her to lunch. Arriving at his office, she saw the deference everyone gave her when she said she had a luncheon appointment with him.

"Oh, Miss Kwan, I'm to show you in the second you arrive," one of Mark's secretaries said.

Samantha followed her into Mark's huge office.

"Goddamn it, Dooley, I want some action," Mark was yelling at a distinguished-looking man who sat uncomfortable in a chair before Mark's desk. "What the hell do you think you're here for?"

"Right, Mark," the man said, and he stood, preparing to go.

"Oh, Samantha. Do you know Senator Nathan Dooley? Senator, Miss Kwan."

The man hurried out a moment later.

During lunch, Samantha noticed that Mark seemed to know intuitively what she might be interested in. Later, she realized he might just have brought up certain topics because she was Chinese. Whatever the way, Mark was clever.

"What do you know about the Chinese Triad that runs Chinatown?" he asked.

"Not much."

"I could tell you every bit of real estate they own, what they are going to buy next, what kind of properties they need, and whether they are paying in dollars or gold."

"And just how can you do that?"

"Because Minotaur does most of the buying for them," he replied, laughing.

She later realized she had let herself be fooled by her response to his power. She believed he would respond to her in the same way and give her information on the Chans. So she gave him what he wanted and let him exercise power over her. Sexual power. He did so in a way no man ever had before. Each time they met, he invented newer, stranger means of domination. He chose a different place each time. Finding chinks in her armor, the things no one else knew she feared, he used them to show her weakness, demanding her submission. Until the last time.

She vividly recalled it was after midnight; the street was dark. She was wary as she approached the art gallery on East Sixty-fifth Street wearing a fitch coat over a simple black dress. The tapping of her high heels and the rustling of leaves in the night wind were the only audible sounds. She felt instinctively that Mark would go farther tonight than he ever had before. She did not know if she could give him what he wanted. Her body tensed.

When she reached the front door of the gallery she found the door slightly ajar, as Mark said it would be. She entered and closed it behind her, hearing the lock click into place. The hallway was dark, and she opened a door at the other end, entering a large, softly lit room filled with art objects. African masks and spears decorated the walls. Smooth Haitian mahogany statues stood about the room.

Along one wall a door swung open, and she walked through it. Samantha found Mark sitting in an oversized chair wearing jeans and a Ralph Lauren sports shirt open to the waist. He was alone.

Feeling a wave of relief, she went to him and kissed him as her hand caressed his chest. "Love me?" she asked.

"Always," he replied.

He crushed her against him, so that she felt the heat of his body, the pounding of his heart. "Will you do anything for me? Anything?" he asked.

Her uneasiness returned. Trembling slightly, she wondered what he had in mind.

"Yes," she finally replied.

"Beautiful Samantha," he whispered, running his fingers through her hair. "I have a surprise for you tonight."

"What is it?" she breathed.

"Come with me," he said.

Samantha followed Mark through the gallery and to a door that was so well hidden in the wall that she didn't notice it until Mark pressed a button. The door slid back, showing carpeted steps leading to a room below.

"Go down," Mark ordered.

Slowly, Samantha walked down the steps and into a warm, softly lit room that was completely covered with silky beige carpeting, even the walls. She noticed the ceiling was soundproof.

In the center of the room were two large oiled walnut posts with two metal rings attached at the bottom and two about six feet from the floor. There was a table at the far end of the room, and a large mirrored wall opposite the steps.

"Take off your clothes," Mark said from somewhere above her. Glancing up, Samantha saw two speakers embedded in the ceiling. She believed Mark must be watching through the mirror. The thought excited her, and she threw her fitch on the floor. A small smile spread across her face, and she slipped her dress over her head.

As usual, she was braless. Glancing in the mirror with amusement, she peeled off her panties, all the while staring at her reflection, knowing that a man she could break in two was watching.

"Go to the table," Mark ordered.

Samantha walked across the room, her firm body feeling the warmth of the air. Her feet caressed the silky carpeting.

"Put on the collar," he said.

On the table in front of her was a dog collar attached to a leash. Picking it up, she felt the hard leather, placed it around her neck, and buckled it shut, the leash dangling down her back between her buttocks.

"Now put on the mask."

Recoiling, she looked at the leather mask before her. There were nostril and mouth holes for breathing. But none to see through. Trembling, she lifted the soft kidskin mask. Her heart was pounding. For the first time since she was a child, sweat caused by fear broke out on her body and she looked around wild-eyed as panic gripped her. Once she had told Mark how terrified such masks made her ever since the same kind of hood had been placed over her father's head when he was killed.

Mark was deliberately using her fear. Breathing deeply, she forced herself to become calm.

"Very well," she said, uneasily.

Slowly, she brought the mask over her head. Except for a glimmer of light entering from the opening next to her throat, she could see nothing.

From above, she heard the soft hush of the door sliding open. Someone came down the steps. Then another. And another. On the rug, the sounds of their feet were light. *They must be shoeless,* she thought, wondering if they were men or women. Someone took the strings at the bottom of the mask and naked flesh brushed against her. Whoever it was drew the strings around her throat and tied them, plunging her into darkness.

Someone took hold of the leash down her back and pulled her forward. Making a fist, she was about to lash out.

"No!" came Mark's voice.

She let her hand fall to her side. Without protest, she was led across the room. Her right arm was raised and she felt her wrist being tied to one of the iron rings on the post. Then the other wrist, forcing her breath from her as she was stretched between the pillars. Next, her right ankle was similarly bound. Then the left.

Suddenly, hands were delicately stroking her body. She shuddered as she felt some kind of oil poured over her shoulders. Her nipples grew rigid as the oil slithered over them. She gasped as the streams moved down her belly and buttocks, between her legs.

The hands were all over her again, kneading her, rubbing the oil all over her, over every inch of her body. She gasped again as fingers gently probed between her thighs and buttocks. No longer able to help herself, she was gasping with pleasure. As the fingers probed, she writhed and began moaning.

"Oh, please," she whispered, not knowing whether she was asking them to stop or to continue. "Oh, please."

Time stood still. Seeing nothing, she could only feel, with her entire body. Utterly mindless. Suddenly, the thongs binding her hands were cut. She slumped to the floor, kneeling and panting.

Before she realized what was happening, a man mounted her from behind. The oily hands continued stroking and probing. When he was done, another took his place. Then another.

Seeing nothing. Feeling everything. She no longer cared that Mark was humiliating her. She just knew she didn't want it to stop.

"Please," she moaned. "Please."

She didn't know how long she'd been lying on the soft carpet. Slowly, she became conscious that no one was touching her anymore. Then she heard a voice.

"Take off the mask," Mark said.

With arms that felt leaden, Samantha removed the hood. Even the soft light momentarily blinded her. When her eyes became accustomed to the light, she realized she was alone. She hadn't heard the men exit.

*   *   *

After a long pause, Samantha raised her head. She had not told the women the story as it had just flashed through her mind, but rather in a clinical fashion, not revealing her lust of the moment.

"Several weeks later," she summed up for the sisters, "I received a note from Mark telling me to check out a movie on Forty-second Street. Mark had made a porno flick out of what I went through. My face was never shown, though. Only a woman in a mask. But he said he had another film, the unedited version, one showing my face. I told him I'd kill him!" she said. "I still don't know why he would betray me. Maybe he just hated all women."

Darleen looked drained when Samantha finished. "This is all my fault. I think Mark was trying, in his own deranged way, to get back at me through you."

"I'm sorry I started this whole thing," Joy said. "But since I have, I'd better tell you that Mark was also blackmailing me with a videotape."

It had happened one spring night about a year and a half ago. Mark called her from his office to tell her he had an important story for her, "one that hasn't been told before." Though something told her not to see him, she dismissed the notion. Christ, he was in a position to give her a prizewinner, if he wanted to. Plus, he had helped her land her current job.

She knocked on his office door. It was seven thirty in the evening, dead time between her five and eleven o'clock news programs, and Mark's secretaries were already gone.

"Come in," he called.

She entered and put her coat on the couch and her handbag on the floor before she sat in front of Mark's desk. He had treated her cordially on prior occasions, but now he didn't bother.

"You've been a naughty girl," he said with a laugh.

"Come on, Mark. Don't waste my time. What's this hot story?"

The obnoxious grin he had been wearing since she arrived broadened. "I want you to do a story on Minotaur Development Corporation—a very *favorable* story."

Joy looked at him as if he were crazy. "Darleen did say you

had gotten strange," she said. "She didn't tell me you were a fucking lunatic."

At the mention of Darleen's name, his face darkened, and his eyes became angry. "Don't talk about her," he snapped.

Gathering up her pocketbook and coat, she prepared to leave. "What in God's name gave you the idea I'd ever do a puff piece on Minotaur?"

"There is a very good reason," he said. "I want you to watch something."

He pressed a button on a remote-control device, and the television set on the opposite wall flickered on. Startled, Joy recognized the interior of the room on the screen.

It was her bedroom.

Fascinated, she watched the bedroom door open. Her mouth opened in shock as three people entered—herself, a man, and a woman. The man was tall and dark-haired, the woman petite with red hair. Both were very good-looking.

She recalled the evening vividly—it had been only a week ago. She had attended an awards dinner at the Waldorf-Astoria, one of the few she attended during the year. And she wouldn't have gone that night, if the station manager hadn't begged her to accept a plaque on behalf of the station.

When she sat down, she believed the night could be salvaged. She was sitting between a couple who were in their late twenties. She knew them slightly from various cocktail parties, and she recalled from a *New York* magazine article that they had what sounded like a kinky sex life. Strange they would show up at a gathering like this, but she was glad they had.

"Count and Countess Padruski!" she said. "Thank God you came. The night promised to be a total bore."

"Joy, I am also delighted," the count said, looking at her appreciatively.

"And me," the countess said, leaning over and kissing Joy. As she did so, she rested her hand lightly on Joy's exposed shoulder.

Throughout the meal, Joy found herself the focus of their attention. In retrospect, they were very practiced at seduction, touching her independently and sometimes together while others at the table were oblivious to what was going on. Joy enjoyed herself immensely, especially when each of them ran their hands up her thighs. She found herself more excited than she had been in a long time. Just before they reached the top of her legs, she held their hands in check.

"I think we had better go back to my place," Joy whispered.

Once in her apartment, Joy, always discreet, closed the drapes. She turned and eyed the couple mischievously. "Would you like a drink?"

"I have had enough food and drink for one evening," the countess said.

"May I see your bedroom?" the count asked.

Still wearing his overcoat, he went into her bedroom. A minute later, he returned. "I just wanted to make sure you had a king-size bed."

He extracted a small vial of cocaine from his pocket. "Beautiful women first," he said.

Joy bent over and rapidly snorted two lines. Instantly, the room became brighter. She felt gayer. The countess did the same and passed the straw to her husband.

"Now, children," he said, "let's make love."

Joy's reverie was broken by Mark's laughter. As she watched the TV screen, she saw herself lying naked, the count kissing her breasts while his wife licked her. On the screen, Joy's eyes were closed and her mouth was open. She looked blissful.

Suddenly, Mark turned the TV off. "There's no sense in seeing more," he said. "You do remember, don't you?"

"How did you get this?" she demanded.

Mark looked at her coldly. "Don't be naive. The count owes me a lot of money. Small cameras are wonderful, aren't they?"

"Why did you do this?"

"I told you. I want a piece on Minotaur."

"And if I refuse?"

"We both know how skittish TV executives are about scandal. Particularly involving an anchorwoman."

Joy was furious, almost as angry with herself as with Mark. For years, she had been discreet about her sex life, just so this would never happen. "I could kill you," she hissed.

Darleen gasped aloud at the look of hatred on Joy's face. Then Joy glanced up, startled. While recounting her story, she had gotten lost in it, as though it were happening to her again. She looked around the room at the sisters, who were hanging on her every word.

She caught herself and sat back with a mischievous smile. "So now we know what the bastard did to me." Looking at Deborah, she said, "Now, Deb, it's your turn."

Deborah took off her glasses and wiped them nervously. "I've told the story of how he messed up my marriage so often, I sound like a broken record." Glancing down at the floor, she added quietly, "What I never told anyone was that he compromised me on the job."

"Good Christ, how?" Joy said.

"Later, when I have more time," Deborah said.

"How awful for you," said Darleen.

Joy turned to Aida. "Now we can hear from the Bell Jar."

"Cut it out," Aida said crossly.

"What did he do to you?" Joy said mercilessly.

Aida looked up warily. She had been listening to the sisters talking and commiserating, but for the most part, she was lost in her own thoughts. And she wasn't about to reveal them now.

"What was it?" Joy repeated.

Anxiously, Aida got up and left the room. She hurried to the bathroom and locked the door. In desperation, she shook the contents of her handbag onto the floor. Finally, she found the brown leather case that looked like a small wallet. She took out a small mirror, then extracted a tiny plastic bag, and shook the white powder onto the mirror. Using a gold razor blade, she quickly formed the powder into two lines. Taking the short gold straw from the case, she inhaled the cocaine. Almost immediately, she felt the rush. Her cares fell away.

Upon re-entering the living room, Aida was talkative and almost gay, which caused the other sisters to look at her closely. "Well, none of this matters anymore, does it?" she asked. "After all, the wicked witch is dead!"

When he took off his earphones, Sullivan was exhausted. "Jesus," he said, turning to Mays.

"Heavy duty, my man," Mays said. "Any of them could have offed the son of a bitch."

"Well, we know one thing," Sullivan said.

"What's that?"

"They didn't do it together."

Eighteen

Sitting in the big leather chair behind the desk in what had been Mark's office, Darleen watched the gray sky darken. Wondering what would happen next, she was terrified some evidence damning her would turn up. God, what if Joy was right? What if she had killed Mark? She couldn't have! If only she could remember what had happened.

The familiar office struck her as somehow strange now. Then she realized with a start that she had never sat in Mark's chair before, never saw the room from this vantage point, even though she had spent hours with Mark poring over business deals. Until the rupture in their marriage, Mark had enjoyed discussing business with her, and she had enjoyed learning. There were times, she thought ruefully, that Mark told her she understood more about what was going on than he did.

The first time he told her that was on their honeymoon. Darleen had never traveled anywhere, and when Mark asked her where she wanted to go on their honeymoon, she had told him Martinique.

"A beautiful place," Mark said, "but why there, when the whole world is our oyster?"

"I've taken French since I was a sophomore in high

school," she said, "and I want to see if anybody understands me. I love the water, and beaches, too."

Since neither she nor Mark had large families, they decided on a small wedding. Yet, she had found it lovely. They were married at the altar of St. Thomas's on Fifth Avenue. Lilies of the valley were everywhere because she had told Mark it was her favorite flower. The only guests were the sisters and a couple of old school friends of Mark's, one of whom gave her away while another was the groom's best man. Emmanuel Saunders hadn't come, having gone to Europe on business.

Mark and Darleen left immediately for Martinique. They arrived on the island on a flight from Miami, where they had to fly from New York. Darleen fell in love with the almond-shaped island from the first moment she saw it from the air.

"Isn't it beautiful?" she whispered to Mark.

He delighted in how everything was new and wonderful for her. "This is the island of Empress Josephine," he said. "In fact, in her youth, Madame de Maintenon, who was Louis XIV's mistress, lived here."

"Okay, how do you know so much?" Darleen asked.

"I've sailed down here ever since I was a boy."

Mark had reserved a private villa, but before they got there Darleen was reminded once again of how easy money made one's life. While other passengers groped with their baggage after leaving customs, a local man wearing a freshly starched tan uniform came up and took their bags from a porter.

"How are you, Mr. Saunders?" he said.

"Fine, Joseph. I haven't seen you in quite a while. This is my wife, Darleen."

"Very pleased to meet you, Madame," he said. "If you will follow me, I have a car waiting."

The car was an air-conditioned white Mercedes. With Joseph driving, they were whisked to their villa, where the staff also called Mark by name, and the service was impeccable. But Darleen was embarrassed by having servants at her beck and call. The bedroom and the veranda had an exquisite view of the blue waters of the harbor. They spent their days snorkeling, sailing, sunbathing, and playing tennis. At night they dined and made love and fell asleep to the rustling of palm leaves.

Toward the end of their month, Mark looked at Darleen.

"Today, we'll do something a little different. Dress up elegant for lunch."

"What do you mean?" she said, laughing expectantly.

Mark pointed out of one of the bedroom windows toward the harbor. "See that yacht?"

Darleen saw a magnificent yacht gently rocking about half a mile off shore. "How could I miss it?"

"That's Nicky Niarchos's," he said. "That's where we are having lunch."

Darleen accepted everything Mark said at face value. But she continued to find her new life-style incredible.

Three hours later, a motorboat picked them up at the marina and deposited them on the Niarchos yacht.

"Mark, how are you?" someone called out. "How's Emmanuel?"

"He's fine, and I'm terrific," Mark said to a muscular, tanned man with wiry gray hair. "Nicky, this is my bride, Darleen."

"Bride! That's wonderful!" He kissed Darleen's hand. "I'm sure you'll make Mark very happy. By the way, Mark, I'd like to talk to you a bit later on. But for now, enjoy yourselves."

As they wandered about the boat, Mark introduced her to more people whose names she knew from gossip columns or plaques on hospitals and museums around New York. The boat itself was breathtaking. There was a dining room with chandeliers. The art on the wall consisted of original Picassos, Klees, and Rauschenbergs. The utensils and serving trays for the buffet lunch were sterling silver.

"This is a floating palace," Darleen marveled.

"I try to make things nice," Niarchos said with fake modesty as he came up. "Mark, there is still that matter of the property at Second Avenue and Fifty-first Street. . . ."

"Yes, Darleen and I were discussing that on the way down," Mark said. "You know, Nicky, three million dollars is steep for that section of the city."

"Sorry, Mark, that's the lowest I'll take," Niarchos said. "Come on. It's too gorgeous a day to waste time like this."

Mark had told Darleen that his father wanted the Niarchos deal sewn up. He wouldn't take no for an answer. The problem was the asking price; Emmanuel said it was too steep, unless they got more for the money. As she listened to the exchange, Darleen suddenly remembered something that Mark had told her that made any property much more valuable.

"Would you guarantee air rights from surrounding properties if you get your price?" she asked Niarchos.

The shipping magnate looked at her shrewdly. "Okay. Sure. Why not."

Shaking his head, Mark looked at her and smiled. "Deal."

The men shook hands.

"Pretty smart, little girl," Niarchos said appreciatively.

When they were alone a few minutes later, Mark pulled her to him and kissed her. "Very clever. I think you belong in this business more than I do."

Now she thought about the business, Darleen realized that she had learned a great deal about it over the years and had helped Mark reach a lot of decisions. At last, an idea she'd always fantasized about was within her reach.

Her reverie was broken off when Tony Dragonetti walked into the office. He was surprised to see her.

"Why, hello, Mrs. Saunders," he said. "I sent you a note telling you how sorry I am about Mark, but I'd like to tell you once again."

"Thank you, Mr. Dragonetti."

He was about to leave, but she asked him to stay. The request made Dragonetti nervous.

His encounters with Darleen over the years had been minimal. Some cocktail parties and dinners Mark took her to, as well as a couple of office social functions. Then there were the times she was poring over development plans with Mark. From what she had said on those occasions, Dragonetti thought she had a pretty good grasp of the business.

Dragonetti had liked Mark ever since Mark was a young guy, and he was glad when he got married. Obviously, Mark was crazy about the lady. He bought her everything, took her everywhere, and seemed to rely on her judgment. It was funny, though—as much as Mark liked Darleen, old Emmanuel seemed to resent her. But that had changed.

A couple of years ago, Mark had started treating Darleen as if she didn't exist. The same way old man Saunders used to treat Mark himself. Even the same belittling meanness. Dragonetti had never been able to figure that one out. But then, around that time, Mark had started behaving like a first-class prick with everybody. Still, he had acknowledged Dragonetti's value, something Emmanuel never did. To Emmanuel, executives were to be fucked over like dime-a-dozen bimbos, Dragonetti thought disgustedly.

Dragonetti looked up. What did the beautiful widow want with him? Was she going to give him shit about something? He wished he had a Maalox at hand. "Life's a motherfucker and then you die," he muttered to himself. It was his mantra.

Dragonetti wanted to ask what had been on his mind since Mark's death, so he could start protecting his ass. "Mrs. Saunders, can I ask you something?"

"Of course."

"It's common knowledge that you inherited Mark's fifty percent of the company. What's going to happen to Minotaur now? You going to sell it out to Emmanuel or one of the other princes?"

"It's strange that you should ask that, Mr. Dragonetti. I was just formulating my plans for Minotaur."

The way she said it struck Dragonetti as authoritative and very calculating.

Then she floored him. She put him in a bind he wasn't expecting. One that placed him in direct conflict with Emmanuel Saunders and showed that Darleen Saunders was a lot tougher a cookie than he had ever thought she was.

"As you know," she went on smoothly, "the other half of Minotaur is owned by my father-in-law. I'm sure he has deluded himself into believing he can run this huge company again. But he is older now, and since that terrible accident he has not been on top of things. Therefore, I intend to make you president of Minotaur Development Corporation. And I'll be chairman of the board."

Dragonetti was speechless.

"But I have one condition," she said. "You will teach me every aspect of this business. If you hold anything back—*any-thing*—you're out on your ear. Oh, and just to make sure you don't deceive me, I intend to touch base with other real estate people in town. As you know, my husband knew everyone. Any questions?"

Dragonetti stood there dumbfounded. Widow Saunders versus Emmanuel. A face-off. Nobody had ever done that before. When Mark had wanted to do something the old man didn't approve of, he had gone around his flanks, taking the shit later. Why the fuck was she doing this? Had she planned it all a long time ago? Did *she* kill Mark?

"Mr. Dragonetti?"

He looked at her, realizing he had been thinking so long he'd just let her stand there. "Yes?"

"I want your decision today."

Dragonetti felt sick. Choose between Emmanuel and the widow? How the hell was he going to pay all his goddamn bills if he made the wrong decision? What the fuck had he done to deserve this?

"Life is a motherfucker and then you die," he muttered.

"What?" Darleen asked. She saw what a state she had thrown the poor man into, but she didn't know what to do about it. She wanted to say something nice and give him more time to think—but she knew she couldn't.

"You'll have my decision shortly, Mrs. Saunders," he said.

Dragonetti knew he wasn't staring into the face of one of those pampered poodles that so many wives of rich men became. There was a steeliness he hadn't noticed before. Perhaps she really could pull it off.

Minutes later, in his office, Dragonetti pondered his choice. If Emmanuel came back unchallenged, Dragonetti and every other fucking executive would be treated like an errand boy by the arrogant bastard. Dragonetti burned with anger when he thought of how Emmanuel had routinely humiliated him.

What could he lose if he swung in with Darleen Saunders? His job, of course. But then, he'd never *get* the fucking job if he sided with Emmanuel. Still, when Emmanuel Saunders was crossed, he went into uncontrollable rages. Like when he kicked the shit out of that crane operator.

He picked up the intercom. "Betty," he barked to his secretary. "Tell Mrs. Saunders I'm on my way."

Darleen waited tensely. She needed Dragonetti more than he realized. Nonetheless, she looked composed when he entered, almost as if his decision were irrelevant.

He smiled broadly, and this time he was the first to extend his hand. "Mrs. Saunders, I accept," he said, thinking he'd probably just fucked up his life.

Darleen felt like running around the desk and kissing him. Instead, she shook his hand and said, "Thank you, Mr. Dragonetti. I'm sure we will work very well together."

"Now," she continued, "let's get down to business. We have to get the board members' approval, and we haven't much time before Monday's meeting."

"They think Emmanuel's going to run the company again," Dragonetti said.

"Yes, but from what my husband told me, a lot of them don't care for Emmanuel. How will they feel about me heading the company with you as my right hand?"

Dragonetti reflected for a moment. He knew the other directors respected his judgment. On more than one occasion, he had tempered Mark's enthusiasm for a screwball project. In addition, he had run interference for the directors with Emmanuel, deflecting the old man's wrath from them to himself. Like the time Emmanuel ranted at his board because they approved the resale of a property that had just been acquired, one Emmanuel had wanted to hang on to.

"Mr. Saunders, that was my fault," Dragonetti told Emmanuel. "It made sense to get rid of it at that price. I talked everyone else into it."

Emmanuel had turned to him, eyes blazing. "Dragonetti, you're through."

However, one director spoke up. "No, Emmanuel," Randolph said. "Dragonetti was right."

The two men glared at one another. Mark quickly called for a vote. Mark abstained, but Randolph and the other man he had appointed backed Dragonetti. Only Emmanuel's appointees—Armante and Fitzgerald—supported the old man.

"Mrs. Saunders, here's what we've gotta do. Forget about Armante and Fitzgerald. They're in Emmanuel's hip pocket. We've got a good shot at the others. Call Randolph first. I know he's got an axe to grind with Emmanuel. . . ."

Dragonetti shot Darleen a cynical look. "You know you gotta give perks."

Darleen looked at him. "I think I know what you mean, but would you please explain?"

"We aren't dealing with nice guys. You know Mark didn't trust them, so he even videotaped his meetings with board members as well as clients!"

"No, I didn't know that," Darleen said.

"You wouldn't. He didn't even tell the old man," Dragonetti said. "Feel under the edge of the desk top near your phone."

Darleen reached where he said and felt a button.

"There's another one in the boardroom right by Mark's chair at the head of the table. He used to tape them before he showed up at board meetings to see what they were sayin' about him."

"And the perks?" Darleen asked.

"Yeah, sorry. You gotta buy these guys' votes. Promise them something big. Like, I know Fitzgerald wants the company to go public, and he wants to do the underwriting, which will give him a fortune. . . ."

Darleen listened intently, interrupting with questions every now and then. "So Mayhew lives way over his head and has an expensive girlfriend," she said. "We should be able to help him, shouldn't we?"

Dragonetti was impressed with some of the ingenious solutions she came up with and he laughed.

Darleen smiled. "What do you find so amusing?"

"Emmanuel's always talking about Machiavelli. He could take a couple of lessons from you!"

Darleen glanced at the clock and looked startled. "Thank God, we've wrapped this up for the moment. I have an appointment."

Detective Sullivan had called, wanting to see her again today. She had suggested dinner because it would be less formal, less threatening. While she was with Dragonetti, she had been able to forget about the horror of Mark's death. Now her palms moistened, and she felt short of breath. What could she possibly tell the detective?

"You okay, Mrs. Saunders?" Dragonetti asked.

Darleen shook her head slightly and smiled. "Yes, thanks."

As Dragonetti was about to go through the doorway, she called out, "You aren't a bad Machiavelli yourself!"

Nineteen

Sullivan climbed out of a cab at the address on Eighty-seventh Street, between Lexington and Third avenues. He was wearing a freshly pressed brown tweed suit, pale yellow shirt, and striped tie. The restaurant Darleen had chosen was a little German place, the kind he liked.

He immediately saw her at a table in the rear, but she didn't see him. She was staring at her hands folded on the table in front of her. The pose conveyed dignity—as well as a great deal of sadness.

Darleen was wearing a gray wool Geoffrey Beene dress and a heavy silver bracelet with matching earrings. She had deliberately not worn a fur since she felt Sullivan would view a fur as a way of flaunting great wealth. Not that it should matter what this detective thought of her. Suddenly, she felt a presence and looked up.

Sullivan smiled down at her. "Sorry—I didn't mean to startle you."

"No, please sit down. I'm just so preoccupied that . . ." She looked flustered for a moment and blushed. She saw that he was spruced up, and couldn't help feeling pleased that he may have done it for her.

Sullivan was stumped. The blush had to be genuine; he had never known anyone to fake one. So how could anyone who blushed so easily be a vamp? This was, after all, a poor girl who had worked her way through school, not some jaded little tease.

A slut? Hardly. A murderess? That was another question. Sullivan found himself very curious about the lady. "Mrs. Saunders," he began.

"Please call me Darleen."

"Okay, Darleen, and my name is Brian," he said smiling. Thinking again about Carter's demand that he charm the lady, he felt the guilt rise again. "I've had a long day, and you did, too." Signaling the waiter, he said, "I'm going to have a drink. Would you care to join me?"

They accepted menus from the waiter.

"White wine," she said.

"Bourbon on the rocks," Sullivan ordered.

Darleen put down the menu without looking at it.

"Not hungry?" Sullivan asked.

"I know what I want. Wiener schnitzel."

"Peasant food," he said, with mock surprise.

"Betrays my background, I'm afraid," she said, smiling ruefully.

"And what might that be?"

Darleen looked at him wryly. "I guess I'm the classic rags-to-riches girl."

"Surely, there's more to it than that."

"There is, but my life seems like a pattern of tragedy when I look back on it. My father died shortly after I was born. And my mother died shortly after I became a scholarship student at Sarah Lawrence." Darleen looked up wistfully. "My mother was a wonderful woman. Her dream was to see that I graduated from college so that I could live the kind of life she never had. A Golden Life, she called it."

"How about college?"

"To make a long story short, I threw myself into my studies, figuring it was one area where I could shine. It was there I met the sisters—the women you have as murder suspects—there that I had any real friends."

"Then you met Mark Saunders, and he offered the golden

dream," Sullivan said—somewhat sarcastically.

Darleen looked at him wearily. "Oh, I was dazzled by Mark. Of course, some of the allure had to do with his money. But he was also very nice, not at all what he became later." Darleen paused and wiped tears from her eyes. "If only he had believed me instead of his father," she said, more to herself than to Sullivan.

When he looked at her, Sullivan didn't think he had ever seen so much suffering in anyone's eyes. He was about to ask her what she meant, but he didn't want to push her, or to let his personal feelings overcome his professional demands.

"Hard as it may be to believe," she said, "right now I don't care much for the life I lead."

"It's not hard for me to believe it *at all*."

Sullivan spoke with such conviction that Darleen looked startled. When he perceived the expression on her face, he smiled ruefully.

"I didn't mean to upset you more than you already are. It's just that I'm all too familiar with that big-money crowd."

"How's that?" Darleen raised an eyebrow and looked perplexed.

"My mother is Theresa Bingham."

"Oh, my," Darleen said, with a smile. "A powerful lady in the art world."

"Barracuda is the description most people use when they refer to her," Sullivan said dryly.

"Then how did you become a policeman?" Darleen asked curiously.

"I guess my story is riches-to-rags," he said with a laugh. "My stepfather was a wealthy industrialist, and I received all the advantages money can buy. Prep schools. Yale. I pleased my mother by dressing the J. Press preppy way she adored, traveled with the very rich—whose power, Mother informed me, would rub off on me. My wife, Paige, dabbled in art. She was the kind of rich princess my mother thought I should marry. In a nutshell, I came to the realization that rich people often aren't very nice. When I learned about ten years ago that my real father had been a cop, I chucked the ways of the wealthy and followed Dad's footsteps. My mother disowned me. My wife divorced me."

"Brian," she said with a smile that faded quickly as she thought of what she had to say. "I know I told you that I would prove I had nothing to do with Mark's death, but truthfully I'm not sure I can."

Haltingly, she reconstructed her actions on the night of her husband's death as well as she could. Right up to waking up in a strange bed and not knowing how she got there.

"Not a pretty picture," she said. "And it doesn't speak much for my moral standards. But believe me, I was never unfaithful to my husband before that night."

Sullivan quickly evaluated the facts as presented: Her friend Aida left her stranded. Her drink was apparently doctored. A strange man picked her up. The rest of the night was a blank. She awoke in a strange apartment. It almost sounded like someone was trying to frame her. And yet, he couldn't help wondering how she could have been so goddamn dumb. Rich and powerful, why had she put herself in such a vulnerable position?

"How about your friend Aida? Isn't she any help?"

"Not for anything that happened after midnight."

Darleen now was trembling. Sullivan thought she was going to cry, but she took a deep breath and pulled herself together.

"Darleen," he said slowly. "I'd like to help you. But to be honest, I'm not sure I can."

"Does that mean you're going to arrest me?" she asked terrified.

Sullivan knew that was exactly what Carter wanted. But the possibility of a frame couldn't be ignored. Neither could the tapes and letter that implicated the other women. Nor, increasingly, could his feelings for Darleen.

"For now, let's assume somebody else killed your husband. How about this guy you woke up with? What can you remember about him? About where he lived?"

She started shaking her head. "I don't know..."

"Please, Darleen. Think!" Sullivan said, thinking to himself, don't let Carter nail you. "When you left his apartment, what part of town was it in? Was there anything unusual about it? Anything unusual about him?"

"All I can remember is that it was in SoHo, right around Houston Street."

By the time Sullivan ceased pressing her for information, he realized that either he had gotten everything she knew, or she was very clever. "I didn't mean to upset you," he said genuinely.

"I know," she replied softly. "I guess I'm just beginning to believe that whole horrible thing is real. Until now, I didn't feel anything . . . *oh, God, how I wish Mark had believed me instead of his father!*"

"About what?"

She shook her head and reached for her pocketbook. "Please take me home," she said. "This has been a very long day."

Sullivan motioned for the check. "Of course," he said.

During the taxi ride to Saunders Tower they were both silent. When the cab stopped at the front entrance, she looked at him thoughtfully. Almost absentmindedly, she started getting out.

"Will you call—if you find anything?" she asked, her tone demanding.

He reached out and touched her arm. "Can I call even if I don't?"

For the first time during the evening, she smiled. Pulling her coat around her, she opened the door. "Yes," she said.

Sullivan slumped back and wondered. "Now, who's using who?"

SATURDAY

Twenty

"Oh, Tommy, it's no big deal. Just a couple of days on Fire Island."

"I know, Martha. I can't help it. I don't ever want to be away from you."

Tommy Winslow ran his right hand through his thick black hair. He was a gangly, nice-looking young man of twenty-two. A straight nose, full lips. Dark, serious eyes. Though it was very cold, he wore only a heavy wool muffler around his neck and a thick sweater under his corduroy sports coat, because he didn't have an overcoat.

Sitting next to him on the bench in Central Park was Martha Hendrick, a girl he had known for two months and desperately wanted to marry, although he didn't know how he could ever afford to do so. He was from Iowa, and he'd just entered Columbia Law School, where he had a scholarship.

Until now, he had never had a girlfriend, and he had almost thought he never would. He was too serious. Didn't know how to joke with girls and say the kinds of things they liked to hear. He respected girls too much, which was another problem. He used to see drunken fraternity types in college who treated the really good-looking girls they were with like shit.

Grabbing them and making obscene remarks to them. And going to bed with them. Girls he would gladly have died for.

Then along came Martha, and the world that to him had always seemed lonely and dismal suddenly became bright and warm. He had met her accidentally on the steps of the main public library on Fifth Avenue. Not looking where he was going, he tripped over her, sprawling down the steps and cutting his forehead.

Martha was alarmed. "Are you all right?" she asked fearfully. "It was all my fault."

He wound up laughing at how seriously she took what had happened, recognizing that usually he would have behaved like her. "Would you care for a cup of coffee?" he asked shyly.

He was amazed when she accepted. More amazed when he found himself talking to her almost nonstop, much of his loquacity stemming from his loneliness. He found out she, too, was alone in New York. They were suddenly allies in thinking of themselves as hicks in the big city.

They met the next day, and the next, and started going to movies at night. One night Martha came back to his apartment and he made love to her. Embarrassed, she confessed that she was a virgin. He experienced relief because he was, too.

Now, he was irked that she'd been invited to Fire Island without him. He had come to take it for granted that they would do everything together. He was jealous, but not wanting to admit it.

"Oh, Tommy," Martha said. "I'm not leaving you. I'm just going out for a couple of days with Joy, the woman I told you about."

"I know. It's just that I don't want to be away from you," he repeated.

Martha was concerned, but she smiled. She almost gave in to him. But that was her biggest problem. Doing what everybody wanted her to do. So they would like her. Think she was nice. "Look, silly, we need the money. Plus, I've heard so much about the island, I'd like to see it for myself. You know I grew up around the ocean and beaches, and you know how much I miss the seashore. I have a feeling it will be a little like home."

Tommy didn't tell her he was afraid she would meet another guy out there. Somebody sophisticated with a lot of money who would make him look like a nerd. "Okay," he said. "Have a good time."

Martha leaned over and kissed him. "I'll be back before you know it."

He warmed under the kiss. "No you won't," he grumbled.

Twenty-One

John Cummins sat in the cramped office of the Lower East Side community council in a dilapidated red-brick tenement on Ninth Street near Avenue C. He was late for the appointment, having spent a sleepless night debating whether to come, whether to quit his job. He considered himself a coward, experiencing the familiar leaden feeling of being unable to do what he wanted to.

The little speech about ethics he gave Fitzgerald until he was chastized sounded tinny in his memory, still leaving a metallic taste in his mouth. The irony of him preaching ethics. He who did base acts out of fear. He couldn't look Charlene Duncan in the eyes while he spoke to her. He merely repeated what Fitzgerald had told him to say.

"As you know, we would like to relocate the people in the area," he said. "And, uh, while many people will have to be relocated to different boroughs, we, uh, thought we'd get you a nice rent-controlled apartment in a very good location."

Charlene Duncan looked at him craftily. An intense, painfully thin woman with frizzy black hair, she had been making life as much hell as possible for these real estate developers. She was the head organizer for nearly one thousand residents of the area who were going to be shoved out of their homes because a greedy developer could turn their apartments into luxury cooperative apartments.

She knew how powerful she was. One word from her and every fucking tenant would sit where he or she was, stop paying rent, hang ON RENT STRIKE sheets out their windows, and not move without a court order, which could take years. She knew that the more she busted the developers' balls, the better her payoff would be to see that the relocation went without more hitches.

"And just where would that be?"

Through various holding companies controlled by the law firm, apartments were warehoused around the city for such occasions. Money was too crude a bribe. But in New York, a desirable apartment was worth its weight in gold.

Cummins wiped his glasses nervously. He could envision himself getting disbarred. Disgracing his mother and father. Winding up some sleazy ambulance chaser. All because of the way business was done in New York and of his lacking the guts to say no.

"Uh . . . Central Park South."

For a minute, Charlene was tempted to look for another way to break his chops. See what else she could get. But she suddenly realized there was nothing else. Her eyes lit up like the dollar slot machine in Vegas. Her face contorted into a wolflike smile. Squirming in her seat, she thought she might have an orgasm.

How about that. Very good location. The little jerk had just offered her the moon. Central Park South, one of the most fashionable, most desirable addresses in the city. In a fucking rent-controlled building.

"Mr. Cummins, tell whoever the hell you represent that we have a deal."

Twenty-Two

Aida peered fearfully past the chain lock on her front door. It was about noon and a crumpled, somewhat nice-looking guy stood outside. "Yes?"

"Miss Miller, my name's Detective Sullivan. Can I speak with you about Mark Saunders's death?"

A troubled look clouded Aida's face. She shut the door and undid the chain. Terrifying thoughts filled her head. *Why is he here? Why come after me?*

She had slept late and was now dressed only in a blue silk dressing gown. Her hair was down, and she wore no makeup. He face was still a little puffy from just having climbed out of bed. With her dark hair and liquid movements, she looked like a sleepy panther.

By the time Sullivan brushed past her, Aida was in control of herself, ready to act like someone else. "Try to find a place to sit," she said. "Sorry the place looks like an unmade hotel room. Actresses are on the road so much we have little time to fix up our homes."

Sullivan thought her description was accurate. There were no personal effects around that indicated anyone really lived there. It did look like a hotel room—an expensive one. The walls were pale green, the carpet oriental, and the du:ty furniture Chippendale. He shoved a coat aside and sat down.

"Do you mind if I ask you something personal?" he said.

"Shoot."

"I don't recall you having made it big in anything. How can you afford to live like this?"

"All this was bought with a trust fund that was set up after my parents died. They were killed in a car crash years ago in England."

"Why were they in England?"

"Sir," Aida said in an aristocratic English accent, "I am half British. My father was a peer of the realm. A penniless peer, I'm afraid, who married a wealthy American dowager who made his life hell. You see, Mother wanted ever so much to be married to a man with a title. She didn't notice until it was too late that my father had been raised to do nothing. My mother held the purse strings and *never* let him forget it."

"How did you wind up over here?"

"I was at Sarah Lawrence when they died," she replied. "After graduation, I saw no reason to go back. All of my friends were here."

"The sisters?"

"You know about the sisters?" she said, giving Sullivan a slightly quizzical look. "Then you must be the same detective who went to see Darleen."

"That's right."

"Is it true, then, that we are all murder suspects? Like in some bizarre Agatha Christie novel?"

"Let's just say I'm collecting alibis."

"That calls for a drink," she said, walking to a bar in the corner and pouring herself a Vodka straight up. "How about you?"

"A little early for me."

Aida took a long pull on her drink and set it down. "Now, why would I kill Mark Saunders?"

"You tell me," Sullivan said, disliking her flip manner.

"What do you want me to say?"

"For one thing, last year you threatened him in public," Sullivan said.

"Oh, so you know about that," she said lightly. "No, that

was something else. It was nothing, really. Will you excuse me for a minute?" She went to her bedroom hurriedly and closed the door. She was shaking as she vividly recalled what had caused her to threaten Mark's life.

When Mark had called her, it was the first time he had contacted her since his marriage to Darleen. "I have something for you that will help you," he told her over the phone. "Can you meet me tomorrow evening?"

"Name the time and place," she told him dryly. "I haven't worked in so long all I have is time."

She met him at "21". Though she had often heard Darleen say how badly Mark treated her, he seemed now like the decent young man Aida had known more than ten years ago. After listening to him, Aida wondered whether Darleen might be making up those stories.

"Aida, I'm backing a play. Not just *any* play—the new Neil Simon. It's something I've always wanted to do."

"That's terrific, Mark," she replied. "But really, I can't handle anyone's success tonight. My own achievement level has been zero, lately."

"That's all about to change," Mark said.

"Come again?" She felt a flicker of hope about what he might say next, but she extinguished it immediately. No, she told herself, that was an impossibility.

Then Mark turned the flicker into a roaring flame. "Aida, I want you for the lead!"

She tried to act nonchalant, but as she lit a cigarette, her trembling hands gave her away.

"I'm serious," Mark said.

After two months of staying away from drugs and still feeling on cloud nine, Aida showed up at the Butler Theater on the day rehearsals were to begin. But when she tried to enter, the guard told her he didn't have her name on his sheet.

"There must be some mistake," she said. "Call Matt Clawson, the director."

While the guard headed down the hall, Aida slipped in and saw Mark sitting about ten rows down, watching actors and actresses up on the stage. "Thank God, you're here," she said to him.

Startled, Mark looked up. "What are *you* doing here?"

"What do you mean? I'm the lead, remember?"

Mark began laughing. "Good Lord, Aida, you didn't take me seriously, did you?"

She looked at him in disbelief. Then, as what he'd done dawned on her, she glared at him with hatred and fury. For some insane reason, he had concocted an elaborate practical joke at her expense, to humiliate her.

"You bastard!" she screamed. Her shriek was so piercing the actors on stage stopped and stared into the auditorium. But Aida was oblivious to them. All she could see was the cruel smirk on Mark's face.

"You dirty, filthy bastard!" She threw herself on him. "I'll kill you! I'll kill you!" she shouted, gashing his face with her nails until he was able to grasp her hands and hold them down at her side.

The door guard rushed over and grabbed Aida and dragged her out. As she was led away, she heard Mark apologizing to the cast. "The woman is obviously crazy."

The sound of Detective Sullivan rapping on her door snapped her out of her reverie. She opened it, looking like a startled deer.

"Are you okay?" he asked.

"Just a little dizzy for the moment. I'm all right now."

"You haven't told me yet why you threatened to kill Mark Saunders," Sullivan pressed.

"I told you, it was nothing," she said, her voice suddenly airy again. "Just a case of artistic differences."

Sullivan studied her for a moment. She obviously wasn't going to give him a straight answer, which made her as much of a suspect as Darleen. He'd try another line of questioning.

"What time did you leave Palladium on the night of his death?"

"About eleven thirty or quarter of twelve."

"Why did you and Mrs. Saunders go there?"

"To dance. That's all, for God's sake."

"Why did you leave so early?" he pressed.

Aida looked up and involuntarily flushed. "I didn't feel well, so I went home."

"Can you prove that?"

"Christ almighty, ask my doorman."

"And you have no idea who Mrs. Saunders left with?"

"She was dancing with several different guys. Ask her."

"You told her someone doctored her drink?"

"I told her it *looked* like somebody did something funny with her drink. I don't know for sure if it was doctored."

"Do you know anything else that would help this investigation?"

Aida stood up and walked over to the door. She wrung her hands nervously.

"Yes. I think you should know that Mark had hit her that night. She'd taken a lot of verbal abuse, but she said that was the last straw."

Sullivan's face remained impassive, but he felt himself growing angry. Why hadn't Darleen told him Mark had slugged her? Didn't she think he'd find out? Did the last straw mean that Darleen had *intended* to kill her husband?

"Go on, Miss Miller."

"There's no more. I'm late for an audition as it is."

Sullivan left, and Aida went into the bedroom and opened the top drawer of her bureau. Taking out a brown vial, she unscrewed the plastic cap and used the small spoon inside to scoop up some of the white powder. Holding one nostril, she snorted the cocaine.

Sullivan, meanwhile, shook his head in disgust as he walked back to his car. He had found still more reason to think Darleen might be guilty.

But Aida also looked guilty.

Twenty-Three

In his car, Mays asked the dispatcher if she could put him through to Sullivan. He figured he'd catch him before Sullivan interviewed Deborah Bartley, so they could compare notes.

"Detective Sullivan isn't back yet," a woman's voice said.

"Tell him I'm going to Fire Island."

Suddenly, Captain Carter's voice broke in. "What the hell are you going to Fire Island for?"

"A suntan," Mays muttered disgustedly. Then, "Tell Sullivan that Joy Livingston's at her beach house."

"When am I going to have an arrest?" Carter demanded.

Mays flicked off the radio without answering. He took a pair of field glasses from the trunk, figuring he'd while away the boat ride watching fishermen. Goddamn shame Sullivan had to miss his fishing trip, he thought. He joined the handful of passengers boarding the white ferry.

Another passenger was Martha Hendrick, who was wearing khakis and running shoes and a Villager blouse under her pale blue angora sweater, a present from her parents last Christmas. Her red nylon windbreaker crackled in the wind.

The day was sparkling as the ferry made its way from Long

Island. The sun was glittering and the sky was a rich blue with traces of wispy clouds. Though it was windy, Martha stood on the top deck and looked out over the water, her red hair ruffling in the breeze.

She wanted to see Fire Island so much, but she was worried that she would embarrass herself. What if Joy was moody and different from when she was in the city? Worse, what if Joy found Martha boring? What if some of Joy's rich friends were there? Should she act like them or the hired help? *If only I were sophisticated,* she thought, her stomach in a knot.

As the boat approached the dock at the Pines, Martha spotted Joy smiling and waving in welcome. Joy was wearing yellow slacks and a matching sailing jacket. Martha couldn't help thinking how beautiful she looked in the sunlight.

"No cars on Fire Island, so you have quite a trek in front of you, young lady," Joy said, after giving Martha a hug. She grabbed Martha's weekender tote bag from her and slung it over her shoulders. Martha grabbed it back again.

"I'm in good shape," Martha said with a laugh.

"Yes, indeed you are!" said Joy, looking at her appreciatively. Martha knew her face was red. She felt stupid all over again.

Using his binoculars, Mays observed the greeting and decided not to give himself away, but instead to keep them under surveillance for a while. Christ, he thought, he had to do something. The next ferry back wasn't until the evening.

The women walked along the unpaved street, with Joy making easy conversation. Did Martha have any specific plans for the future? Had she seen this movie and that play? All of Martha's anxieties melted, and she found herself chattering away, telling Joy about her home on the Jersey seashore, and how much she loved the beach and the ocean.

When Joy put her arm through hers, Martha felt like they were the best of friends.

They had been walking for a while, and the more built-up part of the island was left behind them. Then a modern glass and cedar shingle beach house loomed ahead, sandwiched between enormous dunes and the shimmering ocean.

"Well, here we are," Joy said.

They approached the structure that looked as if it had been

sculpted to blend into the surroundings. "It's beautiful!" Martha said.

They stepped inside. Martha gaped at everything she saw. The house was like a loft split-leveled into sections. None of the various living areas were walled off; rather, they were separated by being on different levels and finished off in different textured wood and stones.

The galley kitchen off to the right was all stainless steel. The sunken living room had a glass-and-stone beamed cathedral ceiling and a large flagstone fireplace. A massive glass wall created a moving mural out of the ocean.

"Sheds a lot," said Joy, laughing as Martha bent over and stroked the silky goat hair carpeting.

Joy took off her jacket and Martha saw that she was braless, her full breasts shaped by a tight lavender sweater. She felt Joy press the palm of her hand against her lower back, gently pushing her toward a redwood platform between the living and sleeping quarters. Inset in the platform was a large sunken tub. Towering potted ferns secluded the area from the living room. The ceiling was a huge tinted-glass dome.

"Watch," Joy said.

She pressed a button and the tinted glass became clear, showing the sky above in its natural color. "I'm not sure how these things work, but they're marvelous," she said.

Next, she took Martha by the hand to the sleeping quarters. In the center of the open area was a huge circular bed low to the floor. Oak dressers and closets were built into polished oak walls. There were huge windows everywhere—a sensuous, soaring cathedral.

"I'm so isolated out here there's no need for curtains," Joy said.

Next, Joy showed Martha the guest quarters. There were built-in closets that were disguised as a wall, plus a queen-size bed.

"I figured it was easier to give guests something traditional rather than put them in another hedonistic merry-go-round bed," she said, laughing. "Say," she added. "Let's get in some sunbathing while it's still light out. I told you to bring a bathing suit, didn't I?"

"Yes, and I did. But isn't it too cold?"

"No. The sun is bright, and there's a little cove down in the dunes that blocks the wind."

Joy went back to her sleeping area, Martha toward hers. *Thank goodness,* Martha thought, *there are no sophisticated friends here! This is going to be great.*

She turned and realized Joy was taking her clothes off and putting on a bikini. Martha looked for a moment and blushed, feeling like she was peeking. Turning away, she stripped and put on her suit, too.

Joy came over wearing a fluffy white terrycloth robe and carrying another. "Put this on. You'll need it until we get down there."

While Mays watched through his binoculars, Joy led Martha between the steep dunes as the wind billowed out their robes. After five minutes, they came to a small shelter about six by ten feet that gave a view of the water. The surrounding dunes blocked the wind.

Joy spread out a blanket, took off her robe, and stretched out. She patted a place next to her and Martha followed suit, luxuriating in the warmth of the sun, such a contrast with the cold breeze that was blowing all around them.

Sitting up, Joy said, "Be a good girl and unhook me."

With fumbling fingers, Martha unhooked Joy's bikini bra. Joy turned and faced her, her left breast brushing against Martha. Martha felt an electric shock go up her arm.

"Turn around," Joy said, poised to unhook Martha's top.

Martha was going to beg off, but suddenly that feeling of being a hick came back. "All right," she said, turning her back to Joy.

Joy untied the strap around Martha's neck, her fingers lingering for a moment beneath the younger woman's hair. Then she undid the clasp on her bikini bra. Martha's skin prickled at the touch of Joy's fingers.

"Now," Joy said. "Let me have a look at you." She slowly turned Martha around. "God," Joy said. "They're perfect."

Martha hunched over and clasped her knees. Would she ever stop blushing?

Joy took a bottle of suntan lotion out of her robe pocket. "Your tan lines tells me you don't go topless much. Let me put some of this on you."

"No, uh, I'll do it myself."

Martha felt funny spreading the lotion over her breasts, and was glad Joy was on her stomach and not watching. Her nipples hardened as her hands applied the cream. At the same time, she felt daring and sophisticated. The vast ocean made her feel open and free. She giggled. Tommy would be shocked if he knew what she was doing. Maybe she wouldn't tell him.

As Joy and Martha talked comfortably, Mays watched them through his binoculars. He admired their bodies, wondering if Livingston was getting it on with the young one. He wished he could hear them.

"How did you become an anchorwoman?" Martha asked.

"Through hard work," Joy said. "After I graduated from Sarah Lawrence, the only TV job I could get was weathergirl for a small station in Greensboro." She paused for a wry smile. "Believe me, weather in Greensboro is pretty damned boring.

"Then I got a big break. One day we were so short-staffed they had to assign me to cover a shoot-out between Klansmen and Communists. You might remember it. I was the only reporter able to get near the gunmen. I gave a live report with bullets whizzing over my head, and it paid off. I sent a copy of the tape to each of my best friends. One, Darleen Saunders, gave it to her husband, and he passed it along to a network executive who thought I was hot. Two months later, I was in New York."

She paused again. "A lot of people think TV women got where they did on their backs, but in my case it's not true." The sun started going down, and Joy shivered. "I guess we should head back," she said.

Martha looked over and saw the sunlight shimmering on the film of sweat on Joy's throat and breasts. Looking down, she saw the same on her own breasts. Joy put her robe on and stuffed the halter into her pocket. Martha did the same, enjoying the feel of the rough terrycloth against her breasts. But by the time they got back to the house, they were both shivering.

"Thank God we're here," Martha said. "I'm freezing."

"Let me get us something nice and warm to drink," Joy said.

Several minutes later, she returned with two large brandy snifters. Her robe opened, and her breasts swayed softly as she bent forward to hand a glass to Martha. "This is the only thing that really takes the edge off a day like this," she said.

They sat in two oversized leather chairs and watched the sun go down. "I like to make a big production out of dinner," Joy said. "Get dressed up. Candlelight. Good wine. Good music. I hope you'll indulge me."

"It sounds wonderful," Martha replied. "But—I didn't bring anything nice to wear. I'm sorry. I—"

"Oh, don't worry. We're about the same size. I'll lend you something."

The brandy sent a warmth through Martha's entire body. She felt like a pampered kitten, drowsy in the evening sun.

"Why don't you take a nap, and I'll fix dinner," Joy said. "I love to cook, but I can't stand having anybody hovering over me in the kitchen."

"Okay, if that's the way you want it," Martha said languidly, not feeling like moving.

"I'll leave some lovely clothes out for you," Joy said.

While Martha slept, Mays paid Joy a house call. Joy seemed initially more annoyed than frightened by his visit.

"So you think I killed Mark Saunders," Joy said, after he sat down and told her about the tape Saunders gave them.

"I didn't exactly say that," Mays said. "But that tape does mean something, doesn't it?"

"I guess it does, but I *do* have an alibi. I was editing a tape that night for a special news report. Now, if you have any more questions . . ."

They sparred verbally for another twenty minutes. Finally, Mays checked his watch. "My ferry is leaving soon. If there's anything else, I'll reach you in the city."

"And you did say that tape will not find its way out of your possession, didn't you?" Joy asked, somewhat anxiously.

She seemed to keep steering the conversation toward the tape and away from the rest; Mays wondered how strong her alibi was. "Don't worry," he said, and left.

When Martha awoke, the sky was dark. Checking her watch, she realized she had slept for an hour. Mozart was playing from the stereo, and she could hear the crackling of logs in the fireplace. Quickly, she showered and washed her hair, dried herself with a big, fluffy towel, and looked at the clothing Joy had left on her bed.

Everything matched. There was a beautiful, ice-blue silk gown that zippered down the back, a pair of lace panties, stockings, a garter belt, and high-heeled shoes. Martha looked in the mirror before putting on the dressing gown. She had never worn a garter belt and stockings, but she could tell they looked sexy on her. She wondered what Tommy would think of them.

When she entered the living room, she saw a small table set for two. Candles were lit. A wine bottle sat open. The dancing light of the fireplace cast flickering shadows everywhere.

"Well, here you you, sleepyhead," Joy said.

Turning, Martha saw that Joy was wearing a replica of the gown she had on, except that it was an emerald green that matched her eyes. She realized Joy's undergarments also must match her own. Joy's delicate silk gown fell in soft folds from the points of her nipples and rippled over the curve of her hips.

"I hope I didn't hold up dinner," she said apologetically.

"You're in luck, you naughty girl. Nothing's spoiled."

Joy walked across the room and appraised Martha from head to toe. "I must say, that looks stunning on you. Absolutely beautiful."

"You look beautiful, too," Martha found herself saying.

Taking Martha by the hand, Joy led her over to the fireplace, sat down on the floor, and pulled Martha down next to her. She reached over to a coffee table and opened a silver cigarette box and took a joint out.

"To enhance the meal, I like to smoke a little," she said. "You do do grass, don't you?" Joy asked, as if everyone in the world did.

Joy lit and inhaled deeply. Martha took the joint and did the same. By the time they finished the joint, Martha was feeling mellow. The flames in the fireplace were more brilliant. The carpeting felt silkier.

"I'll put dinner on," Joy said.

"There must be something I can do," Martha said.

"Just sit and look beautiful. You will serve tomorrow night."

Martha went to the table, brushing her feet through the piles of the rug. She sat and stared at the heavens and the ocean. The black sky looked like velvet, the stars like diamonds. She felt like she could touch them.

The meal was sumptuous. A celery remoulade, accompanied by Château Mouton Rothschild 1965, suffused Martha with warmth from her mouth up to her head and throughout her whole body. Then a cup of lobster bisque with a sherry base. Cornish hens stuffed with wild rice and mushrooms was the main course. For dessert there was chocolate mousse, accompanied by a Bordeaux d'Youen. Martha found herself luxuriating in every taste, differentiating each, letting each morsel slide down her throat.

"I can't believe an evening can be so perfect," Martha said. "I feel like a pampered poodle."

"Close your eyes," Joy said.

Martha automatically shut them tightly.

"Listen to the sound of the ocean."

The rolling sound of the surf became more audible as Martha breathed deeply and let it wash over her while Joy walked around the table to her. Martha felt Joy's warm hands on her neck, smoothing down to her shoulders and pressing deep into the muscles. She gasped at the silky brush of her own gown as it moved across her nipples and over her belly and thighs.

"I have an idea," Joy whispered. "Let's give each other a massage."

Joy led her past the sunken bath to her bed. She turned back to the girl.

"Help me off with my gown," she said.

As if in a trance, Martha pulled the zipper down to where it stopped below Joy's buttocks. In one slow motion, the gown slid off Joy's body. She was wearing emerald stockings, panties, and garter belt.

"Turn around, Martha," Joy whispered, touching her gown. "You won't be able to give a massage wearing this."

Obediently, Martha turned. Trembling, she felt Joy unzip her gown, which, too, slid to the floor. Warm air enveloped her, leaving her feeling more pleasantly exposed than she ever had in her life. When she turned, Joy was facing her.

Joy's nipples were erect. She took a step toward Martha and their nipples touched. Martha felt her nipples harden in response, and she took a step backward. Was this all right? Why was she confused?

Lying down on the silver silk sheets on her bed, Joy whispered, "Lie down. Just relax."

Martha obeyed. Joy's hands were gentle and sensitive. The softness of the sheets and the motions of the massage felt like a dream. Martha rolled over and looked up at the incredibly soft glow of starlight rimming Joy's hair and brushing the curve of her cheek. How soft she looked. How lovely.

Joy brought her face close to Martha's and kissed her gently on the lips, her hand cupping her breast. Martha gasped. What was Joy doing? And what should *she* do, now? How could she get up? She'd embarrass Joy terribly, and hadn't she undressed and lain down as if this were all right with her? And besides, she didn't want Joy to take her hand away. It felt so *good*. She wanted more.

She reached up to touch Joy's shoulder almost as if to push her away, and found herself sliding her hand down Joy's arm and reaching to touch Joy's breast and hips. Reaching down, Joy put her hand over Martha's and slid off her emerald panties.

"I won't take off yours," Joy said. "That is up to you."

Martha turned away in confusion. Joy kissed her on her flushed cheek and lips, running a finger down her thigh. Then Martha felt herself kissing Joy.

She felt Joy's tongue and teeth everywhere on her body. Her breasts, navel, between her thighs. She began moaning and trembling. She began stroking Joy's body, and kissing her everywhere, doing to Joy whatever Joy did to her. Her body arched and shuddered as Joy's hands and mouth explored her. Whimpering, she removed her panties so Joy could have what she wanted.

"Oh God," she moaned to herself. *What am I doing? What's going to happen to me?*

Twenty-Four

It was three P.M., and Deborah was in her office in City Hall Annex across the street from City Hall, boning up on a meeting of the Board of Estimates.

Kay Edelman, another of the seven women among the thirty-five city council members, poked her head into Deborah's office. About five feet five inches tall with reddish hair, Kay was thin and had nervous energy to burn. "Slaving away again on Saturday, huh?"

"What else?" Deborah replied.

"Can I borrow your secretary for a little bit? I'm so short of staff I have to kiss my own ass."

"Sure," Deborah replied with a laugh.

A moment later she was interrupted again by a man who rapped twice on her open door. "Excuse me, Mrs. Bartley. My name is Detective Sullivan. Your maid told me you were working here. I have some questions to ask you about Mark Saunders's death."

His visit wasn't a surprise. Since Darleen had told the sisters they were all suspects in the case, Deborah had been expecting an official caller.

"Please, sit down," she said.

"I'll come to the point," Sullivan said. "Among Mark Saunders's personal effects was a letter from you."

Deborah leaned back in her chair and smiled at him rue-fully. "Written more than a year ago in a moment of intense anger, Detective," she said. "But I am not a murderess."

"Why did you write it?"

"Look, I've told half the world already. Mark and I had an affair and... our lives were getting very complicated. Mark was an egotistical bastard who told my husband that he was not the only one I was sleeping with, and Stephen filed for divorce. Case closed."

As she said the words, Deborah remembered how her own ego had gotten her into the mess with Mark. It began shortly after Mark was named head of Minotaur. He called, saying it was important that he see her, and suggested they meet in the Rose Room of the Algonquin Hotel.

When Deborah entered the Algonquin she went to the old-fashioned reception desk to see if there were any messages for her, having left word at the office about where she would be. The clerk, like the hotel itself, was genteel and a little dowdy, but comfortable. With its drawing-room furnishings and shiny brass and gleaming woodwork, the hotel gave off the aura of a bygone age when people with money had more time to appre-ciate their world of privilege.

At the entrance to the stately dining room, Deborah saw Mark sitting at one of the white cloth–covered tables. He looked concerned.

An elderly waiter led her across the room and held her chair for her. Mark looked up and smiled through his frown.

"Is there anything wrong?" she asked.

"Wrong? No." He paused. "Let me be blunt, Deborah. You know the political clout the real estate princes have. They're looking for a politician to back, someone smart who has the potential to go a long way. You know the gubernatorial race is coming up in another two years."

"Yes, but what does this have to do with me?" she asked.

"I want you as our candidate for governor."

Deborah's heart raced. What Mark proposed seemed like the answer to a dream. For a long time, she had been looking for a way to make that leap from the political rank and file, and now Mark Saunders was handing it to her on a silver platter.

"I appreciate your confidence in me," she said trembling—and thinking how good he still looked. She admitted to herself she still had a thing for him.

During dinner, he brushed his leg against hers and pointedly touched her hands, arms, and thigh, while telling amusing stories about business and politics. She had always found Mark sexy. Now, he was irresistible. Each touch made her quiver.

At the end of the meal, he pressed something into her hand. "Meet me in a few minutes," he whispered.

She looked down and saw that he had given her a room key. She flushed with pleasure and excitement.

A short while later, they were in bed making love. Afterward, Mark poured out his problems with Darleen. He said he couldn't trust her, but wouldn't elaborate on that. He implied some nobility on his part for refusing to say why. Deborah wanted desperately to believe him, to take away the guilt she felt about betraying Darleen's friendship.

Deborah broke all the rules she had set for herself years ago regarding sex—rules against romantic involvement with anyone she knew.

Only after Mark asked her to help him did she have doubts. She remembered the occasion vividly. When Mark appeared at the hotel room, he was anxious. His dark eyes were brooding and looking at her beseechingly.

"My father thinks I'm going to fail," he said. "God, I am."

Deborah cradled his head in her arms. "Is there anything I can do to help?"

"Yes," he said hesitantly.

With feigned reluctance, he revealed he must find out who was bidding on a certain city construction project and how much the bid was. They both knew such information was secret, and only a few people could gain access to it. Deborah realized that her success might well hinge upon Mark's.

"I'll help you," she offered.

Mark got what he needed. In the end, however, he pushed her for more and more information, and he stopped being manipulative about extracting it from her. "Get it!" he ordered.

"No," she finally replied.

"If you don't," he said, "kiss your marriage and political career good-bye."

Her marriage blew up one afternoon when Stephen burst into their bedroom when she was in bed with a trick. He had come home because Mark had told him to go home immediately if he wanted to find out what his wife was really like—a whore. Ever since then, she had worried about how he meant to harm her career.

"So," Sullivan continued, "your story is that you threatened him because he broke up your marriage?"

Indignantly, Deborah replied, "My *story*, Detective, is the truth!"

"The *whole* truth?" asked Sullivan, remembering that Deborah's letter made pointed reference to Mark's jeopardizing of her political career as well as ruining her marriage.

The question unnerved Deborah, but she remained outwardly calm. "Yes, the whole truth."

"Very well," Sullivan said, noting that now Deborah—like Darleen and Aida before her—was holding something back.

"Where were you last Wednesday night?" Sullivan asked.

"At the Waldorf for a Democratic fund-raiser," she replied swiftly.

She went to a filing cabinet and handed him a flyer. "Here's the program, with most of the names of those who attended. Just about anybody on the list knows me and will tell you I was there. And, in anticipation of your next questions, it didn't break up until about one thirty, and I got a ride home with Deputy Mayor Calvante."

"Very neat and tidy," Sullivan said dryly while glancing at the list. "Do you have any idea who might have killed him?"

"Check the telephone book," Deborah said blithely. "As you must have gathered by now, in the past few years Mark had become a son of a bitch."

As he left her office, Sullivan thought that the lady seemed a bit too sure of her alibi. He knew what those fund-raisers were like. Huge affairs with hundreds of people milling about. It would have been easy to slip out for a half hour without being noticed.

Although pleased with the way she had handled the interview, Deborah wasn't smiling as she looked out at lower Manhattan's grimy facade. That damn letter! How stupid of her.

She was still trying to remember exactly what she had written when the phone rang. "I've got something you want, Missus," Cookie Garcìa said. He laughed harshly. "Not what you usually want, but you're gonna pay for this, too."

"What are you talking about?" Deborah asked, fear suffusing her.

"Go home and check your wall safe. Some files are missing. The ones dealing with Minotaur Development."

"Dear God," Deborah gasped silently. Wasn't one blackmailer enough?

"How much?" she asked.

"Ten thousand dollars."

In spite of her predicament, Deborah smiled. The little chiseler. There were people who would pay millions for those papers. "Where and when?" she asked.

Cookie chose Sheridan Square, a busy intersection in Greenwich Village, apparently counting on crowded streets as an easy way to escape if she went to the police. *As if that were a possibility under the circumstances,* she thought.

"All right," she answered coolly.

After hanging up, she debated her options. She could ignore the little shit, but he *might* do something reckless.

She believed she had no alternatives. She picked up her phone and dialed a number. "Mr. D'Angelo, this is Deborah Bartley. . . ."

After she outlined the particulars of her problem, the line was silent for a moment.

"You got a bad habit," the Buddha's voice rumbled. "You oughta buy a bigger shredder for your office. It might be cheaper in the long run."

He laughed at his own joke, while Deborah's hand trembled as she hung up.

Twenty-Five

Sullivan returned to his apartment at six o'clock. He was bone-tired and frustrated as hell.

Throwing his suit coat on the sofa, he pulled down his tie.

He flicked on his television set and he went into the kitchen for a beer. But before he could pop the top, he heard a voice that sent him racing back into the living room. He stood staring at the TV in disbelief.

Captain Carter was on the screen wearing an insipid smile. "We have arrested a murder suspect. She is Darleen Saunders, the wife of the deceased."

The camera cut to a clip of Darleen being led by police from Saunders Tower. Her face was white and grief-stricken.

"Shit!" Sullivan exploded, wishing Carter were within reach so he could strangle the simple-minded son of a bitch.

Grabbing his coat again, he ran out of the apartment. Minutes later, he walked into headquarters and saw Carter just as Carter noticed him. Carter ducked into his office and shut the door. Sullivan doggedly followed him inside.

"Don't you knock?" Carter snarled, refusing to look Sullivan in the eyes.

"Why'd you do it?" Sullivan asked wearily.

"Do what?"

"For God's sake—arrest Darleen Saunders."

"I don't have to answer to you, Sullivan."

Suddenly Sullivan glared at him, his anger radiating like heat from a blast furnace. "Carter, this is my fucking case. You tell me what's going on, or, so help me, you'll go out the window like Mark Saunders."

Carter's tone became more reasonable. "Now, take it easy. I was going to tell you about her arrest but I couldn't find you. Honest."

"But why arrest her now? We don't have any hard evidence."

"Something came up. Pathology found a piece of pin on what was left of Saunders's body. They could tell that it was a large gold horseshoe. And it belongs to Mrs. Saunders."

Sullivan looked skeptical.

"C'mon," Carter said. "We've got the pin. The night guard can place her at the scene. And with hubby dead, she gets half the company."

Sullivan looked at Carter and then turned away. "You still moved too fast," he said angrily.

"Jeez, Sullivan," Carter said, seeking to understand. "Emmanuel Saunders has friends all over. You can't believe the pressure I'm under to wrap this thing up."

Sullivan sighed. "Where is she?"

"In the holding pen."

"Christ, why there?"

"Because the press would be on my ass if I gave her special treatment."

"Yeah, yeah," Sullivan said, walking away disgustedly. He had to admit that the pin was incriminating. But who was to say one of the sisters hadn't taken it so she could frame Darleen? Everything was too pat.

Slowly, Sullivan walked downstairs to the holding pens—the airless, smelly jails where cops warehoused people being held for arraignment. "Where's Mrs. Saunders?" he asked the sergeant on duty.

"Try the first cell."

Sullivan walked through the huge metal door that led into the pens in the basement. The stale air stank of Lysol, vomit, and urine. The light was dim. When he looked past the bars of the first cell, he immediately saw Darleen sitting by herself. She sat with her mink coat pulled tightly around her, as though warding off the prostitutes and junkies behind bars with her. Her face was distraught.

"Darleen," Sullivan called softly.

She glanced up and ran over to the bars. "Get me out of here. Please. For God's sake, get me out!"

She pressed against the bars and clutched his jacket. "I can't stand it. I'm losing my mind in here."

Sullivan looked worried. "Hold on, I'll have you out in a minute."

He went back to the sergeant on duty and told him he was taking Mrs. Saunders to an interrogation room. Another cop followed him back inside and opened the cell.

When she came into the harsh light in the corridor between the cells, her eyes, red-rimmed from crying, sought Sullivan's. "This is a horrible nightmare," she said, starting to weep again.

They didn't speak while Sullivan led her upstairs and into one of the interrogation rooms. He wasn't sure what to say. He wasn't sure about anything anymore.

Turning and facing him, Darleen started crying softly. "Brian, I swear I lost that pin. But I guess I could have found it and not remember. I may even have gone back to the Tower that night. I just don't know."

"No, I don't believe you did it," he said slowly. He thought to himself, *This woman is smart, and somebody smart would come up with a better alibi than amnesia. Convenient amnesia, at that.*

With a start, he realized he believed what he'd just said and thought.

But what if he were wrong? He knew his heart went out to her. What if his feelings were affecting his professional judgment? Maybe he was hunting for a killer when she was right here, under his nose.

Darleen sat in a chair and suddenly looked much smaller. Defeated. Sullivan had to restrain himself from running over to her and taking her in his arms. Instead, he walked up to her and put his right hand over hers and said gently, "Are you okay?"

"No! First they arrested me at my apartment and led me out past those horrible newspeople who started screaming questions at me. Then they fingerprinted me and put me in that terrible cell."

"I'm afraid you'll be going over to Manhattan Criminal Court for arraignment," he said. "Who's your lawyer?"

"Mr. Fitzgerald."

"The guy on Minotaur's board?"

"Yes. He—he could help me for now, and if I go to trial he will get me a top criminal lawyer."

Several minutes later, Fitzgerald entered the interrogation room. He looked coolly at Sullivan, and then spoke to Darleen.

"Mrs. Saunders, don't say anything at all to the police. I am not a criminal lawyer, but I can get you through the arraignment. After that, I will see that you have one of the best legal minds in the nation defending you."

"Thank you for coming," she said. "But Detective Sullivan is on my side."

"Oh, really?" Fitzgerald said cynically. "Listen, I've brought a certified check for one hundred fifty thousand dollars in case bail goes that high, which it shouldn't," Fitzgerald said.

They rode the six blocks to the Criminal Court in a police car. Fitzgerald had a blue binder in his hand that was stamped COMPLAINT. Beneath that was written one word, MURDER.

As soon as they entered the hallway of the courthouse, newspeople swarmed around them. Television reporters jammed microphones in front of Darleen's face. Camera lights nearly blinded them.

"Why'd you do it, Darleen?" one yelled.

"Why didn't you use a gun?"

"You going to write a book about it? Like Jean Harris?"

"Have you sold the movie rights to your story?"

Sullivan became furious. He got in front of Darleen and began shoving the reporters out of the way. "Can't you act like human beings?" he yelled.

Then a big cameraman tried to stand in front of them. Sullivan shoved him out of the way, using the weight of the camera on the man's shoulder to throw him off balance. "Next time, bozo, I'll arrest you for obstructing justice!"

By the time they reached the courtroom, Darleen was sobbing and holding her ears to drown out the din of reporters' questions. Inside, Darleen and Fitzgerald sat at a table to the right of the judge, while an assistant district attorney sat to the left. The judge, a concerned-looking man of about sixty, had a round, pink face and thinning white hair. He was kindly but firm.

"Do you have a lawyer?" he asked.

"Yes," she replied.

"All right, then," he said. "Let's proceed."

The district attorney told the court that Darleen was charged with the murder of her husband, Mark Saunders. "We contend that the crime was premeditated and we are asking a bail of one million dollars."

Fitzgerald got to his feet. "Your Honor. The defendant has no previous arrest record. The evidence against her is circumstantial. She is a respected citizen who is involved in many charitable activities. We ask that she be released on her own recognizance."

The judge looked at both lawyers and then at Darleen. "Bail is set at fifty thousand dollars. Mrs. Saunders will remain in custody until bail is posted. Next case."

Over Fitzgerald's objections Sullivan sat with Darleen for the next hour and a half while the lawyer arranged the bail. "I know this is trying," Sullivan told her at one point, "but you will have to go through it again soon, because the case is a felony."

"What do you mean?" she asked.

"A felony is a case for which the maximum sentencing is usually more than a year. That means you'll be arraigned before the State Supreme Court. Then the case will probably go before a grand jury."

Finally, Darleen was free to go. Before rushing down the courthouse steps, she paused and looked at Sullivan. "I want to thank you for everything," she said.

"I didn't do much."

"You were there, and that was enough," she said. "I feel so

alone right now that I don't know what to do. If I go back to the apartment and see everything that reminds me of Mark I think I'll scream."

"Well, if you feel like company, how about me?"

Darleen looked at him and smiled. "Mr. Fitzgerald told me to stay away from you."

"What do you want to do?" asked Sullivan.

"I need to talk," she said.

Sullivan hailed a cab, ignoring the reporters. He gave the driver an address on the Upper West Side. "Where are we going?" she asked.

"The only place that we won't be hounded by reporters."

"Where's that?"

"My place."

"Are you sure we're doing the right thing?"

For a second he glanced away, then looked straight into her eyes. "No," he said, laughing self-consciously. "But what the hell, how much worse can things get?"

Twenty-Six

Sullivan's phone was ringing insistently as he struggled to unlock his apartment door. Darleen found his predicament amusing.

"Well, you wouldn't make a good burglar," she teased.

"Very funny." The door swung open and he bolted toward the phone. "Have a seat," he called out.

He flicked on the lights and grabbed the phone. "Where have you been, man? Fire Island?"

While talking, Sullivan checked on Darleen. She was absorbed in looking at his paintings. He continued in a low voice.

"While you were playing Peeping Tom, Carter arrested Darleen Saunders. Yeah, I know it was stupid. Have you interviewed Kwan yet? I know it's late, but you've got to do it tonight. No time to explain. Just meet me at the station in the morning, and we'll compare notes. Thanks."

He hung up just as Darleen approached him. "I'm impressed," he said, looking around. "Terry Winters, Eric Fischel, Francesco Clemente," she went on, naming some of the artists whose paintings and etchings were hanging on the walls. "Even a photo by Cindy Sherman."

Suddenly, she wheeled and faced him, a gleam in her eyes. "Now, I know," she said.

"Know what?"

"I *knew* I had seen you before. You were at the Birnbaum Gallery a few weeks ago."

"Guilty," he said with a rueful smile.

He glanced at the paintings. "Don't get the idea that cops are paid well. Collecting is something I do on a very limited budget. I bought that Terry Winters piece at his first show three years ago for two thousand dollars."

"Now it's worth ten times that," she said.

"I put a lot of time into choosing art. I painted a little myself in college, and my ex-wife was an artist at one time."

Sullivan took her coat and went toward the closet. "But I'm forgetting my manners. What would you like to drink?"

"White wine?" Darleen smoothed her maroon jersey wrap dress.

"I think I can swing that."

Sullivan went into the kitchen and returned with a bottle of California white wine and two glasses on a tray. He sat on the sofa, leaving a distance between them, and handed her a glass.

"Darleen, I have a confession to make."

She looked at him curiously. "What?"

"Part of my job was to try to get close to you. I know it's loathsome, but my captain was convinced from the outset that you were a murderess and I guess I was, too."

Darleen smiled bitterly. "I should have known," she said softly, unable to hide the hurt in her tone. "And now?"

"Now? Now I think you're innocent."

"Why?"

"I believe I'm a good judge of character. You didn't do it. Period."

Darleen stared at him angrily. "Is this just part of the game? You come on to me and then entrap me. Is that the idea?"

Sullivan's voice was sober. "You're right to be angry. No, this isn't part of some game."

Darleen hugged herself and started crying. "I feel so alone and so frightened. Nothing is the way it seems anymore. My

God, what if I *did* kill him! What if I go to prison!"

She looked at him. "You don't know what it's like. Mark changed so much. He began treating me like dirt. I kept hoping he would change, but he kept getting worse, and I grew more afraid."

As she spoke, Darleen vividly recalled a particularly humiliating incident at the Museum of Modern Art.

The occasion was a special black tie dinner party for patrons and movers and shakers in the art world as well as for political leaders, when MOMA reopened after extensive renovations.

When Darleen and Mark climbed out of the limousine at the gallery's front door, he stumbled, and Darleen realized he was already drunk. Once inside the glass doors, they went their separate ways to talk with various friends and associates.

The ground floor was a multicolor swirl of silk of designer dresses worn by the bejeweled women moving among formally attired men. Only some of the designers, such as Calvin Klein and Bill Blass, wore colored dinner jackets, and Scotty MacKenzie, who was an investment banker, looked like a Highland soldier in his tartan kilt, which was always his formal attire.

Twenty minutes after their arrival, Darleen, wearing a floor-length backless mauve silk Galanos, was talking to Jerry Cunningham, with whom she was on the boards of Lenox Hill Hospital and the New York Public Library. She always enjoyed talking with Jerry, a nice man in his early fifties who was always trying to get the poorer communities involved with the city's major cultural institutions. His wife, Kay, was a charming woman whom Darleen knew from her work with the Cancer Care Center.

Mark approached them, and Darleen braced herself because she could tell how drunk he was. "Well, well, isn't this cozy," Mark said, trying to use amusement to mask hostility. "You and Darleen spend a lot of time together, don't you?"

He towered over Jerry Cunningham and he put his arm around the man's shoulders. "I know what you'd like to do with Darleen, don't I, Jer?" he said loudly.

"Enough, Mark," Darleen said quietly.

Other people around them looked on as Cunningham tried

to remove Mark's arm. "I think you've had enough to drink, Saunders," he said.

"You do, do you? You think I've had too much to drink and you want to fuck my wife."

Darleen was mortified. Her face turned red, but she tried to maintain her composure. She knew the stories that would spread like wildfire through the Upper East Side tonight as a result of the incident, but that wasn't what bothered her. It was the sense of betrayal she felt.

Cunningham, flushed, pulled away. "I'm very sorry, Darleen. Good night."

"I'm leaving, Mark, and if you know what's good for you, you will, too."

Mark looked around at the crowd watching. "What can a guy do with a wife like this?" he asked.

Most people turned their backs on him and wandered away.

Darleen left, and for the first time she seriously considered divorcing Mark. Yet, even then, she blamed his father more than Mark for what had happened. She knew Mark was in a great deal of pain because of his inability to confront his father. Still, she stayed, knowing she was blameless for what had happened to cause the break between them.

Now Darleen looked at Sullivan. "When you told me he was dead, I felt a great sense of relief. Now, do you still believe I'm innocent?"

"What were you going to do?"

"File for divorce. It would have been difficult, and Mark would have fought me, but I had to."

"Why?"

"I couldn't stand my life or myself anymore," she said angrily. "And that last night he even hit me." She doubled over with her fists to her eyes, and wept so hard that her shoulders shook. All the pent up emotion of the past several days unlocked and came pouring out in a torrent.

Sullivan drew nearer and held her. "I know what it's like to be in a loveless marriage and to hope against hope that it will change. I didn't have the courage to leave my marriage. Paige walked out on me. As much as our marriage was a disaster, I still felt like a failure when it ended. I still do."

He held Darleen closer as the shuddering cries racked her. He looked down and stroked the shimmering hair, gently quieting her. "It will be okay," he said softly. "Everything will be okay."

"No, it will never be all right, as long as Emmanuel can hurt people the way he does," she said.

"What do you mean?"

"Brian, I'm going to tell you something that I have never told anyone but Mark. It's how Emmanuel ruined my marriage by turning Mark against me."

"What are you talking about?"

She hugged her arms across her chest, as though feeling intense cold. Then she started telling Sullivan the secret she had never shared with anyone, not even the sisters.

The incident was etched vividly in her memory, as if it had happened the previous night, not three years earlier. She was dining with Emmanuel Saunders at Mandragola, while Mark was on a business trip to Houston.

The dining room was high-vaulted and dominated by a huge gilt-framed mirror over the mantelpiece. The table was long, with places set at each end for Emmanuel and herself. Darleen had always felt uncomfortable sitting at that table when the only diners were she, Mark, and his father. Since Emmanuel insisted on evening attire no matter how many people dined, Darleen wore a coral silk gown that she'd bought while shopping in Paris several weeks before. This evening, staring at Emmanuel twenty feet away while dining in such a formal fashion struck her as ludicrous.

From the start, Darleen wished she had never said she would stay the night. During dinner, Emmanuel drank even more than usual, staring intently and silently at her while a servant refilled his glass, then motioning that he continue topping off her glass.

Finally, Emmanuel broke the silence. "You remind me of Marissa," he said, the words escaping with a bitter sigh.

Knowing the story of Marissa Saunders—and how she had left Emmanuel for another man shortly after Mark's birth—Darleen tried to change the subject. "Mark didn't make it clear why he was going to Houston. Is it to buy that new office building?"

"Ah, I forgot that you have an interest in the business. Yes, yes, he went about the office building. There you do differ from Marissa. She never took an interest in the world of real estate, but in every other way you are just like her. Beautiful . . . willful . . . Eve in the Garden of Eden waiting to destroy Adam! The curse of man is woman. Woman, the betrayer!"

Flushed with anger, Darleen pushed her chair back from the table. "I won't listen to your insults," she said quietly. Turning to the maid, she said, "Please, call a taxi for me."

As she left the table, however, she felt woozy, realizing for the first time that the wine had gone to her head. The maid took her arm. "Are you all right, Mrs. Saunders?"

"No," Darleen said, trying unsuccessfully to clear her head.

On Emmanuel's order, the maid helped Darleen to the room she and Mark used when at Mandragola, a large, airy chamber with a king-size four-poster bed. The maid slipped Darleen's clothes off, and Darleen slid naked between the satin sheets, feeling an overwhelming sleepiness enveloping her.

She didn't know how long she'd been asleep before the door, half-opening, awakened her with a click. For a moment, the hallway light silhouetted a figure. Then the door shut. She peered into the darkness but saw nothing. Unsure whether anyone came in, she stretched toward the lamp on the bedside table. But before her hand reached the switch, her arm was seized in a powerful grip.

"You're just like all of them," a voice broke through the silence. "You don't care who comes to your bed."

"Emmanuel!" she shouted. "Get out of here!"

While his one hand continued holding her, his other pulled the sheets away, exposing her nakedness in the moonlight streaming across the bed. She tried getting up and twisting away, but he grabbed her shoulder, forcing her back, his arms pinning her to the bed, the sour smell of wine on his breath.

"No! No! Don't! Please! Don't!" she begged.

A moment later, Emmanuel's silk robe was pressing against her breasts, his weight crushing her, his right leg pushing between her legs.

"You are for all men," Emmanuel gasped and plunged into her.

After he was gone from her room, Darleen called a taxi herself. Still crying, she dressed and met the cab at the front gate and went back to her and Mark's apartment. The next day, when Mark returned from his trip, he found her sitting on the couch, weeping.

"Your father," she cried. "He—he—"

"He what?" Mark asked. "Damn it, Darleen, has something happened to Emmanuel?"

She curled her knees to her chest and circled her arms around them and began rocking back and forth. Briefly, she told him what had happened the previous night.

Looks of horror and dread spread across Mark's face. He held his hands to his mouth as if he had just witnessed someone being shot. "*My* father? Are you crazy?"

"He did," she said in a small voice. "He did!"

Mark stalked across the room angrily and picked up the phone. He began dialing, then slammed down the receiver. When he turned, there was hatred on his face. "I know you despise him," he shrieked. "You would do anything to get me to hate him. If you think I believe this, you're crazy!"

While listening with a mixture of embarrassment, anger, and love, Sullivan looked at her full of heartsick concern. "After I was raped," she said, "Mark treated me with contempt, just the way his father treated all women. In fact, he became like his father in just about every way."

Looking at Darleen, Sullivan ached for her. Gently placing his hands on her shoulders, he kissed her.

Tears streaming down her face, she backed away from his embrace. "I really do hate Emmanuel."

As much out of passion as compassion, he lifted her off the couch and carried her into his bedroom. Speaking softly to her, he undressed her. Kissing her, he stroked her tenderly and then more passionately, until finally, when he entered her, he crushed her to him as if he were welding himself to her. She shuddered and responded with a kind of abandon she'd never felt before, as if she were racing away from everything that was bad in her life.

Later, she ran her fingers tenderly through his hair. He rolled over and kissed her again, more gently as his mouth moved to her breasts and stomach and between her legs. She was as moist as ever. She tried to pull him toward her but he resisted. "No, Darleen, let me," he said.

In all the years of their marriage, even when everything was all right between them, Mark had never put her satisfaction before his. Instinctively, she trusted Sullivan's tenderness because she could feel that it was tinged with love. Darleen felt a warmth toward Sullivan that she had never felt toward any man before. She moaned, and when he entered her again, she felt more giving than she ever had in her life.

In time Darleen fell asleep. But Sullivan found himself wakeful and restless. He looked at her curled like a child next to him and he knew he was falling in love—and he felt sad when he wondered where it might lead him.

"No!" she cried out in her sleep, twisting as though trying to get away from someone. "Please! No!"

Sullivan enveloped her in his arms and crooned to her softly. "Everything's all right, Darleen. Everything's all right."

She opened her eyes sleepily and smiled at him and drifted off to sleep again. He held her closely until her tremors stopped.

As dawn broke, Sullivan got up and went to the window. He was thinking about his parents, about his ex-wife, about that whole world of the rich that he had sworn never to re-enter. As much as he might love her, she was still from that world. What was he going to do?

Could he stand to be without her? Having finally found love, how could he let her go?

With a sigh, he went back to bed, but he didn't fall asleep.

Twenty-Seven

After Mays hung up with Sullivan, he kicked himself for having agreed to interview Samantha Kwan tonight. He'd already put in a long day. His hours on Fire Island might have warmed his loins, but the rest of him still ached from the cold. He sneezed and bitched that he'd probably gotten pneumonia.

"Fuck it, let's go," he muttered to himself, grabbing his black leather jacket and heading off to Kwan's SoHo loft.

While Mays drove to SoHo, Samantha finished getting ready for the night ahead. Her boyfriend, John Ming, was sitting in the living area when she entered; her lithe body was encased in a skintight black bodysuit and black leather boots.

He looked somber. "You're ready?"

"Yes."

Just as they closed Samantha's front door and ran around the corner to Spring Street, Mays pulled onto Lafayette Street. Climbing out of his car, he followed them around the corner just in time to see them pull away in a black Porsche. Running back to the Dodge, he jumped in and raced in the direction they were headed.

"Damn," he muttered, "I should let her go and talk to her

tomorrow. Why the fuck did I tell Sullivan I'd question her tonight?"

He followed them for a few blocks, the Dodge blending into the night traffic. But the Porsche ran a yellow light, and Mays had to make a quick decision. He decided to run the red, but when he almost sideswiped another car, the driver leaned on his horn. He could see the Porsche driver glance back and speed up.

"Shit," Mays grunted, furious at having been spotted.

Following the Porsche's taillights, Mays raced across Delancey Street, turned left on Clinton, right on Houston, and right on Columbia. He slowed down and banged the steering wheel with his fist.

"Lost the bitch!" he yelled.

Fifteen minutes later, Samantha crouched on the roof of the old four-story red-brick tenement building on the Lower East Side, her silent motions a counterpoint to the plaintive drone of a foghorn blaring somewhere in the nearby East River. She could no longer see the river because of the rolling fog.

Checking her watch, she felt a steady calm. Finally, the years of training and intense concentration were soon to translate into action.

Catlike, she crouched behind a foot-high ledge, scanning the street. The neighborhood was desolate. Few people ventured into the dark in this part of New York. The sound of the foghorn had subsided. Other than the night wind, she heard little. A saxophonist played sad jazz somewhere below her. A police siren screamed blocks away.

Suddenly, Samantha tensed. A black Cadillac limousine glided up to the front door of the building. Two large Orientals got out of the front seat and looked up and down the street. Then one opened the left rear door. A small, older Chinese man emerged. With the two larger men at his sides, he walked toward the building. At the front door, one of the men took up a vigil while the other accompanied the smaller man inside.

Taking a deep breath, Samantha pulled a black ski mask over her face. Silently, she opened a trapdoor and crept down a dirty, trash-littered stairwell. The piercing stench of garbage made her wonder why the Chan underworld met furtively in such fetid places, like rats.

The building was empty except for the night visitor and those who had been awaiting him. On the second floor, she heard voices arguing loudly. Looking down the hallway, she saw a bodyguard lounging outside a doorway. About six feet tall and stocky, he wore a suit and overcoat. Leaning down, she took a piece of newspaper from the floor, rustled it, and moaned softly.

The guard's head jerked up. Stealthily, he moved down the hallway. Samantha took a thin-bladed dagger out of her boot. At the last second, she stepped in front of him and jammed the knife into his windpipe, and, in a second quick motion, into his heart. Hot blood spurted over her as he pitched forward. She eased his body noiselessly to the floor.

Silently, she stole up to the doorway and peered through the keyhole. Sitting around a table were the old man from the limousine and two middle-aged Orientals. Talking excitedly, they pointed to a sheaf of papers spread open before them.

Quickly, Samantha removed from her belt a metal star with razor-sharp blades. Bursting through the door, she threw the star at the middle-aged man across the table. As he looked up in astonishment, the star tore across his throat. In a blinding motion she smashed the man nearest her in the temple with her fist and broke his neck with a karate chop.

The old man pulled a knife from inside his coat and with surprising swiftness lunged at her. Grabbing his wrist, she kicked him with all her might in the stomach. He crashed to the floor. He looked up at her in glassy-eyed terror, blood streaming from his mouth.

Using the slim knife with which she had attacked the guard, she leaned down and slowly slit his throat. "Mr. Chan," she hissed. "The Kai-chungs are being avenged."

Picking up the papers that had fallen from the table, she folded them and placed them in her belt. She didn't see one stray document that was trapped beneath a body on the floor. Leaving the room, she closed the door behind her, silently climbed the stairs, and raced along rooftops to the last of the row of tenements.

Pulling off her ski mask, she climbed down the fire escape

and hurried to where Ming had parked the Porsche, inside an abandoned warehouse. She got in and kissed him passionately. Then, she flicked on the dashboard light and began to examine the papers.

The top line read: MINOTAUR DEVELOPMENT.

"Good!" she said with a catlike smile.

"Is everything okay?" Ming asked.

"Perfect. I have the drawings. Everything is as planned."

A half hour later, Samantha and Ming entered the Jade Tea restaurant. Their beauty attracted attention. Samantha was almost translucent in the black silk kimono she wore. An elegant dark blue suit covered Ming's muscular body. He had parked the Porsche as close as possible to the entrance. A band of Kai-chung youths watched over it.

Ming was fairly well known as a photographer in Chinatown. What few knew was his ranking status in the Kai-chung Triad. Only Samantha knew about the .44 Magnum strapped to his chest in case anything went wrong tonight.

The restaurant was bright and busy. Waiters bustled nervously from table to table. The walls were papered in red watered silk. Chrysanthemums were in vases on the tables. The night's murders had already had an effect. Men on either side of the door carefully screened everyone entering, looking for weapons, for people they didn't know—trying to find the unknown.

Samantha followed the maître d' to a table. Ming followed her. Both of them acted calm, smiling warmly at one another, giving no indication that tonight they were partners in death.

Casually, Samantha surveyed the room. As she was told, Mao Chan, ironically nicknamed the Red Chan since he was as unlike Mao Tse-tung as possible, held court in a large booth in the rear. His braying laughter rose above that of the men and women around him, who all laughed a second or two after Mao began his booming giggles.

There was no mistaking Mao. Even without his trademark tuxedo, he would have been readily identifiable. About five feet eight inches tall, he was built like a sumo wrestler, he wore his long gray-streaked hair almost to his shoulders. Gold and diamond rings glittered on all his fingers. On either side of him sat beautiful girls no more than seventeen years old wearing traditional silk robes.

At least a quarter of the restaurant was given over to Mao's people. Table after table of men and women nervously looked at everyone in the dining room; everyone seemed suspicious. As an added precaution, only one waiter was allowed to tend to the demands of Mao and his entourage. Mao was a creature of habit, even when he thought he was in danger. The setting was the way it had been described the previous night to Samantha and Ming.

In addition to being careful, Mao was arrogant. The latter outweighed the former. He ate at the same restaurant at the same time every night. His own restaurant. Telling everyone that the Jade Tea served the only edible food in Chinatown. Ordering ahead every night for the dishes he wanted. Letting the world know his movements. Now, as he always did, he sat in the rear near the restrooms.

Samantha and Ming were shown to a table along the right wall. Fortunately, it gave them a clear view of Mao.

"You look very beautiful this evening," Ming said.

"Thank you. And you look quite dashing."

"And Mr. Chan looks remarkably healthy," he said, laughing slightly.

"A bit overweight and stupid, though, don't you think?"

"A bit."

They both laughed. Making light of being in the heart of the Chan empire excited them. Yet the banter also eased their own fears. Calming their nerves, they sat in the heart of the dragon.

Suddenly, there was a crash. A dozen men around Chan jumped to their feet, revolvers in their hands, staring around wildly.

The diners froze, looking aghast at the men. A waiter who had tripped and dropped his tray rose to his feet, staring in terror at the men who had guns pointed at him, screeching at them in Chinese and making apologetic bows in the direction of the Red Chan.

An ashen-faced Mao, looking as if he had been shot, smiled. He yelled, "Foolish old man!"

Suddenly, Mao began laughing, giggles swelling from his

enormous chest. The men and women around him began laughing, too, pointing at the waiter who crept away in humiliation.

The armed men sat down, putting away their weapons. The restaurant noises resumed. People at several tables quickly motioned for their checks, paid, and left. Most diners, however, went back to their meals, thinking of the stories they had to tell when they got home.

Neither Samantha nor Ming had much of an appetite, and they ate little of the course they'd ordered. Touching hands with Ming across the table, Samantha was actually reassured by the gentle touches of the strong man sitting opposite her.

"Are you sure you want to do this now?" Ming asked.

"Yes."

From her purse, Samantha extracted a small, insulated canister, like a section of a straw. A puff of cold air came out of it when she removed the cap. Carefully, she removed a tiny dart made of ice and only a quarter of an inch long. She inserted it in the tube and placed the tube in her mouth.

"Be very careful, beautiful Samantha. You know how dangerous the poison is," Ming said.

Rising from her seat, Samantha walked toward the restrooms. When she was a step beyond the Red Chan's table, she pursed her lips and blew. The dart pricked the side of Mao's neck. It was done in an instant, never breaking her stride.

Mao slapped at his neck as if he had been stung by a mosquito. Turning around with an annoyed expression to look at his hand, he could see nothing but a drop of water. Curiously, he looked up at the ceiling as though expecting to see it dripping, and then he placed his hand back on the thigh of the girl next to him and laughed at the joke he had been telling.

In the ladies' room, Samantha flushed the tube down the toilet and left. She walked nonchalantly back to her table and sat down. "How much time do we have?" she asked.

"About ten minutes," Ming replied. He signaled to the waiter for the check.

Several minutes later, they were outside. Samantha felt exhilarated by a strange sense of power. The power over life and death.

They walked to the Porsche, seeing no one around but

knowing the car—and they—were being watched by dozens of eyes. Once in the car, Samantha pressed herself against Ming.

"You are a very remarkable woman," he said. "As remarkable as you are beautiful."

Samantha looked into his eyes and touched his face. "I feel like this is the beginning of my life," she said.

At the restaurant, Mao Chan suddenly felt dizzy. His eyes blurred, and his heart began pounding. He gasped for air and tried to stand up. Swinging his arms wildly, he tried to scream—but nothing came out. His entourage looked on, not knowing what to do. Only Jimmy Lo, the manager, went into action. Rushing to the front desk, he screamed, "Call a doctor."

By the time Lo returned to Mao's table, it was too late.

The Red Chan's face was slumped in the plate of Peking duck in front of him, his eyes glassy and staring up in wonder. His heart had stopped ten minutes after Samantha walked by his table on her way to the ladies' room.

When the Porsche stopped in front of her loft, Samantha looked at John beseechingly. "Don't leave me tonight."

"No. I won't."

In her loft, the sight of her familiar apartment struck Samantha as almost eerie. She felt changed. She expected the world to look different. But everything in the loft was as she'd left it only a few hours ago. She walked over to the bar.

"I need a drink," she said. "I'm sure you do, too."

"A Stoly on the rocks."

"In honor of Red Chan?"

"To forget the bastard and the rest of the Chans."

After handing him his drink, Samantha took hers and walked into her bedroom. She took off her clothes and put on a gray silk kimono decorated with silver cherry blossoms. "John," she called.

Having removed his coat and tie, Ming entered her room and walked up to her. Placing his hands on her shoulders, he slid the robe down her body. Stepping back, he unbuttoned his shirt and took it off. When he bent over to remove his shoes, Samantha admired again the tattoo on his back.

She walked around him. With awe, she realized now the tattoo was identical to the brand-new one on her back. Reaching out, she brushed her hand across his back. Then, with trembling fingers, she began tracing the design, watching with fascination as the blues, greens, reds, and yellows seemed to become more vibrant under her touch. The dragon moved as if alive as the muscles on Ming's back responded to her touch.

Naked, he turned and held her. She shivered as he moved his fingers over her back, delicately stroking her. Feeling the mark that was placed there for all time. Feeling it come alive under his touch. His touch became almost unbearable as she quivered and flinched under his every stroke. Finally, she experienced the pleasure as it radiated between her legs.

She thought of the boy in the back of the tattoo parlor as she moaned.

Lifting her in his arms, Ming placed her on the bed. "Let me be your first and only lover since you became a Triad Dragon tonight."

SUNDAY

Twenty-Eight

On Sunday morning, Martha awoke slowly. The daylight hurt her eyes. She heard the dull, muffled roar of the surf and the murmuring of voices. The rich smell of coffee filled the air. Her mouth was dry. She closed her eyes again as thoughts of last night rushed into her mind. Had she been dreaming?

She realized she was lying in Joy's bed, the silver sheets pulled around her. She was naked. Suddenly, burning with shame, Martha whispered, "Oh, no. God, no."

Joy walked in, holding a cup of coffee. "Thought you might need this," she said, leaning over and stroking Martha's hair.

Martha pulled away, averting Joy's gaze. Joy decided not to push it.

"Why don't you take a bath, then give me a massage," Joy suggested lightly. "Oh, and there's someone here I want you to meet."

Martha turned on the hot water and was about to step into the tub when she heard Joy in the other room say loudly and indignantly, "Don't be ridiculous!"

With the water covering her sounds, Martha tiptoed to the door and listened.

"That's not an answer," a male voice said. "Joy, did you kill him?"

There was silence. Then the man said, "You can tell me. As soon as I saw that that brute Saunders was murdered, I said to myself, Why, my Joy has killed the bastard."

"You really think I did it, don't you?" Joy said.

"Don't forget, my dear, I know you better than anyone. I know your childhood, your passions, and your capacity for revenge. Remember that young woman you brought here last year? What was her name? Connie? You did get quite cruel with her when she wouldn't perform for you."

"Why would I have killed Mark?"

"Are you forgetting that you told me he was blackmailing you? I believe at the time I said to myself, Jacques, poor Mark hasn't heard the last from my Joy."

"And what if I did kill him?" she said playfully.

"It would make you much more desirable, my dear. I don't think I've ever made love to a murderess before."

Joy laughed.

Martha listened with dread. She recalled that Joy was a friend of Saunders's wife. What was this about a girl named Connie? Had Joy killed her, too?

In the shower, all Martha could think about was getting away from them. Then it occurred to her that she couldn't just bolt. Joy would have her fired, and she needed the money for school. Maybe if she just gave Joy a massage, she would be allowed to leave. "Please don't hurt me," she whispered.

When she came out of the shower, Martha found Joy lying on the rug with a towel draped over her buttocks, just as she did when she wanted a massage at her apartment. After dressing, she knelt down and mechanically began massaging Joy's back.

"You are a dear," Joy said, patting Martha's knee affectionately. "A beautiful little dear."

Joy rose, put on a robe, and steered Martha into the living room. The man sat quietly. Tan and lean, he was almost beautiful. He rose gracefully, took Martha's hand, and gallantly kissed it. "Ah, Martha," he said. "You are as exquisite as Joy said."

Joy broke into a soft laugh. "Martha, this charming rogue

is Jacques Levy, one of my oldest and dearest friends."

"Not *that* old," he replied, giving Joy a mock scowl. "In some circles, forty-four is considered quite young."

Turning to Martha, he said, "We are going to the beach. But we will wait until you have something to eat."

"No thank you," Martha replied. "I really ought to be getting back to the city."

"Nonsense," Jacques said, placing his arm familiarly around her shoulder. "I am so pleased that you are here. We must become great friends."

Martha twisted out of his grasp. "Really, no," she said, her voice now shaking as she backed away from them and toward the front door. "Three's a crowd and all that, right?"

"Oh, dear," Jacques said. "I believe I have given you offense."

"No, no. My job is done. I just think you'd rather be by yourselves."

Running back to the bedroom, she grabbed her clothes and haphazardly stuffed them into her tote bag. At the front door, Martha was suddenly certain that Joy Livingston was a killer. She fumbled for the handle, swinging it open, then ran down the road, back toward the ferry. Furious, Joy watched her go from the window.

Twenty-Nine

"Hell of a way to spend a Sunday," Mays called out when he saw Sullivan entering One Police Plaza.

"Sorry about making you work," Sullivan said.

"It's not just that."

"Then what?"

"That Kwan bitch," Mays said. "Just as I got to her apartment last night, I saw her and some guy jump into a Porsche. I followed her, but she spotted me. I lost her in Alphabet City."

"I hope you had better luck on Fire Island," Sullivan said.

"Froze my nuts off out there."

The big detective then filled Sullivan in on Joy and Martha, giving him more details than he'd been able to last night over the phone. "It was like the spider and the fly," he said with a laugh. "Only, Spider Woman lost her cool."

"What do you mean?"

"I rattled her when I mentioned that film. I got the impression she'd have done just about anything to have gotten it back."

"Or to have gotten back at whoever blackmailed her with it?"

"You got it," Mays said somberly. "Her alibi was that she stayed late at the studio looking for clips for a story."

"Does it check?" Sullivan asked.

"No. Before I came in this morning, I went by the TV station. The only people who might have seen her last Wednesday night don't remember her being there late, but they say she could have been. I got the feeling the lady wasn't truthful."

Sullivan looked perplexed. "Frankly, I got much the same impression with Aida Miller and Deborah Bartley."

Quickly, he recounted his questioning of both women. "Miller was completely erratic, while Bartley was just too smooth."

"What about Lady Saunders?"

"Darleen?" Sullivan said.

"Oh, so it's Dar*leen*, now."

Sullivan looked embarrassed. Mays raised his eyebrows and laughed. "Well, well, detective . . ."

"Knock it off."

When Mays continued looking at him questioningly, Sullivan felt he should explain himself. "Look, I've spent a lot of time with Darleen Saunders. She claims that she doesn't know what happened the night her husband was killed."

"And you believe her?" Mays asked matter-of-factly.

Sullivan hesitated for a split second before replying, "Yes."

Just then, another detective entered the office. His name was Joe Peters, and he was short and stocky. The sleeves of his white shirt were rolled up, and the collar was open, with the tie down a notch. He was carrying a large sheet of drafting paper.

"Sullivan. Mays," he said, nodding at each man. "Since you guys are working on that Saunders murder, maybe you can help me out."

"What do you need?" Mays asked.

"There were some murders in Chinatown last night. The heads of the Chan Triad were knocked off. Real old-style Ninja-type stuff. Karate. Poison darts, we think. I haven't seen that shit for years."

"What's that got to do with Saunders?" Sullivan asked.

"Look at this," said Peters, spreading the paper out on the desk.

"What is it?" Mays asked.

"Some kind of blueprint. For a real big building project in Chinatown."

"I still don't see the connection," Sullivan said.

"Look at the name. Here," Peters said, pointing.

Mays glanced at the name. "So it says Saunders. So what?"

"This was found last night under one of the bodies in the Triad killings," Peters said. "There were three of them. Long Chan, who was one of the heads of the Triad. A guy named Sammy Ling, who is a big developer in Hong Kong as well as being into narcotics, prostitution, and a ton of other shit. And Won Lo, assistant to Charlie Liu, a member of Minotaur's board of directors."

"How's Liu mixed up in this?" Sullivan asked.

"I thought you guys knew," Peters said. "Liu is the Chans' investment banker."

"Where'd you say these guys were murdered?" Sullivan asked, suddenly very attentive.

"In one of those old tenements in Alphabet City."

Mays shot him a strange look. "*Exactly* where?"

"Avenue C, just off Houston."

"What time?" Mays asked.

"We figure they bought it about ten o'clock."

"I wonder . . ." Mays said lowly, to himself.

"Anyway," Peters said, "I just wanted you to know that Saunders was mixed up with the Chans. Whoever offed them might have offed him, too."

"Thanks," Sullivan said. The only thing Sullivan could think of was that, if Peters was right, Darleen was in the clear. There was no way that she could have killed anyone last night. She wasn't Bruce Lee, for Christ's sake. And she had been with him.

Peters left, and Mays immediately grabbed his coat and started pulling his tie up to his neck.

"Where you going?" Sullivan asked.

"To see Samantha Kwan."

"A few minutes ago you were bitching about working on Sunday. Now, you're acting like a damn bloodhound."

"Remember where I said I lost Kwan last night?"

"Alphabet City."

"What I didn't tell you was that it was Avenue C, just off

Houston. I lost her around nine thirty, just before those Chan dudes got wasted."

"Jesus Christ," Sullivan said.

"Now, which of the sisters could be described as a Ninja?" Mays asked, rhetorically.

"Get over there fast," Sullivan said.

Thirty

Samantha stood in the shower, soothing, warm water cleansing her body. But she was unable to wash away memories of last night. She still smelled the putrid odor of the tenement. She felt the hot, sticky blood on her hands. "You always live with the deaths you bring to others," she remembered her uncle once telling her.

Her door buzzer sounded. Turning off the water, she wrapped a large towel around herself and darted to the intercom on the wall near the loft door.

"Who is it?"

"Detective Mays. NYPD."

Her heart beat faster, and she looked warily around the room. Deliberately breathing slowly, she said, "Just a minute, please."

While she pulled on a black silk kimono, Mays stood in the cold muttering to himself. "I freeze my buns off every time I have to see one of these women."

Samantha pressed the buzzer that unlocked the front door. A few moments later she heard the elevator rising. "Stay calm," she told herself. "If they were after me for last night they would have sent ten squad cars and surrounded the building."

When Mays reached her door, Samantha stood at the peep-hole. "Show me your badge," she said.

Mays pulled out his wallet and flashed his shield. Two tumbler locks were undone, and the door swung open. The first thing that struck Mays when he saw Samantha with her wet hair wrapped in a towel was how innocent and vulnerable she appeared. That she was a martial arts expert who could cut him down in seconds seemed all wrong—until he saw the calluses on the outer edges of her hands.

She led him into the living room. He was conscious of her firm body outlined beneath the silk kimono. She obviously wasn't wearing anything else. Thinking of the film he had seen of her with those three guys, he almost groaned. "The sexy sisters," he muttered.

"What's that, Detective?"

"Nothing."

Samantha sat in a chair and looked at Mays expectantly as he sat opposite her.

"Miss Kwan, I'm here about Mark Saunders's murder. Where were you the night he was killed?"

Samantha smiled to herself, but the look she gave Mays was serious. "I was working late. You can check the logbook at the front desk at *Chanèle* magazine. That's where I work. I didn't get out that night until close to one in the morning."

While Mays made notes, she paused and unconsciously rubbed her hands as though wiping off something unpleasant. "Darleen Saunders told our group that we are all suspects. Why me?"

"Miss Kwan, we have the porno tape Saunders made of you. Was he blackmailing you?"

Samantha looked away. "No," she said. "I don't think Mark really knew what he was doing other than lashing out at those closest to Darleen."

Mays closed his notepad. "Miss Kwan, where were you last night?"

Samantha looked at him coolly. "I had a date. Any particular reason for your asking?"

Not sure how he should pursue this line of questioning, Mays decided he had to be direct, even though he didn't want to be. "There were some men killed last night. Two were heads of the Chan Triad that runs Chinatown."

"And because I'm Chinese I must have something to do with it?" Samantha said with an amused smile. "Please, Detective, I give you more credit than that."

Mays felt she was toying with him, playing a cat-and-mouse game. *Goddamn,* he thought, *if Joy Livingston is the Spider Woman, Samantha Kwan is the Cat Woman.*

"What do you know about a big development project in Chinatown? The one the Chans and Saunders were doing together."

"Why should I know anything about such a project?" she asked, without missing a beat.

"Because you're Chinese," Mays said sarcastically. "Did Saunders ever mention it to you?"

Wariness veiled Samantha's eyes when she answered. "No, Detective."

Looking pointedly at her watch, she asked, "Is that all?"

Mays rose from his chair determined to check out the lady's alibi. "For *now*, Miss Kwan."

After he left, Samantha went into her bedroom, knelt down, and pulled a sheaf of papers from beneath her bed. When she stood, she was staring at the architectural drawings she had taken from the meeting last night.

While examining them, she was able to confirm that the plans were what Mark had talked to her about, the big deal he had been making with the Chans. She felt she had to know the plan's full scope if she were to prevent its completion and assure the ruination of the rest of the Chan Triad.

Picking up her telephone, she dialed hastily the one person who might be able to help. "Mrs. Saunders, please," she said when she got an answer.

A moment later, Darleen was on the line. "Darleen, I have something here I want to drop off at your apartment tonight. I want you to find out how big one of Mark's deals was. It might even help you at your meeting tomorrow morning. How? Well, just your *knowing* about it may make that Mr. Liu on Minotaur's board skittish as hell. Yes, it seems that he was in with Mark on this big waterfront project, and it wasn't entirely on the up and up. . . ."

Thirty-One

Martha Hendrick was lying on her bed, listening to someone pounding on her door. She had no idea how long the
banging had been going on.

Since coming home from Joy's earlier in the day, Martha
had been unable to get out of bed. She was ravaged by two
emotions: humiliation at what she had done and terror at what
she had overheard. Every time she shut her eyes, she heard
Joy and Jacques discussing Mark Saunders's murder. Had Joy
done it? Was Martha next?

The banging on the door continued. What if it's Joy? she
thought. What if she's come back for me?

Finally, she heard a voice calling, as though from a long
way off. No, it wasn't them. Dragging herself from bed, she
went like a sleepwalker to the door and opened it.

"Damn it, Martha! What's going on?"

Tommy Winslow was frantic. His blue eyes were pained,
his brow creased with worry.

"Oh God, Tommy. Hold me," Martha said, sobbing.

Tommy was shocked by her appearance. There were huge
black circles under her eyes, and her clothes looked slept in.

"What happened on Fire Island?" he asked.

"Joy Livingston's a murderer."

"Oh, come on."

"No! I heard her."

"Who did she say she had killed?"

"A girl like me," Martha said. "And that big real estate developer, Mark Saunders."

Tommy stared into her eyes. Her fear told him she wasn't lying. "Come on," he said softly. "I'll make coffee and you can tell me everything."

Three hours later, Tommy was standing in front of Sullivan and Mays at police headquarters. He cleared his voice. "Uh, excuse me. Are you detectives Mays and Sullivan?"

Mays and Sullivan broke off their conversation and looked up. "Yes," said Sullivan, his exasperation noticeable.

"I was told you are handling the Mark Saunders murder."

Sullivan threw a pencil down on his desk. "Sit down, son. What can we do for you?" he asked wearily.

Tommy sat tentatively. "Look, my girlfriend—her name is Martha Hendrick—was on Fire Island this weekend with a TV newswoman, Joy Livingston. . . ."

The detectives exchanged glances. "What of it?" Mays asked.

"Martha's in danger," Tommy said.

"Why?" Sullivan asked.

Tommy hesitated and then spoke up determinedly. "She overheard Miss Livingston talking with some guy named Jacques about the Saunders murder."

"So what?" Mays asked.

"Martha heard Jacques say Joy did it. Joy killed Saunders."

Sullivan turned to Mays. "What the hell is this?"

"Where's your girlfriend?" Mays asked.

"I put her on a bus home to south Jersey," Tommy said. "She was terrified that Joy and this Jacques were going to come after her. You see, she also overheard them talking about another girl who Joy had out to Fire Island. It sounded like she was murdered, too."

Sullivan raised his eyebrows skeptically and looked at

Mays. "Give me your girlfriend's name, address, and phone number," he said.

Tommy gave them the information and stood up, ready to leave.

"We'll get back to you and your girlfriend if we have to," Sullivan said.

"What do you mean, if?" Tommy demanded. "I tell you who killed someone and about someone else who knows about it and is terrified and—"

Before he could finish, Sullivan exploded. "We're not playing games here, kid. You've got a suspect. So do a lot of other people. Get in line!"

Mays took Tommy by the arm and steered him toward the door and away from Sullivan. "What the detective means is that we can only check out one lead at a time."

Captain Carter, who had observed Sullivan's outburst, came up to Sullivan's desk. "What's going on here?"

"Just somebody with information about another suspect in the Saunders case," Sullivan said.

"Impossible." Carter said. "We've already got our murderer." And he stomped off.

"What are we going to do about Martha Hendrick?" Mays asked.

"I'll call her later," Sullivan said. "Miller is the one we want."

Thirty-Two

Darleen stretched out in her bathtub and luxuriated in the warm water. She felt exhausted.

She had spent hours talking with Minotaur directors and hadn't gotten a commitment out of any of them, not even Randolph. Dragonetti had warned her that none of them would tip their hands before Monday's board meeting. Being careful businessmen, they were waiting to see how the meeting unfolded. She was grateful for the soothing bathwaters and the calming sounds of classical music coming from the speakers built into the chamber's walls.

During the past few years, Darleen had used the bathroom as a refuge of sorts from her problems with Mark. It was a vaulted room with a skylight roof that Mark had had John Saladino design from scratch while they were on their honeymoon. When she first saw it, she couldn't believe it. The room was so sensuous, it appeared almost decadent. But somehow the effect was tasteful.

The tub was ten feet by ten feet of white marble sculpted in the shape of a seashell and sitting on a raised marble platform in the middle of the room. The walls were mirrored. The floor peach marble. The fixtures gold.

One mirrored wall hid a large-screen television and the stereo equipment. Towering potted palms and ferns were about.

Following Dragonetti's advice, she had offered each of the three board members not under Emmanuel's control something they wanted badly.

To Randolph, she promised that his bank would be the sole underwriter when Minotaur's stock went public, which she said would be within a year. Randolph personally stood to make at least three million dollars on the transaction. To Horace Mayhew, the ex–Landmarks Commission chairman who Mark had controlled by threatening to fire him, she had promised a lifetime contract. To Charlie Liu, the Chinese-American businessman and civic leader, she promised a multimillion-dollar oceanfront property in the Hamptons that his family had long tried to buy. Maybe whatever Samantha had would help her sway Liu, she thought.

Now, tired as she was after making the phone calls, she knew she couldn't rest. The need to clear herself of murder drove her on. Grabbing her coat, she headed for SoHo. She was meeting Sullivan in fifteen minutes. "We must find that apartment," she said to herself.

Fifteen minutes later, she pulled her peacoat tightly around her. Her hair blew wildly as a piercing wind tore down Houston Street. Looking everywhere and seeing nothing familiar, she muttered, "I know it's here. I *know* it's here."

Turning a corner, she ran right into Sullivan. She was startled, but she quickly recovered, and she grabbed his arm, smiling. "There you are," she said.

Sullivan was subdued. His quietness made her uneasy.

"What's wrong?" Darleen asked.

Sullivan looked at her, knowing all the pain she had been through and not wanting to give her any more, but at the same time unable to help himself. "Us. *Me*," he said exasperatedly.

"But last night—"

Gripping her shoulders and staring into her eyes, Sullivan said, "Goddamn it, Darleen, I feel more for you than I ever did for anyone," he said. "But I can't let my emotions dictate how I do my job."

Darleen felt the strength she had willed over the past few

days drain away. Her shoulders sagged. "You think I'm guilty, don't you?" she said flatly. "Even though last night—"

"No," he said wearily. "Darleen, I love you. That's why we're here. I figure that if I can find the apartment you woke up in, I'll find the guy you woke up with. Without him..." His voice trailed off.

"Without him what?" she asked frantically. But a moment later she listlessly answered her own question. "Without him I don't have much of a chance, do I?"

Sullivan didn't answer. "Come on," he said, taking her arm. "Let's see if we can jar your memory. If any of these buildings look the least bit familiar, let me know."

They walked together for thirty minutes, covering a half a dozen blocks off Broadway. At last, she said, "It's no use. I don't recognize anything."

Frustrated, Sullivan said, "Darleen, there must be something. Think about the *inside* of the apartment. Maybe that will help."

"Like what?"

"Do you remember what floor the apartment was on?"

"I remember it wasn't on the first floor because I had to walk down two—no, three flights of stairs. Oh, wait. I remember there were these awful posters on the walls."

"What kind of posters?"

"Clint Eastwood, Humphrey Bogart. That kind of thing."

"Can you remember anything else?"

"The guy was swarthy. Hispanic, I think."

"Puerto Rican?"

"I think so."

"Don't stop now. What else do you remember?"

"Well, I remember sitting there in bed thinking how enormous the windows were."

"Like a loft?"

"Yes, I believe it was."

"A Puerto Rican in a third-floor loft with movie posters," said Sullivan thoughtfully.

"A *filthy* loft," she added. "Is that enough to work with?" she asked hopefully.

"Sure," he said, hiding his uncertainty.

"What do we do next?"

"*We* do nothing."

"But I want to help you!"

"Then go home. I mean it. How would it look if *we* found this apartment?"

"Like a setup?"

"Right. I can just see some public defender having a field day with that."

"All right," she said.

Sullivan put Darleen into a cab. She stared at him anxiously out the back window until the cab disappeared around a corner. He took a one-hundred-eighty-degree turn and muttered, "If he's here, I swear I'll find him."

For the next two hours, Sullivan tried building after building, asking superintendents, tenants—anyone—whether they knew of a third-floor Latin lover with a Dirty Harry fixation. Finally, on his nineteenth building, Sullivan got lucky.

The building superintendent was an Indian or Pakistani, a skinny guy who stood barely five feet tall.

"Who've you got living on the third floor?" Sullivan began.

The super just shrugged. He wouldn't look Sullivan in the eyes. Probably doesn't have a green card, Sullivan thought.

"Guess I'll have to take you to the station house," Sullivan said bullyingly. "Give you a background check and—"

Before he could finish his sentence, the man almost shrieked. "Yes! Yes! There is such a fellow on the third floor. I show you!"

Sullivan nodded. They walked up the three flights and the super knocked on a door. No one answered.

"Open it," Sullivan ordered.

The super pulled a ring of keys from his back pocket and opened the door. A loft. On the walls, posters of Clint Eastwood and Humphrey Bogart.

Bingo!

"When's he due back?" Sullivan asked.

"Don't know," the super said. "He comes in and out. All times. Day and night."

"What's his name?"

"Garcìa."

Sullivan checked his watch. It was a little after seven o'clock. "Go about your business," he told the superintendent. "I'll wait for him here. Oh, and if you see Mr. Garcìa come in, you know nothing. Got it?"

"Yes! Okay! Yes!"

When the door shut, Sullivan walked around the room trying to figure out what Garcìa was all about. There wasn't a book, magazine, or newspaper in sight. Marks of a transient. The furniture was rickety, and the refrigerator was about empty. A bottle of Tequila was on the counter. A lot of empty beer cans were in the trash.

The only expensive goods in view were a stereo, a twenty-five-inch TV, and a VCR. But the closet was full of flashy clothes.

Suddenly, Sullivan heard the scape of a key inserted in the door lock. Moving silently behind the odor, he took out his Dan Wesson .357 from the holster by his right hip.

An instant later, Cookie Garcìa found himself staring down the barrel of Sullivan's pistol.

"Who . . . who sent you, man?" he said, his voice cracking.

"Police," Sullivan said. "Arms against the door. Spread your legs."

"A cop? Is that all?"

"It's enough, Garcìa," Sullivan snarled, flattening Cookie's nose against the door. "Now spread 'em!"

Cookie sneered, but he did as he was told. Sullivan frisked him and, finding him clean, put his revolver away.

"Sit down," Sullivan ordered.

"Sure, bro'," he said, laughing. "But I ain't got all fucking night."

"That's where you're wrong, kid."

Sullivan paused. Time to gamble. "If you don't want to talk here, I'm going to book you for receiving stolen goods. Your buddy told us how you came by that stereo and TV."

Cookie looked up. That fucking Fernando Rivera. Couldn't he do anything right? *Why do things always get fucked up? Everything was going so good. Shit*.

"Must be big, if you're ready to deal," Cookie answered calculatingly.

"It is. To me, anyway. I want you to tell me what you were doing Wednesday night."

"Oh, man," Cookie said laughing. "I can't remember what I did *last* night."

"I'll help you," Sullivan said, disliking the little greaser more and more. When he thought of Darleen in bed with this creep, he felt like strangling him. With an effort, he kept his voice steady.

"That was the night you went to Palladium and messed around with a lady's drink and brought her back here. A very classy lady."

Suddenly, Cookie looked fearful again. His eyes darted from side to side, as if he was trying to figure where he could run. He knew he shouldn't have gotten into that shit.

"I don't know what the fuck you're talking about, man," he said angrily.

"Sure you do, Garcìa. Because if you don't, I'm going to book you for accessory to murder." Sullivan glared at him with such unadulterated rage that Cookie gulped hard. "The lady's husband was killed that night. She's been charged with the murder. You, my boy, are her alibi."

Sullivan paused again to drive in what he was saying. "Of course, if the lady killed her husband, your really are an accessory. People saw you leave Palladium together."

Cookie put the fingers of his right hand to his mouth and started gnawing on them. "I know what you're talking about. But I swear, I wasn't involved in no fucking murder."

Rapidly, Cookie began telling how Darleen wound up in his apartment that night. It had started a couple of days earlier.

Cookie had gotten a call from a guy.

"Who?" Sullivan demanded.

"I don't know," Cookie said quickly, skating over the lie. "Nobody like that gives his name."

"What did he want?"

"He set up a meet with a woman. She showed me the picture of another woman. Told me to meet her at Palladium and dance with her friend. She gave me some shit to put in her drink. Told me to bring her back here because somebody was gonna make a movie of us in bed."

Sullivan winced at the details. "Did you ever see the woman again?"

"Yeah, sure."

"What do you mean, yeah, sure!"

"She was with her that night at Palladium."

Sullivan stared at the greaser. Suddenly, it began to make sense. Aida! Darleen's messed up friend had set her up.

"What happened after you left Palladium?"

"I got her back here. But I was so spaced out that I passed out on the bed."

"Did the movie guy ever show?" Sullivan asked.

"Couldn't tell you. When I woke up the next morning, I was alone."

"Did you get paid?"

"Yeah. A grand in the mail."

Sullivan quickly sorted things out. Much of Garcìa's story jibed with what Darleen had told him, but there was something odd about it. It was all a setup. That much was clear. But why had Aida conveniently left so all this could take place? To kill Mark Saunders?

Sullivan knew that a clever prosecutor could say that Darleen hired Aida to set the whole thing up herself. That she planned to go to Palladium. That she didn't take the doctored drink. That, after Garcìa passed out, she left him, killed Mark, and returned, with Garcìa now her alibi.

And, God help him, the prosecutor might make a strong case. *After all*, he thought, *Aida is an actress*. He tried to push the rest of the thought from his mind, but he couldn't. Maybe she and Darleen were partners in crime.

"Okay, Garcìa. I'll be back in touch soon. Don't tell anybody you talked with me."

As soon as Sullivan left, Cookie picked up the phone, his hand trembling. "Mr. D'Angelo, I need your help."

Thirty-Three

The high-vaulted lobby of the Center City Club was crowded when Edward Fitzgerald entered. He scanned the men and saw Cummins standing near the open hearth with a roaring fire opposite the front door. A small smile of satisfaction creased his lips.

Making his way through the crowd, Fitzgerald touched Cummins's shoulder. The young lawyer jumped like a startled rabbit. He turned and held out his hand. The wary expression on his face showed that he didn't know what was up — why the leading member of the firm had asked him to dinner after bawling him out the other morning. Sick to his stomach, he was fearful that he was going to be chastized again.

Fitzgerald read Cummins's reaction and was secretly pleased. He wanted the boy nervous, off-balance. Vulnerable.

"Mr. Cummins, I am so glad you could come."

"Thank you for inviting me, sir."

"Have you ever been to the club before?"

"No, I was just admiring what little of it I've seen so far."

"These columns," Fitzgerald said, pointing to the massive marble lobby columns, "were carved by Irish stonemasons."

Laughing, he added, "The brown stains in them were actually from the workers' chewing tobacco."

Relaxing, Cummins asked a question that all the firm's associates had been wondering about. "Sir, the office was buzzing about your helping Mrs. Saunders at her arraignment. Will you be defending her? If so, I'd like to volunteer to help you."

"No, Mr. Cummins, thank God. Her position is so weak she needs the sharpest criminal attorney in the country."

"Oh. I see."

"No, you don't see."

"What do you mean?" Cummins asked.

"We're not getting her a good lawyer, because Emmanuel Saunders doesn't want us to. We work for him, not for Minotaur. He asked me to get her one of the many inept, high-priced people who populate our profession."

"Isn't that a con—" Cummins bit his tongue, realizing he was about to call his boss on another shameful act. How, he wondered, could Fitzgerald so cavalierly send the woman to her doom?

Fitzgerald led Cummins to the huge, ornate reading room off to the right of the lobby, and then took him upstairs to the walnut-paneled library that looked like it could have been in the Vatican. While showing Cummins through, Fitzgerald kept up a congenial banter, setting his underling more at ease.

"Now," he said, "let's go to the dining room."

There weren't many people in the high-ceilinged room. Fitzgerald asked for a table in the back, away from everyone else, telling the maître d' they would be discussing business and didn't want to be overheard.

At the table, Fitzgerald held the younger man's chair for him, bringing a small protest of embarrassment from Cummins. Instead of sitting opposite his guest, Fitzgerald took the chair immediately to the left, his right leg brushing against the lawyer's left when he sat down.

"How did yesterday go?" Fitzgerald asked.

Cummins looked away and gave a brief rundown of Charlene Duncan's reaction to her new apartment.

"Now, about Friday morning, Mr. Cummins," Fitzgerald said, watching the panic-stricken look return to the boy's face.

"Believe me, sir, I wasn't criticizing you. I—"

"Mr. Cummins," Fitzgerald interrupted. "I imagine I don't have to tell you that you are skating on very thin ice at the firm."

Cummins looked stricken. "I—I'll do anything," he began.

"May I call you by your first name?"

"Of course."

Fitzgerald moved carefully, strategically. Building the pressure on the boy. "John, I'm afraid your overall performance could be better," he said solicitously. "It's not just a matter of Friday morning. . . ."

"Please, sir. I didn't think I was doing that badly."

Fitzgerald reached under the table and patted Cummins's knee. "There, there. I understand that you want to do well and succeed at the best law firm in the nation."

He let his hand rest on the boy's leg, seemingly as an afterthought. Then he gently squeezed Cummins's thigh before taking his hand away. "I am sure there are many other firms that would be pleased to have you."

"But Mr. Fitzgerald, no one has ever complained about my work," Cummins said plaintively.

Fitzgerald gazed at him intently. "Perhaps I'm being too harsh in my judgment. Besides, John, you are an attractive young man. It would be a shame to see you have to leave."

The lawyer looked at him and flushed. "What?"

Fitzgerald leaned closer to Cummins and again put his hand on Cummins's thigh, leaving it there. He felt the boy's leg tremble. "I said you are an attractive young man."

Cummins blushed and didn't know what to do. He began perspiring. Suddenly, his limbs felt immobile. What should he do? If he did the wrong thing, his career was over. Who would ever believe this? He wanted to get up and leave, but he couldn't. He felt paralyzed. God, he felt Fitzgerald's hand inching up his thigh.

"John, I am sure that we can forget your impudence earlier today," Fitzgerald said soothingly. "I always like to help bright young lawyers at the firm whenever I can. As you know, I can do a lot for you. You do know that, don't you?"

"Yes—*yes*," Cummins replied shakily.

"There are many young men at the firm whom I have

helped over the years. Young men who were good to me. Do you understand me, John?"

The attorney gulped and reddened. He adjusted his glasses. "Yes," he whispered.

"Good."

Throughout the meal, Fitzgerald kept returning his hand to Cummins's leg, edging a little higher each time. Feeling the boy trembling, as if he were shivering.

Cummins was afraid to move, not knowing what to do. Dismayed, he felt himself starting to get an erection. Suddenly, Fitzgerald's hand touched his crotch.

"Now, John," Fitzgerald said softly. "I would like you to come upstairs with me where we can talk more privately. Believe me, this will be very good for your career."

Fitzgerald pushed his chair back and got up. "Follow me," he ordered.

Cummins stood and followed Fitzgerald toward the elevator. Moving mechanically. Wondering why he couldn't bring himself to walk out the front door.

An hour later, Cummins walked out the front door of the club. He hated Fitzgerald and felt disgusted with himself for having been so weak. He wanted to put as much distance between himself and the crooked fairy as quickly as possible. God, he wondered, can I ever make amends for what I've done? All because of cowardice.

Suddenly, with a certainty he hadn't felt since he had joined the law firm, he knew what he must do. Stopping at a pay phone, he dialed information. "Mrs. Mark Saunders— Saunders Tower."

He called the number the operator gave him. "Mrs. Saunders?"

"Yes."

"This is a friend," he said tensely. "I want to warn you about Fitzgerald. He and Emmanuel Saunders are hiring an incompetent lawyer to defend you."

"Who is this?" Darleen felt her body go rigid.

"It doesn't matter. But I'm telling the truth."

"I can believe Emmanuel would do that. But Mr. Fitzgerald rushed to defend me when I was arrested."

"Mrs. Saunders, believe me! Fitzgerald does whatever Saunders says. You're being manipulated."

"Please, tell me who you are," she pleaded.

Cummins hung up.

Despite the news, Darleen was composed when she put the phone down. She walked to the window, and making a fist of her hand, shook it toward the east. "I should have expected as much, old man. You never give up, do you?"

Thirty-Four

Aida stared at herself in the mirror. Posing first one way and then another, she gave bad imitations of Meryl Streep. Finally, she looked frightened, and tears started rolling down her cheeks. No longer acting, she let her sobs become shrieks.

"It was *my* part!" she yelled. "*My* part! The bastard stole it from me. I would have been a star. A star!"

Grabbing an ashtray, she threw it against the image of herself, and the mirror shattered. "He deserved it," she screamed. "He deserved to die!"

Just then the phone rang. "Hello," she answered, her voice turning silky. "Oh, Detective Sullivan? Why do you want to come over? Uh, okay."

Slamming the receiver down, Aida began trembling. She went into the bedroom and poured the contents of her bag onto the top of her bureau while she frantically searched for cocaine. Finding none, she pulled open bureau drawers, scattering the contents around like a whirlwind. She ran into the living room, pulling cushions from chairs and the sofa and even looking under the rug, knowing no drugs were there, but hoping all the while.

Finally, she began sobbing again. "God, I can't take it anymore," she said aloud.

She grabbed her address book and her coat and ran out of the apartment. Outside her building, she hailed a cab and sat anxiously in the back as the taxi headed uptown.

"You *sure* you want to go here, lady?" the cab driver asked when she reached her destination, looking at Aida as if she were crazy.

They were in Harlem, on 135th Street between Seventh Avenue and Lenox. It was now nearly nine o'clock, and the sky was dark. Half the buildings appeared bombed out and, from what could be seen in the harsh street light, the others looked like they ought to be. Boarded up windows. Garbage strewn about. Broken stoops, pavement, and doors. Winos huddled in doorways.

The cabbie, a balding man of about fifty wearing a brown leather jacket and blue watch cap, shook his head in disgust. Aida didn't even look at him. She just shoved a ten-dollar bill in his direction and climbed out.

She checked the address against the one in her address book and walked shakily up a stoop that was littered with glass. The front door was unlocked when she pushed it. The hallway smelled of urine mixed with indescribable foul odors, but she didn't notice.

Aida climbed to the second floor and looked for apartment C. She found the door and knocked. No one answered. She knocked louder.

"Who's there?" a low voice called.

"Aida Miller," she said, rubbing her arms, the need for a fix beginning to overwhelm her again.

There was the sound of several tumbler locks being undone, and a chain lock being pulled back. The door opened, and there was Mad Manny in a black silk shirt, black pants, half a dozen gold chains around his neck, and gold rings on each of his fingers. His face appeared snake-like when his mouth pulled back into an ironic grin.

All of a sudden, he began cackling, laughing his crazy laugh. Reaching out, he pulled her inside by the coat.

"I told you you'd be back," he said. "I told you!"

The door slammed behind her, and the locks bolted—a deadening sound. Manny led her down a dark hallway. Another doorway opened into a living room that was all white—walls, furniture, rugs. Five black men were playing poker.

"Come on, Manny," shouted a voice.

"Yeah, man. Why you takin' so long?... Well, hello, Mama."

"Boys, give me a minute to get our next pot ready."

They laughed knowingly.

"You pretty bad to come back to old Manny, ain't you?" he said as he led Aida into another room, to his briefcase on the sofa. Opening it, he extracted a plastic bag of cocaine and poured some on top of a table. He handed a short straw to Aida.

"When you done, come back to me," he said.

She grabbed his arm pleadingly. "Please, Manny, don't do anything to me. Just let me have this and go home."

He suddenly clutched her menacingly. "You gotta pay for what you get in this life." Just as suddenly, he let her go. "But hey, I'm not forcing ya, you know? The choice is yours."

Alone, tormented, Aida wrestled with herself. But each second that passed only heightened her passion for the white powder in front of her. She greedily took the straw and snorted a line. Moments later, she did another. Suddenly, everything looked brighter, better. Breathing deeply, she turned and walked back into the room, momentarily oblivious to the deal she had just sealed.

"Mmmm. *Mmm*," said one card player.

"Where you find her, my man?" said another.

"You made the right choice, girl," Manny said. He looked up at Aida. "Show 'em what you got, sugar."

Aida stood frozen. She felt like running, but there was nowhere left to hide. Manny reached up and pulled the zipper of her red body-skimming dress halfway down. She took his hand away and pulled it the rest of the way down herself. She stepped out of her dress and looked at the men.

Stepping back, she slowly slipped off her bra. Hooking her thumbs in her panties, she pulled them down, turning her back to the men as she did so. After taking off each piece of clothing, she held it up to them like an offering and curled her tongue at the men.

When she was naked, she walked back and forth before them as she took the bobby pins out of her hair and shook it down her back. Finally, turning sideways, she thrust out her chest. All the time smiling.

"Okay," Manny said. "Who in?"

"I'm in, Manny," said one man.

"Me, too," said another.

"We *all* gonna get in," said a third, huskily.

They all laughed. Manny dealt the cards while Aida stood oblivious, with her arm around his shoulder. She had escaped to somewhere else.

Sullivan immediately drove to Aida's apartment. Because his earlier doubts about Darleen were making him furious with himself, he directed his rage at Aida. "Aida," he muttered, "I'll make you confess!"

He parked in front of a building on East Seventy-sixth Street. He took the elevator to the twentieth floor and rang Aida's bell.

No answer. "Shit," he muttered as he leaned on the bell again, then he went downstairs and summoned the superintendent to open the apartment door.

The super, a stocky man about fifty-five years old and wearing khaki work pants and shirt, fiddled with a jangling key ring until he found the one for Aida's door.

"Okay, Detective," he said. "If there's anything else you need, just let me know. I've gotta fix a stopped up drain on another floor. My wife's downstairs, and she'll know where I am."

Sullivan walked through the rooms, looking for a clue to where Aida had gone. He was ill at ease, a feeling he always had in such situations—another part of being a cop he didn't like. Going through someone's home when they weren't there made them unexpectedly vulnerable, he thought, like walking in on someone naked in the bathroom.

Entering the bedroom, Sullivan did a double take. There was a wig on a wig stand on the vanity. Beautiful. Chestnut. The cut was familiar.

As he approached the vanity, he saw a large color photograph of Darleen pasted on the mirror. Her hair in the photo
was the same style as the wig.

As he examined the picture, it dawned on Sullivan that he
wasn't looking at Darleen. The eyes were larger, darker, the
nose was a little more aquiline. The lips were a little fuller.
He knew the woman in the picture. Aida!

The whole thing was eerie. He put the photo back, and felt
like wiping his fingers off, as though he had touched something dirty.

What the hell is Aida up to? he wondered. Did she kill
Mark Saunders dressed up like Darleen in case somebody
spotted her leaving the scene? Even wearing Darleen's pin,
which Mark grabbed before going out the window?

Now Sullivan knew he had to find her fast. Quickly, he
opened drawers and closets. But he found nothing of use.

He went back to his car and headed for the station, thinking about who might know where she had gone. The other
sisters? Theater people, maybe. Perhaps a cabbie would remember picking her up. He radioed in and got a patrol man
assigned to stake out her building in case she returned.

Pressing the button on his police radio, he said, "Dispatcher, find Detective Mays and get him back to headquarters. Tell him we've got a murderer to find."

MONDAY

Thirty-Five

Darleen finished her hair and appraised herself in the mirror of her vanity. Her hair was held in a French twist, both simple and attractive. She had difficulty considering her appearance because of where she had to go early this morning — and because of the meeting she had to attend right afterward.

This was the morning of the memorial service for Mark. Fortunately, Emmanuel Saunders — through the lawyer Fitzgerald — had let her know that he wanted the service to include just the immediate family. She had been depressed when she tried to think of whom else she should really invite; there was no one, really. Mark had cut himself off from his friends over the past several years. Those he hadn't dropped, he had offended.

Having tossed and turned all night, she woke this morning feeling just as tired as before going to bed. Her dreams were flooded with images of Mark. The anxiety induced by his horrible death, along with the thought of what she must face at this morning's board meeting, made her wish the day were already over.

She dabbed a tear from the corner of her left eye. "Thank God Brian called last night, or I'd be in worse shape," she whispered to herself while thinking of how Sullivan had found the awful person she had been with the night Mark was murdered. "And thank God the stranger backed up my story."

Shuddering as if a cold breeze were blowing by, she checked her watch. It was almost seven A.M. Time was running short. She hurried into her dressing room and opened one of the mirrored doors of her closet.

Darleen was wearing a black slip, bra, and panties. Scanning her massive closet, she pulled out several dresses and immediately discarded them. The choice was very important, she knew. Because of the board meeting, it must be one that tipped the balance from a widow accidentally entering the corporate world because of an inheritance to a woman who inherited a company she knew how to manage responsibly.

Finally, she took down two dresses. She held up the gray wool Valentino suit with a peplum and looked critically in the mirror. Next, she held a tailored black Chloe. She slipped into the latter, deciding black was more appropriate.

St. Thomas Church appeared cavernous when she entered. Father Thomas Morrow, who had officiated at her marriage, came over and held her hands. "Are you all right, Darleen?"

"Yes, thank you."

He led her to the first pew to the left, going past the empty coffin in the aisle. Unable to help herself, she began crying, weeping for Mark and for what he had become. Crying for the life together they had lost.

Genuflecting, she entered the pew and knelt. Her hands were trembling; she folded them together as she remained kneeling. Deborah and Samantha had asked if she wanted them to accompany her this morning, but she had explained that she wanted to go through this alone.

The clicking of hard leather soles on the aisle floor distracted her. Glancing around, she saw Emmanuel approaching the front of the church. He entered a pew to the right. For a moment, she felt sorry for him. He looked haggard. His face was drawn. He seemed to have shrunk in stature.

But again she thought of Mark, and her pity turned to anger. Emmanuel was the reason her marriage had become a shambles. The reason her husband came to hate her—because she was a reproach against his weakness.

Father Morrow stood by the altar, facing them, and began, "We are here to remember Mark Saunders. . . ."

At the conclusion of the rite, Emmanuel abruptly left his pew and strode out of the church without looking back. Darleen watched his erect back go through the doors and onto Fifth Avenue, wondering how he could rely on pride even when reminded so profoundly today that it is not how we are perceived but the good we do that lives after us.

She thanked Father Morrow for his kind words and wondered again about Emmanuel. This time, she wondered how he would behave at this morning's meeting. Once again, she felt a strong sense of loss. If only Mark had been stronger.

The sleek, black limousines began gliding up to the front door of Saunders Tower at about 9:30 A.M.

The first board member to arrive was Anthony Armante, retired head of the General Contract Workers, one of the largest construction trade unions in the city. Though the morning was overcast, Armante wore his ever-present sunglasses. A camel-colored cashmere overcoat was buttoned over his massive torso. His hair was thick, curly, and gray. His fleshy face seemed to rest on the white silk scarf around his neck.

Leaning on a cane as he walked from the limo, he radiated authority. A burly, watchful bodyguard followed a few paces behind. The vigilant limousine driver scanned the windows, doorways, and rooftops.

At age seventy-one, Armante was two years older than Emmanuel Saunders, and he had worked on Emmanuel's projects for more than forty years. He was a cautious, careful man. Though the FBI had a folder on him as thick as the Manhattan phone book, his only conviction was for illegal campaign contributions in a congressional race twelve years ago. He had served three months at Danbury, one of the federal prisons known as "country clubs."

There were rumors Armante had taken the fall for his candidate, who had been siphoning off campaign funds to pay for a divorce and a mistress. Now, it was said, this congressman couldn't do enough for Armante and certain of his friends, all Italian, all in organized crime.

Armante fished a gold key from his pocket and opened the

door of the glass tube elevator that ran up the northeast corner
of the building. The elevator held only one person. Armante
appreciated the precautionary measure—and also the bullet-
proof plexiglass. Instinctively, he felt the Colt .45 revolver
under his left armpit. An old-fashioned gun in some respects,
but it was reliable. And he had a permit for it through his
friend the congressman.

As the teardrop-shaped elevator—once dubbed "the largest
champagne bubble in the world" by a *New York Times* architecture critic—sped to the penthouse boardroom, Armante
looked forward to his old friend Emmanuel reassuming control. He had never like Mark. The son lacked Emmanuel's
unpredictable ruthlessness.

When the elevator door slid open, Armante entered a huge,
circular room dominated by a large portrait of Emmanuel
Saunders. The frame was fourteen-carat gold, as were the tum-
blers and water pitcher on the table and the name plates on the
circular golden oak conference table in the middle of the room.

Armante appreciated the way Emmanuel had designed the
room. Symbols were important to people. He himself never
traveled in anything but the right style for his position. Cadil-
lacs, never a Mercedes. Cashmere, never furs. A home on
Staten Island, not a Fifth Avenue apartment. One diamond
ring. The little guys in his union, he knew, appreciated the
fact that their leaders flashed the trappings of power without
living like fucking Rockefellers or pimps.

The next man to step out of a limousine was Mayhew. A
plump, pink-faced little man wearing horn-rimmed glasses
that gave him an owlish look, Mayhew bustled to the elevator
with an air of self-importance, glancing neither to the right
nor to the left.

Mayhew had a Ph.D. in nineteenth-century American litera-
ture from Harvard. His specialty was writers who had lived and
worked in New York City—such as Whitman, Poe, and Crane.
It had given him an academic interest in the city's architecture—
which, in turn, had led to a job with the Landmarks Commission
and, eventually, the directorship. He was fifty-four years old
and, until a year ago, had been married to the same woman for
twenty years, a librarian at Columbia University.

Two years ago, he had met Mark Saunders, who began

inviting Mayhew to parties without his wife. To Horace, the parties were glittering fantasies. He experimented with marijuana, cocaine, and Quaaludes. He found that beautiful young women were attracted to him, not realizing they were just doing Mark's bidding.

Finally, Mark introduced him to a young woman who became an obsession, and an expensive one at that. She liked chic restaurants, clubs, and presents. When Mark offered him a job with a salary beyond his wildest imagination, Mayhew took it. His job was to make sure that Minotaur Development projects got landmarks approval. That wasn't hard. He knew where a little money could be wisely spent. Besides, he had written most of the guidelines, so he knew how to get around them. Mark Saunders had kept him in line by threatening to fire him. If that happened, Mayhew knew his expensive lifestyle — and his mistress — were gone forever.

The next board member to arrive was Randolph, the banker. He couldn't wait to vote against Emmanuel.

When Randolph had been brought on by the board, the appointment was unusual in that it had been made by Mark without consulting Emmanuel, causing a deep rift between father and son. At least initially, Mark had considered Randolph a major addition to the board. Emmanuel considered Randolph a disaster.

When summoned to Mandragola after the announcement of Randolph's appointment appeared in *The Wall Street Journal*, Mark braced himself nervously with several scotches before leaving his office. As expected, he found Emmanuel in a testy mood. But before his father could say anything, Mark seized the initiative.

"A guy like Randolph gives us the kind of eminent respectability we need," Mark said. "Our image will improve a hundred percent. Besides, he's very shrewd, and with his bank's political and military connections, we'll be able to get some of those Defense Department contracts you've always wanted."

Emmanuel's voice rang with disdain. "Prestige! Image! Those are your concerns? Well, Mr. Image Maker, let me show you something."

Emmanuel flung toward him a file folder that bounced off

Mark's chest, the papers scattering on the floor. Angrily, Mark picked up the papers, glaring at his father.

As he read, Mark's expression changed to puzzlement, then to sheepishness.

"Read the fourth paragraph on the second page," Emmanuel ordered.

His voice faltering, Mark began reading: "In his diversification efforts at Metropolis, Randolph is quietly creating the basis for a real estate development company that will become one of the largest in the nation, and a direct rival of Minotaur Development Corp—"

"Why do you think the son of a bitch was so anxious to take you up on your board offer, you fool!" Emmanuel thundered. "This man can learn our every move and ruin everything."

"What am I going to do?" Mark asked, his voice containing the plaintive whine that he had used around his father since he was a boy.

"Have I taught you nothing in all these years?" Emmanuel asked sarcastically. "What would Machiavelli do?" Emmanuel then twisted away from Mark as though the sight of his son sickened him. "Turn your disaster to your advantage," he said quietly. "Feed him false information with the hope that he isn't as brilliant as you believe."

Over the succeeding months, Metropolis entered a series of disastrous real estate ventures. For the first time in his twenty-five years with the bank, Randolph's business judgment was questioned. Finally, Metropolis pulled entirely out of real estate development. Fortunately for Randolph, he successfully pushed the bank into the credit card business. But there was a black mark against his name. It didn't require brilliance to know how it got there. "One down, one to go," he said coolly as the elevator took him to the top.

The last limousine carried Liu, partner with the investment banking house Bachman Bros. Liu had done brilliantly at Princeton, then collected an MBA from Harvard when he was only twenty-one. He was in charge of Bachman's Asian investments. Although most people didn't realize it, his major client was his family. His mother was a Chan. He was a member of the Chan Triad.

Liu was slim, with a shock of unruly black hair. He was

deeply involved in city affairs. He was on the board of Operation Uplift, a city minority hiring program, and was a member of the mayor's Chinese-American civic rights panel. He also had been director of the Chinatown Statue of Liberty Committee, which had raised funds for refurbishment of the Statue.

After the four men were seated, Dragonetti entered the boardroom from the doorway leading from Mark's office. With dark bags under his eyes, he looked like he hadn't slept for a week, which was close to the truth. He took his seat and nodded perfunctorily to those already present.

Then Fitzgerald came through the same door, a smug look on his face. Purposefully, he stopped by each man's seat and shook his hand, chatting for a moment before moving on to the next board member. Though he tried to appear calm, there was an itchiness about him. When he finally took his seat, he carefully adjusted the gold name plate so that it was centered exactly in front of him, scowling all the while as if the plate had done something personal to him by being a little crooked.

Suddenly, all eyes were on the doorway. Darleen Saunders was looking imperiously around the room. She was wearing the black Chloe with a large black straw hat and a dark veil. Outwardly cool, emotionally she was shaking like a leaf.

"Good morning, gentlemen," she said, and strode to her husband's former seat.

The looks were different on the faces of each of the men. Armante was contemptuous. Randolph was sly. Mayhew was fearful. Liu was calculating. Fitzgerald was amused.

Then, once more, all eyes shifted to the doorway. Emmanuel Saunders entered, casting a disdainful look around the room.

"It has been a long time, gentlemen. . . ." he said, pausing and looking at Darleen with wry contempt. "And *lady.*

"For you who may not know this beautiful woman," he continued condescendingly, "this is my son's wife, Darleen Saunders."

Darleen stared back at him coldly. "Thank you, but I don't need you to introduce me. I already know most of them." Pausing, she looked at Fitzgerald. "Why," she added ironically, "Mr. Fitzgerald is finding me a *top criminal lawyer*— isn't that so?"

Fitzgerald looked uncomfortable and tried to make light of her remark. "Good lawyers are hard to find."

"Especially when you aren't looking," she said icily.

Ignoring the exchange, Saunders opened the meeting. "Mrs. Saunders is in the unique position of having inherited my son's share of Minotaur, which makes her a fifty-percent owner."

"Which makes my vote equal to yours," she said forcefully.

Saunders scowled. "A mere formality," he said, with a wave of his hand.

"No," she said. "A reality. Another reality is that my interests, I am sure, don't reflect yours."

This time, Emmanuel laughed mirthlessly. "That sentiment will be of little consequence. I am once again taking charge of the company."

"No," Darleen said firmly. "You are not!"

For the first time, Saunders looked at her with that same wariness he'd had the first time he met her. "What? Just what are you saying?"

"I am saying that you are not up to the demands of running this company. You gave control to Mark because you weren't physically up to the job after your accident. That hasn't changed."

"Just who is supposed to run Minotaur then?" he asked sarcastically.

"A team. Someone with a controlling interest and someone who knows the company inside out," she said.

Everyone in the room sat still. Aware of the importance of the confrontation, each man's eyes shifted back and forth from Darleen to Emmanuel. Calculating eyes sized each of them up as though betting on a racehorse.

Suddenly, Emmanuel picked up the tension in the room. He looked around as though a trap were being laid.

"And who might the people on that team be?"

Darleen inhaled deeply before speaking. "Mr. Dragonetti and myself," she replied.

An incredulous look masked Saunders's face. "You must be out of your mind," he said. "Dragonetti?"

He began laughing and looked around the room, obviously expecting others to share in his mirth. Fitzgerald gave a few obliging chuckles, but no one else joined in.

Acting as if Saunders weren't even present, Darleen made

a formal motion. "I am proposing that Mr. Anthony Dragonetti be named president of Minotaur Development Corporation, and that I be named chairman."

"Second the motion," Dragonetti said quickly.

"So this is your gambit," Emmanuel said. "Well, let's get
this nonsense over with as quickly as possible. "Nay!"

"Nay," said Fitzgerald.

"Obviously, my vote is aye," said Darleen.

"And mine," said Dragonetti, unable to look at Saunders.

"Nay," said Armante, looking kindly at Darleen and adding, "Nice try."

Darleen looked expectantly at the rest of the men, feeling
almost faint from the pressure, wondering whether her induce-
ments to them would be enough.

"Aye," said Randolph, adding with delight, "and they call
them the weaker sex."

Everyone looked at Mayhew, who was nervously drum-
ming his fingers on the tabletop, unaware of the noise it made
in the silent room.

"Aye," he said, a look of stark terror on his face as he spoke.

"Four to three," Dragonetti said happily.

"It's not over yet," Emmanuel growled. He fixed a steely
look on Liu. "Whatever she's offered you, Liu, I'll double it."

Liu looked first at Darleen, then at Emmanuel. It was clear
he thought he was sitting in the catbird seat.

But then Darleen cleared her voice and, staring at Liu,
said, "Maybe this would be a good time to discuss the Waterfront Project."

Liu turned white. He quickly gathered his things, went to
the elevator, and disappeared.

"Four to three with one abstention!" Dragonetti said emphatically.

"No, damn it! No!" Emmanuel said, looking around in disbelief.

"On with the meeting," Darleen said calmly, feeling for the
first time that she was in control of her world, not the other
way around.

Thirty-Six

Cookie stood at Sheridan Square in Greenwich Village in the park on the little island that gave the square its name. His hands shoved into his jacket pockets, he was wearing shades and looking cool.

He passed the time despising the dumb fucks on their way home from work. The guys in suits coming out of the subway station with briefcases growing out of their fucking arms. He hated the freaks who walked around in their shitty costumes and hair colored green, purple, and orange. He was glad to be getting the fuck out of New York for a while. It was too goddamn weird and cold. He wanted to see the fucking sun again.

Checking his watch, he saw he was a little early. The manila envelope was under his arm. He told Deborah Bartley ten A.M. Maybe he ought to be *real* cool, and fuck her for old times' sake. But the idea seemed like too much trouble.

He hardly paid attention to the guy who sidled up next to him and asked him for a light. Cookie was going to tell him to fuck off—until he saw how big the bastard was. As he reached for a light, the guy spoke, and Cookie felt as if an icy hand had squeezed his heart.

"You're Cookie, aren't you?"

Cookie looked up. The man's eyes were hidden behind black sunglasses. He wore a hat and his collar was pulled up, so it was impossible to make out his face.

Turning to run, Cookie realized there were two guys, just as big, blocking his way. Suddenly, he felt a fiery pain in his back. In terror, he looked at the men in front of him. Each held a knife that slid through Cookie's jacket, touching his chest.

The men shoved Cookie over to a black limousine that glided up next to them. One man opened the door and pushed Cookie inside, next to an enormously fat, bald man. Another got into the back seat on Cookie's other side, while the third got in next to the driver.

"Give us the papers, Cookie," the fat man said in a loud, rumbling voice. He squeezed Cookie's right hand until the bones started crunching.

"Sure, Nicky." Cookie handed them over. Suddenly, he began cringing and shaking as though he were freezing, even though it was warm inside the limo.

Thirty-Seven

"Tony, we've done it!"

The meeting had just ended, and Darleen's face was radiant. She felt like dancing around her office, she was so happy.

Dragonetti was impressed. The lady, it would seem, had taken to the business like a duck to water. Imagine, getting the best of Emmanuel Saunders.

"Well, Madam Chairman," he said, his drawn face breaking into a grin. "What's our first order of business?"

She suddenly became serious. Reaching into a desk drawer, she pulled out the blueprint that Samantha had given her. "Tony, what do you know about something called the Waterfront Project?"

Dragonetti's face sank. Just when everything was going so well. "Why, nothing," he answered, the truth painful to admit.

"I want you to look at these and tell me what you think," she said, handing him the blueprints Samantha had given her.

"Okay."

As Dragonetti turned to leave, a man wearing a chauffeur's uniform was led into Darleen's office by her secretary.

"Mrs. Saunders, I'm sorry, but he wouldn't leave it outside. He said he had to deliver it to you personally."

The driver bore an enormous spray of roses in the shape of a horseshoe. "Compliments of Mr. Lipsky," he said, setting the flowers on the floor by her desk and leaving.

"God, it looks like I won the Kentucky Derby," Darleen said excitedly.

"You know who Lipsky is."

"Yes. One of the princes."

Opening the card, she read the message aloud:

> *Congratulations, Mrs. Saunders. Do not make the same mistake your husband made.*
>
> *Lipsky*

She handed Dragonetti Lipsky's note.

"Whatever does this mean?" she asked.

"I don't know." Dragonetti's stomach was churning. "But whatever it is, we'd better find out. Lipsky is nobody you want to mess with—none of the princes are."

Suddenly, Darleen's secretary came back into the room, this time trailing Sullivan.

"Hello, Brian," Darleen said, smiling. "Are you here to congratulate me, too?"

"About what?"

"Why, I just became chairman of the board."

"That's wonderful," he said, his mind elsewhere.

"Please see to *both* these matters," she said to Dragonetti.

"Of course," Dragonetti said. As he left, he closed her office door.

Alone together, Sullivan got down to business. "Do you know where Aida is?"

"No. Why? Is it important?"

Quickly, he told her about finding Garcìa and how the greaser had said that it was Aida who had paid him to doctor her drink.

"You're kidding?" Darleen gasped.

"There's more," Sullivan replied, then told her about the wig and picture he had found in Aida's apartment. "Do you know why she was dressing up like you?" he asked.

"I haven't a clue."

"It looks like she killed him and set you up to take the fall."

"I don't believe it!"

"Oh, come on," he said. "We both know she is capable of it."

Darleen didn't answer; tears welled up in her eyes. Just then her intercom buzzed. "Yes?" she inquired of her secretary.

"A call on line two for Detective Sullivan," the secretary said. "It's his partner. He says it's urgent."

Darleen handed the phone to Sullivan.

"What's up?" Sullivan inquired.

"They just found Cookie Garcìa's body," Mays said.

"Murdered?"

"You got that right."

"Give me the address. I'll meet you there." He got up and started for the door.

"Is Aida dead?" Darleen asked, anticipating the worst.

"No. Just her accomplice."

Twenty minutes later, Sullivan and Mays were at a construction site at Thirty-second and Lexington.

"Is this a Minotaur project?" Mays asked as they made their way to the body in the middle of the lot, under some loose two-by-fours.

"No," said Sullivan, checking the signs.

"Maybe Garcìa's death isn't related to Saunders's," said Mays.

"Don't bet on it," Sullivan said.

A uniformed officer told them that appparently Garcìa had been pushed from one of the top floors.

"Any witnesses?" May asked.

"No. But we found this in his back pocket."

He handed the detectives a pocket calendar. Mays looked first, skimming the pages while Sullivan walked to the lobby.

"Check this out," he said to his partner when Sullivan returned.

Sullivan paged through several months. Just about every weekday had a woman's name, address, and telephone number. Some days two.

"Get a load of the addresses," said Mays. "They're all on the Upper East Side. Looks like a call girl's calendar. Our boy must have been running himself a service."

"Damn," said Sullivan. "Guess who our boy had an appointment with the day after Mark Saunders was killed?"

"Who?" Mays asked.

"Councilwoman Deborah Bartley."

"And guess who he had an appointment with earlier today?"

"Councilwoman Bartley."

While driving to City Hall, Sullivan said to Mays, "I think I'm losing my fucking mind."

"How d'ya figure that?"

"Last night after I saw Garcìa, I thought Darleen might really be guilty. God knows, I didn't want to believe that. But it looked like she and Aida had planned the whole thing together. Then, I go to Aida's apartment and see how Aida was dressing up to look like Darleen. I figure Aida planned the murder herself, hoping to make it look like Darleen had done it. But now we've got a link to Deborah. Shit, I don't know. Maybe it's Deborah and Aida who got together to kill Saunders."

"Our problem," said Mays, "is that whoever killed Saunders, the others were on the verge of doing it, too."

"Yeah, maybe you're right. But, damn it, in my heart I know that Darleen is innocent."

"That's just the problem," said Mays.

"What is?"

"You're using your heart too much."

Wearing a heather tweed suit, Deborah looked coolly efficient, which was exactly the opposite of how she felt as she looked at the policemen sitting in her city council office. With sheer will power, she stopped herself from collapsing.

"I have to ask you again, Mrs. Bartley. Did you know Diego 'Cookie' Garcìa?" Mays asked.

"Yes, I knew him," Deborah said evenly. "He was a dog walker. I have an Afghan."

Mays looked at her with bored insolence. "Lady, we know what the kid was," Mays said. "We're not here to pass moral judgment on you, but to solve a murder. What's it going to be? Here or One Police Plaza?"

"All right. You've—you've made your point." Deborah sighed deeply and sat at her desk. "Yes, I knew Mr. Garcìa."

Briefly, she told them about hiring him through the Yellow Pages. About how he came to her apartment once a week. She tried to keep the whole sordid business as matter-of-factly as possible.

"When did you last see him?" Sullivan asked.

"Last week."

"Then why," Mays demanded, "did he have an appointment to meet with you today?"

Deborah looked up sharply. The color drained from her face and she couldn't speak for a minute. "How did you know that?"

"Lady, Garcìa was very precise about his appointments," Mays said. "Now, why were you going to meet him in Greenwich Village?"

"He called up and wanted to talk. I didn't want him coming to the apartment again, so I told him I would meet him at Sheridan Square."

"What did he want?" Sullivan asked.

"I don't know," Deborah said softly. "I never kept the appointment."

"Just suppose, lady!" Mays said. "I say you kept that appointment. I say you killed him. . . ."

Deborah rose silently. She was breathing fire, but her voice was still calm. "Either arrest me or get the hell out of my office! You're forgetting who you're talking to, detectives."

"Where's Aida?" asked Sullivan.

"I haven't the vaguest idea."

"For your sake," Sullivan said, "you better hope she turns up. Alive."

Moments after the detectives left, Nicky D'Angelo entered through a side door. He'd obviously heard everything.

He held out a manila envelope toward her. It contained the papers that Garcìa had stolen from her. "I believe you lost this," he said.

She went to take it, but he swiftly pulled it away. "Mrs. Bartley, before you get this we must talk about your obligations."

"What do you mean?" she asked.

"We both know how valuable this material is," he continued unperturbed.

Deborah flinched and shut her eyes. Quickly, however, she regained her composure. "Mr. D'Angelo, what is it you want?"

"It's payback time, Deborah. Time to pay me back for what I've done on your behalf."

"Oh, dear God," she groaned.

"It's not so bad," D'Angelo said. "At least we know that you didn't kill Mark Saunders."

"We? How do *you* know that?"

D'Angelo ignored the question. "Deborah," he said instead, "the first thing we would like your help with is securing a liquor license for a certain restaurant owned by a friend of ours."

Deborah paused. "That can be arranged," she said coldly.

"We would also like a Park Avenue address for a certain construction project in which we have an interest that is being built on East Seventy-eighth Street."

"So you can charge Park Avenue prices because of the address?"

"Perhaps."

"That can be arranged, too."

D'Angelo handed her the manila envelope. "That will be all, *for now*."

"What do you mean, for now?"

D'Angelo just stared at her for a moment before walking away.

TUESDAY

Thirty-Eight

Sullivan and Mays were at their wits' end. It was now just after midnight. They'd been at it all day and all night, and they still didn't have a clue to Aida Miller's whereabouts.

They racked their brains for what else they could do. They'd asked the sisters and Aida's theater crowd. They'd left word with the cab companies, checked the airports, train stations, bus terminals, and car rentals.

Nothing.

Then their phone rang. At first, Mays couldn't make out what the caller was saying because there was so much noise in the background.

"I said I'm a cabbie and I'm calling from a pay phone at Fifty-third and Broadway," the caller repeated. "My dispatcher said you might be looking for a fare I had last night."

"What's your name?" Mays shouted.

"Mike Potts. I picked her up in front of her apartment last night."

"What street?" Mays quizzed.

"East Seventy-sixth."

"Bull's-eye!" Mays said to Sullivan.

Sullivan put on his coat and waited for Mays's next cue.

"Where'd you drop her off, Mr. Potts?"

"At 135th and Lenox. Smack in the middle of Harlem."

"Did you see her go into a building?" asked Mays.

"Yeah. A brownstone on the corner."

On the ride up to Harlem, they got cops in a cruiser to read off the numbers of the corner buildings.

"Thanks," Mays said into his microphone. "Now we can check out who lives there."

"Don't bother," the voice came back.

"Explain," said Mays

"Three of those buildings are bombed out. The fourth's Mad Manny's hideaway."

"Mad who?" said Sullivan.

"Manny," the beat cop replied. "Small-time drug dealer and pimp. Apartment C."

"Thanks for your help," Mays said, and then he said to Sullivan, "Looks like our actress is a user."

Twenty minutes later, Mays wheeled the car in front of Mad Manny's address. The tires crunched glass and rubble. "Man, I hate coming to this section at night, and I'm big and black," he said.

Sullivan checked his watch. Two o'clock. "Let's hope the creep is in."

They climbed the steps leading into the dilapidated brownstone. A couple of bleary-eyed winos slowly separated, making a path for them.

Trudging up the putrid stairwell, they stopped before apartment C. Sullivan banged on the door. A search warrant was in his hand in case the slimeball gave them any crap about why they were there.

"Open up, Manny," Mays roared. "Before I break the door and your head, too!"

The command was answered with silence. Mays held up his hand, raised his index finger, and shouted. "One!" Then his thumb. "Two!"

Suddenly, they heard scurrying feet and a toilet flush.

"There go the drugs," Sullivan said disgustedly.

A moment later, there was the clatter of a chain lock being

taken off and the tumble of bolt locks being opened. A sullen Mad Manny opened the door.

"What you want, man?" he said, staring at the detectives with unabashed hatred.

Mays walked through the door, shoving Manny back with his bulk as he did so. The smaller man scrambled along the hall like a spider as he tried to keep out of the big man's way.

"You ain't got no right barging in here, man," Manny yelled. "No right."

Mays looked at him wearily. "Manny. Manny. Why does looking at your ugly face make me want to punch it?"

Mays's right hand shot out and grabbed Manny by his neck chains, pulling the man close to him. Mays edged forward. His left foot covering Manny's right shoe, he brought down the full force of his three hundred ten pounds.

Manny's face twisted with excruciating pain as Mays shifted his weight slightly on the drug dealer's arch. Tears welled up in Manny's eyes.

"My foot," he whined. "You breakin' my fuckin' foot!"

"You're on the guy's foot," Sullivan said, sounding bored, as if Mays didn't know it.

"Oh, so I am," Mays said airily, shifting his weight once more before taking his foot away.

Sullivan walked around the living room, poking into a closet, opening a drawer in an end table, lifting up cushions on the sofa and a chair.

"We're looking for someone," Sullivan said, "a woman named Aida Miller."

The detectives monitored Manny's expression. At the mention of Aida's name, the look in Manny's eyes flickered from sullenness to wariness and fear. The son of a bitch knew where she was all right.

"Don't know what you talkin' 'bout," Manny said, his voice belligerent—but his eyes desperate.

"Sure you do," Mays replied menacingly.

Grabbing Manny again, he twisted the gold chains until they cut into the man's neck. This time, he stomped on Manny's foot. A gagging scream escaped the dealer.

"Where is she, asshole?" Mays said, stomping down again. The crunch of crackling bone was audible.

"On the street, man! On the street!"

"Where?" the big man barked.

"Ninth and Forty-second."

Mays let go of Manny, pushing him back as he did so. The dealer fell to the floor, crying and gingerly rubbing his left ankle.

"Get your coat, scumbag," Mays said.

Manny painfully got to his feet and hobbled to the living room closet, taking out a long black leather trenchcoat and a broad-brimmed maroon hat.

The windows were rolled up to keep out the night cold as the detectives sped down Ninth Avenue. Hunched in the back seat, Manny lit a cigarette.

"Put it out, fuckhead," Mays ordered.

Hurriedly, Manny ground it out in an ashtray, not looking at either cop as he did so.

"What time did you drop her?" Sullivan asked.

"'Bout eight o'clock," Manny mumbled.

Sullivan shook his head, wondering how messed up she'd be.

The blocks whizzed by. When they hit the lower Forties, Mays pulled the car toward the curb at each block. Shivering, glassy-eyed women wearing hot pants, fishnet stockings, and low-cut blouses ran up when they stopped.

"Need company?" one shouted.

"Forty dollars," said another.

Some boldly reached into the windows when they were rolled down, grabbing at the men's crotches or shoving their breasts inside the windows. Sullivan scanned each group. After shaking his head no at Mays, he rolled the Dodge on to the next corner.

At Thirty-eight and Eighth Sullivan saw a tall, sunken-eyed woman with flowing black hair. She was wearing a blue satin miniskirt, garters, stockings, and a white satin blouse. Her face was heavily made up. Rouge streaked her cheeks. When the car stopped, she came running, pushing her way toward the car with the rest of the hookers.

"Hold it," Sullivan said. "We found her."

Opening the car door, Sullivan held up his shield. "Police," he shouted.

The women scattered. Sullivan raced after Aida, catching her without difficulty because of the spike-heeled shoes she was wearing.

"Let me go," she snarled.

"Come on, Aida," Sullivan said gently.

At the mention of her name, a perplexed look came over Aida's face, as if she were hearing a name from a distant memory and trying to place it.

"Who?" she said, looking at Sullivan with a curious naiveté, at odds with the hardened mask her face was.

"I'm here to help you, Aida," Sullivan said, leading her toward the car.

Opening the back door, he motioned to Manny.

"Get out!"

Manny jumped out of the back. He tried to walk briskly away but couldn't, because he was limping badly. Pausing, he gave Aida a menacing glare.

Mays got out and grabbed Manny by the belt on the rear of his coat, yanking him backward so that he stumbled.

"You ever fuck with that lady again," Mays hissed, "and you'll wish you were dead."

Fear flickered across Manny's face. He backed away and limped down the street as fast as he could.

Sullivan eased Aida into the back seat and got in next to her. Her skirt rose up. She wore nothing beneath it. Sullivan reached over and pulled her skirt down. Feeling sorry for her, yet furious with her, he hoped she could be pulled together enough to help Darleen by confessing and naming her accomplice, if she had one.

One hour later, Aida was wrapped in a blue bathrobe, shaking and crying hysterically. "Leave me alone! Please! Leave me alone! Let me die!"

She was sitting in the living room in Darleen's apartment, the robe pulled around her as if she were freezing. Darleen had given her a hot bath, scrubbing off the makeup and cheap perfume, while Sullivan and Mays had waited.

Darleen started to rush toward Aida, but Sullivan held her back. "Please," he whispered. "I have to find out what she was doing with that photograph and wig."

Darleen looked confused. Torn between wanting to help her friend and listening to Sullivan, she cried and walked to the other side of the room.

"Aida," Sullivan said insistently. "Tell me why you made yourself up to look like Darleen."

Aida began whimpering. "I—I never meant to hurt you, Darleen," she said. "God, I never meant to hurt you."

"What happened?" Sullivan pressed.

"I—I was supposed to dress up to look like her, go to Saunders Tower and let the guard at the desk see me."

"Didn't you realize you were framing Darleen for murder?"

"No! I swear it. I just thought it was another of Mark's stupid orders."

"Orders? What orders?"

Aida began twisting her hands together, squeezing her fingernails into her palms. Haltingly, she began telling them about the bargain she and Mark had struck.

"He gave me drugs," she said listlessly. "He first gave them to me to make up for the cruel way he had taken that Broadway role away from me. At least, that's what he said. After I needed them, he gave them to me only if I did things for him."

"Is that why you set up Darleen at Palladium?"

"Yes."

"Why did Mark want you to do that?"

"I don't know, but it wasn't Mark who told me. He used some guy called the Buddha. He gave me drugs sometimes from Mark."

Mays shot Sullivan a look. "D'Angelo."

"He told me to dress up like Darleen and let the guard at the front desk of Saunders Tower see me, and then to leave. I took Darleen's pin at Palladium and gave it to the fat man outside Saunders Tower."

"D'Angelo might have killed Saunders," Sullivan said. "Or put the pin on his body."

"Why did you do it?" Mays asked.

"I just thought it was part of the performance I was to give that night."

"Performance?" Mays asked.

"I performed for his telescope."

"Telescope?" Sullivan said.

"The one in his office. Mark ordered me to be in my apartment Wednesday nights after midnight. I, uh, stripped for him, while he made videotapes of himself watching me."

"Oh, Aida," Darleen said, biting her lip.

"What do you mean, he made videotapes?" Mays asked.

"He showed them to me a couple of times," Aida said. "He was a video nut. He taped his meetings and sometimes he even taped himself watching me."

"For God's sake, *why*?" Darleen asked.

Aida looked up. "I think he hated himself for what he was doing, and wanted a crazy record of how awful he saw himself become."

She began crying again. "I was performing for him when he went out the window."

"What?" Darleen exclaimed.

"I saw him *die*! Understand? *I saw Mark die!*"

Darleen suddenly looked faint. Mays led her to a chair.

"You're certain you saw him go out the window?" Sullivan asked.

"Yes! Yes!"

Mays looked at him. "You thinking what I'm thinking?"

"It's a long shot," Sullivan said. "But he might have been taping that night."

He walked across the room and knelt down next to Darleen. "I have to get into your office. Are you okay if I leave you for a little while?"

Darleen breathed deeply. "I'm coming with you."

"You sure?"

She nodded.

Turning to Mays, he said, "Will you stay with Aida?"

"Sure, man."

Darleen and Sullivan rode down the elevator, walked through the lobby and entered the corporate side of Saunders Tower. She put her arm through his, and Sullivan could feel her body trembling. When he looked at her face, he saw tears trickling from her eyes.

"Suppose it is . . ." She couldn't finish.

"Suppose it is one of the sisters?"

She nodded numbly and gripped his arm tighter.

Both of them were signed in by the guard. They took the elevator to her office. After unlocking the door, Darleen stepped aside and Sullivan entered.

He walked over to the window, and stood approximately where the telescope had been. Turning around, he scanned the opposite wall. There, looking almost exactly like one of the recessed lights, was the eye of a videocamera. "That's it," he said, pointing toward the ceiling.

Thirty-Nine

Sullivan walked over to the wall and opened a panel beneath the camera. He pressed a button and another panel opened overhead; the videocamera emerged and descended on a metal arm. While Darleen watched tensely, he removed the tape and went to the VCR by the TV in the office and loaded the tape. "Do you want to sit down?" he asked her while the tape rewound.

"I'm too nervous," she said, twisting her hands as she paced.

After pressing the PLAY button, Sullivan stood next to Darleen and put his arm around her. She leaned closer to him, a queasy feeling in her stomach.

Suddenly, a picture flashed on the screen. Darleen felt like screaming. There was Mark walking from his desk to the telescope. He leaned over, his eye pressed against the lens.

A few minutes later, they saw the office door open. Darleen gasped as a shadowy figure raced across the room. At the last moment she saw Mark turn, a look of horror on his face before he was shoved through the window.

Darleen screamed as the figure turned and faced the camera. "Emmanuel! My God, it's Emmanuel!"

Sullivan's mouth was wide open as he stared at the screen. "Jesus!" Snapping to attention, he grabbed Darleen and hugged her as she cried and cried.

"But—I—thought—he—loved—Mark," she whimpered.

After several minutes, Sullivan eased away from her, picked up a phone and dialed headquarters. "This is Sullivan. Tell Captain Carter I'll be downtown shortly to give him the key to the Saunders murder."

He clicked the phone button and dialed again. "Mr. Saunders, please. Tell him it's Detective Sullivan."

Sullivan looked grimly at Darleen and put his hand over the receiver. "You will never have to worry about him again."

Taking his hand away, he said, "Mr. Saunders, I have something urgent to take up with you. I will be at your home as quickly as possible. It bears on your son's death."

Gripping the tape, Sullivan steered Darleen out of the office. "Send Aida home and you stay by a phone," he said. "Mays and I are going after Saunders."

Fifteen minutes later, Sullivan barged into Carter's office and threw the videotape down on the captain's desk. "The Saunders case is solved," he said, a note of triumph in his voice.

Carter continued looking at the papers on his desk. "Okay, guy," he asked nonchalantly. "Which of the women did it?"

"None of them," Sullivan said with satisfaction. "Your pal Emmanuel Saunders killed his own son."

Carter's head snapped up and his eyes narrowed as he stared at Sullivan. "What the fuck are you talking about?"

"Indisputable evidence," Sullivan said, pointing to the tape. "What Saunders didn't realize was that his video-freak son taped everything—in this case even his own murder."

"Christ," Carter said, more to himself than to Sullivan.

"Aida Miller, the actress Mays and I have been chasing, put us on to it."

"Uh, good work."

"We're heading out to Mandragola to pick up the son of a bitch."

"Uh, yeah. Good," Carter repeated absentmindedly.

"Say, Sullivan?" Carter called out as the detective was about to leave.

"Has Mays seen the tape?"

"No. Just myself and Darleen Saunders."

The minute Sullivan left, Carter shut his door and placed a phone call. "Emmanuel Saunders, please," he said, speaking quietly. "Tell him it's Carter."

Emmanuel took the call in his office. "Why, hello, Captain. Do you have something new on the case?"

"You bet I do!"

Saunders's jovial tone turned icy. "What do you mean?"

"Sullivan's coming for you. He just gave me a fucking videotape of you pushing your son out of his office window."

There was a deadly silence on the other end of the line. After a few moments, an older, wearier-sounding Saunders said, "Well, well, well."

Suddenly, Carter leaned back and put his feet on his desk. He enjoyed making old Saunders dance in the dark. "Of course, I could destroy the tape. But that would be tampering with evidence, wouldn't it?"

"What do you want, Carter?" Saunders snapped.

"Now, as I mentioned to you before, I know how much influence you and the other princes have in picking the next police commissioner. . . . " Oil dripped from his voice.

There was a pause as Saunders reassessed his next move. "I understand, Commissioner Carter," he said in a silky tone. "Now, tell me how Sullivan learned of the existence of this tape."

"It came from that drugged up actress. Miller, I think her name is."

"I'll take care of that," Saunders murmured.

"What's that?" Carter asked.

"Nothing," Saunders said, adding, "You will get rid of that tape immediately, won't you?"

"You can bet my future on it," Carter said with a laugh as he hung up.

Without cradling the receiver, Saunders pressed the dial tone button on his phone and immediately dialed. "Nicky, I need a favor. It's Aida Miller. You know what to do."

A moment later he buzzed Marga. When she answered the

intercom, he said, "Those detectives who were here last week are coming back. Please show them in when they arrive."

Saunders's expression was sad when he sat back at his desk. He stared at a picture of Mark on the opposite wall. "Mark, you let greed and ambition blind you," he whispered.

Two hours later, Sullivan and Mays strode into Saunders's office. "You're under arrest for the murder of Mark Saunders."

As Mays read Saunders his rights, he went to handcuff him. "That won't be necessary, will it, Detective Sullivan?" Saunders said.

Thinking of what the man had put Darleen through, Sullivan gruffly said, "Cuff him."

"I hope you know what you are doing, Sullivan," Saunders said. "I just may have your job because of this."

Sullivan couldn't help being surprised by how cool the son of a bitch was. "You're finished, Saunders," he replied.

Less than two hours later, Sullivan and Mays entered One Police Plaza pushing Saunders ahead of them. Carter was standing in his office door and yelled at them. "Get over here, you jerks. And Mr. Saunders, would you mind joining us?"

The detectives looked at each other. "Something's up and I don't like it," Mays said.

When they entered his office, Carter slammed the door shut. "Take the handcuffs off Mr. Saunders and apologize to him."

Sullivan stared at the captain as if he must be out of his mind, while Mays gave Carter one swift, shrewd glance. "What are you talking about?" Sullivan demanded. "We bring Saunders in to book him and you act like he's a goddamn guest."

"If we're lucky, that's the way Mr. Saunders will take it," Carter said. Then, looking directly at Sullivan, he added, "What were you trying to pull with that phoney tape shit?"

Suddenly, a shock of awareness flashed across May's face. "Phoney tape," he said, slowly looking from Carter to Saunders. "Get it, Sullivan?"

"Get what?" Then Sullivan's look of confusion turned to

hatred. "What did he give you, Carter?" he asked disgustedly.
"Money? Political connections?"

Suddenly, Sullivan lunged across the desk and grabbed at
Carter, who looked terrified. "You stinking no-good son of a
bitch!" Sullivan screamed.

Mays grabbed Sullivan and pulled him off. "It won't do no
good, man," Mays said. "Can't you see everything's against
you?"

Carter straightened his mussed shirt and tie. "Get out of
here, Sullivan, or I'll kick your ass off the force for hitting a
superior!"

Mays pulled Sullivan through the doorway and halfway
across the squad room while other cops looked on. Sullivan
yanked free. "I'm okay," he muttered. "I've just got to get the
fuck out of here."

Once outside, they walked half a block before talking.
"Shoulda known Carter was on the take from Saunders.
Shoulda known," Mays muttered.

"That corrupt son of a bitch," Sullivan mumbled, adding to
Mays, "I want some time to myself, okay?"

"You sure you don't want to stay with me?" Mays asked.

"No, I'm okay."

Mays started walking away, but stopped when Sullivan
said something. "What's that?" Mays called.

"I said the rich get away with everything—even murder."

Sullivan knew he had to tell Darleen what had happened
and he felt sick about it. He hailed a cab, and jumped in.
"Saunders Tower."

A half hour later, Sullivan finished telling Darleen.
Slumped on the sofa in her living room, she stood up angrily.
"He thinks he's so goddamn clever," she said. "He
is—he's . . ." She was so furious she couldn't finish what she
was saying. Sullivan had never heard her swear before, and it
made him feel worse for letting what had happened happen.

He looked nonplussed. "Darleen, I love you, but . . ."

Darleen looked at him, and some of her anger died. "I love
you, too. But . . ." She turned toward the window. "I told him
I would ruin him—and I will!"

Unsure what to do—and seeing how upset she was—Sullivan paid little heed to what she said. He was more concerned

with rethinking his own life, which he had to do if he was going to share it with her.

"I've got to get some sleep," he said. "I'll call you later."

"Brian," she said, kissing him good-bye. "I really do love you."

"And I really love you," he said, smiling wryly.

After he left, Darleen walked around her office agitatedly. Then it hit her. She buzzed her secretary. "Please get Mr. Lipsky for me."

A minute later, she heard, "Mr. Lipsky's on the line."

"Hello," she said. "There is something the princes should know. . . ."

Forty

The grandfather clock in Edward Fitzgerald's office chimed nine o'clock, and the senior partner of Fitzgerald, Meehan & Golden was still at his desk, a thin-lipped smile of satisfaction on his face. So engrossed was he in the reports and architectural drawings in front of him that he failed to hear the faint click of his office door opening.

Fitzgerald looked up only when a shadow fell across his desk. When he did, the smile on his face vanished. His eyes opened wide in disbelief, his jaw began trembling. Involuntarily, his right arm came up to his face as if to ward off a blow.

"But . . . but how—?" he said.

Suddenly, the lawyer came to his senses. Pulling himself together, he forced the look of fear from his face and slipped on his business demeanor. Efficient. Congenial. Somewhat arrogant. "This is a pleasant surprise," he began. "I had no idea that you would be here tonight." Fitzgerald looked around the room anxiously as he spoke. Seeking desperately an exit, some way to get past his visitor.

"How could you do it?"

"What? What do you mean?" Fitzgerald asked self-righteously.

"So you were the Waterfront Project."

At the mention of the name, Fitzgerald's face caved in. His mouth and cheeks sank into his face, and his eyes stared wide in terror. Breathing in shallow pants, he felt like air was sucked from his lungs. Suddenly, he looked very old and very frightened.

"No!" he said. "No, you have it all wrong. The deal was to help us all. To—to—"

Even as he spoke, Fitzgerald could hear the lameness of what he was saying. The plaintive tone in which he was speaking. Panic seized him. He grabbed a large letter opener from the desk and threw it at his visitor. He hadn't done anything more physical than play golf a half dozen times a year for more than thirty years. His throw was off-center, and the letter opener thudded on the thick carpet.

Backing away from the desk, he was painfully aware that his heart was thumping. His limbs felt paralyzed. Shutting his eyes, he poked ineffectively at the air in front of him with a fist as his visitor walked toward him.

Suddenly, a strong black-gloved hand seized the knot in Fitzgerald's tie. A fist smashed into his jaw, and pain exploded through his face. He started crying; his knees buckled, and he crumpled to the floor. His head was bobbling as the one hand still holding him by the knot of his tie prevented his sprawling all the way on the rug.

Looking up, he saw the fist descending again. The black blur crashed into the side of his face. He plunged into darkness.

Moments later, Fitzgerald groggily awakened to a nightmare. At first, he didn't know where he was or what was happening to him. Then he realized that he was in his office. Held aloft over someone's head!

Sweat broke out on his face. He looked to his right and saw that he was near the high windows overlooking Park Avenue. He tried squirming loose, but the powerful arms and hands held him fast. As they neared the windows, he suddenly realized what was happening.

Thrashing and screaming, he felt the arms heft him higher, heaving him toward the windows. His heart racing, he watched himself crashing through. The windows shattered as he fell like a stone through the cold night air.

Forty-One

The night was silvery, sending soft light through the massive metal curtains over windows of the Grill Room at The Four Seasons. Automatic temperature controls stirred the air, making the curtains shimmer like radiant veils.

Wearing a navy wool Valentino suit, Darleen sat looking around the table at the sisters. After their drink orders arrived, Darleen paid and left a fifty-dollar tip on the waiter's tray, telling him they didn't want to be disturbed.

"Thanks for coming," she said after the waiter left. "Samantha and I have something here that could help us all and help the city at the same time."

Inwardly, Darleen was seething about Emmanuel Saunders having escaped punishment, but outwardly she was cool. She knew how justice might yet be served.

Joy piped up, "Will this take long? I have to get to the studio."

"No," Darleen answered. "Right, Samantha?"

"Right," Samantha said, and proceeded to pull out the architectural drawings she had taken from the Chan meeting. Briefly, she told the sisters what she knew about the real estate development project, carefully avoiding any mention of how the plans came into her possession. "I asked Darleen to find out what she could about this, since it was a Saunders project. What did you find, Darleen?"

Darleen's expression was serious. "I had my president check it out. He didn't know any more than I did, because it was so secret. But he found out a lot from Mark's private papers. The project is very big—and very shady."

Briefly, Darleen told the background on the Waterfront Project, as it was known. "Massive numbers of people will be made homeless. Much of the plan calls for the redevelopment of Chinatown, although the scope goes far beyond that. The Chinese underworld is involved, and much more."

"But why are *we* here?" Deborah asked, looking at Joy and Aida.

"I was just about to tell you that." Darleen smiled slightly. "Who has made our lives miserable lately? Who tried to blame us for the terrible things *he* did?"

"Emmanuel Saunders, of course," Deborah said, looking curiously at Darleen.

"He was also behind this project, along with Mark," Darleen said.

Samantha looked at Darleen sharply. She was about to say something, but held her tongue. Darleen must know that Mark handled the project behind old Saunders's back. Suddenly, it dawned on her what Darleen was about to propose. She who had savored revenge for so long recognized it in another.

"We have an opportunity to repay him," Darleen said.

"How?" Joy asked.

"By exposing what he was doing," Darleen said. "Samantha has already gotten copies of the plans. Deborah can use her political office."

Thinking of D'Angelo, Deborah flinched, but said nothing.

Turning to Joy, Darleen said, "You can be the greatest help of all."

"How?"

"You can put this story on the air," Darleen said. "It's perfect: big company hurts little people with the help of gangsters."

"You mean wreck the plans?" Deborah asked.

"And ruin Emmanuel Saunders," Samantha added.

"Exactly," Darleen said.

"I missed something," Deborah said. "How will Saunders be ruined? He'll be embarrassed and might face some lawsuits, but what else?"

"The other real estate princes will take care of him!" Darleen said, knowing how seriously the princes looked on double-crossing by one of their own.

The other women, except Samantha, looked at one another conspiratorially. All seemed to smile at once, giving them the look of those schoolgirls they once were.

Joy glanced around the room. "To a new beginning. As sisters."

WEDNESDAY

Forty-Two

Deborah Bartley sat in the chair opposite Joy Livingston
under the harsh TV studio lights, and unconsciously she
smoothed her dress. She was wearing a beige silk dress that
made her look at once feminine and authoritative. It was
nearly 6:30 P.M.

"Don't worry. Everything will be fine." Joy had a reassuring smile on her face as she looked at her sister. She was
wearing a coffee-colored silk blouse and a mauve skirt. She
thought it was funny that this was the first time any of the
sisters had appeared on her *Newsmakers* show, which she did
as a segment on the nightly news.

Deborah smiled as if on cue and tried not to appear nervous. Playing with political dynamite, she hoped her ducks
were lined up the way they seemed to be, knowing nothing
was ever certain in politics. Yesterday's friends could be
today's enemies.

The studio was filled with people. Joy had contacted edi-
tors at the wire services Associated Press and United Press
International; at newspapers like *The New York Times*, the
Daily News, the *New York Post*, and *Newsday*; as well as at
rival television and radio stations. There were also aides to

other council people who had heard something was in the wind. Joe Donovan, a deputy mayor, was in the wings, eyeing Deborah strangely. Mays and Captain Carter stood in the back.

"You know, Mays," Carter said with a small satisfied smile, "this may have something to do with who becomes the next police commissioner."

Reporters from each of the news organizations were seated behind the cameras, staring at Deborah. Challenging her with their eyes, they seemed to say that what she had to say had better be good enough to have gotten them off their asses to come out here tonight.

A young technician came over and clipped a microphone to the front of Deborah's blouse. He looked at Deborah critically and backed up behind the cameras. "Thirty seconds, Miss Livingston," he said to Joy.

Joy gave Deborah a reassuring pat on the hand. "Now we make history, sister," she muttered.

A red light came on the camera.

"Tonight, we look at corruption on a wide scale," Joy began. "The buying and selling of our city without the knowledge of the public. New York is up for grabs, and the greedy are doing the grabbing. . . ."

Late as usual, Aida stepped out of her apartment building. Frantically, she began looking for a taxi to take her to the TV studio. Suddenly, a black limousine glided up beside her and the rear door opened. She looked in and involuntarily gasped.

"Get in, Aida," Nicky D'Angelo said. When she started backing away, his right arm shot out, grabbed her by the throat, and yanked her inside. His hands tightened around her neck as the door slammed shut and the limo sped away.

"—Councilwoman Deborah Bartley is here," Joy continued, "with explosive information on a proposed real estate project that would leave thousands homeless while making millions, possibly billions of dollars for the rich."

Deborah faced the cameras. "Unfortunately, everything you said is right, Joy," she said. "The real estate development project is called the Waterfront Project. It amounts to the rape of our city."

* * *

Samantha and Ming were naked in their bed while watching the drama unfold on the TV screen.

"This assures the destruction of the Chans and the dominance of our Triad with you as its leader," he said.

"Yes," she answered, "and there will be changes."

He looked at her quizzically.

"No more prostitution or drugs to ruin the young people of Chinatown," she said emphatically. "There are other ways of making money."

Carefully, Deborah began explaining the project. The architectural drawings provided by Samantha were shown enlarged on the TV screen. Areas were marked off in different colors to show viewers the extent of the project.

When Deborah finished, there were just minutes left in the show. It was then that Tony Dragonetti walked into camera range, carrying a piece of paper.

"Hold on, sir. Who are you?" Joy said, uttering her lines the way she had rehearsed them.

"Anthony Dragonetti. President of Minotaur Development. I'd like to read a statement."

"By all means," Joy said.

"Darleen Saunders, newly elected chairman of Minotaur, wishes New Yorkers to know that she is forthwith canceling this project. Ms. Saunders was shocked and dismayed to learn that her predecessors—her husband, Mark, *and* her father-in-law, Emmanuel—would have dared to do such a disservice to the people of New York. Thank you."

The show ended, and reporters with deadlines raced to telephones. Others converged on Deborah and Dragonetti like a horde of locusts.

"How did you first get on to this, Mrs. Bartley?" a reporter demanded.

"How much real estate is involved?" yelled another.

In the rear, Carter looked crestfallen. Mays flicked a piece of lint off the captain's suit jacket. "You want a tape of this show, Commissioner—I mean, Captain?" he asked sarcastically.

EPILOGUE

Darleen turned off the television and looked at the clock on her office wall. She felt like an enormous weight had been lifted from her shoulders. In fact, she felt so exhilarated she was embarrassed. *So this is the sweet taste of revenge,* she thought.

Going to a wall mirror, she began fixing her makeup. Brian was coming by shortly and they were going to dinner. She wanted to celebrate—and she wanted him.

Her attention was drawn to the faint hum of the outside elevator. *God,* she thought, *Brian's early and I'm not ready yet.* He had taken to using the director's special elevator, joking that he didn't want her employees seeing her dating a cop. There was the unmistakable shush of the elevator doors opening, and she saw a crack of light appear under the door connecting the boardroom with her office. Suddenly, she felt something was very wrong. Why didn't Brian come into her office?

But then, who else could it be?

Crossing the office, Darleen put her hand on the brass knob of the boardroom door. What was going on? Who was there? It couldn't be one of the directors this time of night. Other than Brian, they were the only ones with gold keys. Something told her not to go in.

Brushing aside her anxiety, she pulled the door open and gasped.

Emmanuel Saunders was sitting at the end of the conference table. A gun was in his hand, pointed at his temple. Lost in thought, he looked up startled. When he saw who was in the doorway, he smiled sardonically. He slowly pointed the gun at Darleen.

"Maybe there *is* a God," he laughed mirthlessly.

Her eyes wide in terror, Darleen took a step backward.

"Get in here, bitch!"

She froze.

"I said, get in here!"

Her heart pounding and her legs almost buckling, Darleen moved like a sleepwalker into the boardroom. Her vision blurred, and the room started to swim as she almost fainted.

At the last moment, she breathed deeply and was able to focus on her captor.

"Wha—what are you doing here?" she managed to ask.

"What does it look like? You've robbed me of everything that was mine! My company! My son! My life!"

Darleen shrank under the intensity of his glare. She had never seen a look of such hatred. With sudden clarity, she knew he was going to kill her. Just as he had killed his son. Just as he had raped her. Her fear turned to anger.

"You demon," she hissed.

Suddenly, she remembered Dragonetti's telling her about the conference table's secret button. She would die, but she would let the world know what a monster the man was.

She edged closer to the conference table, and slumped in Mark's old seat.

"Why did you come back here?" she asked, desperately hoping to buy another minute.

Emmanuel rose from his chair and began pacing about the room like a wild bull.

"That TV show this evening signed my death warrant. But I alone will choose where I die—and that is on the mountaintop I created!"

As he ranted, Darleen slid her hand along the edge of the table and pressed the button that would activate the video recorder. "Why did you kill Mark?"

Suddenly, Emmanuel looked very old and very tired. "That was the hardest thing I have ever done in my life," he said wearily. "But you must understand. The princes would have destroyed both him and me as well as Minotaur if Mark went unpunished for what he had done."

Emmanuel paused and then continued. "The unwritten code among the princes is that betrayal by any of us must be paid for with death. Mark and Fitzgerald were arrogant enough to believe they could do what no one has ever done."

"So you killed Fitzgerald as well?" she gasped.

"Of course. I had no choice. He was a fool." Tears welled up in Saunders's eyes. "But Mark. I had come to love Mark!"

Darleen was at a loss for words. The horror of the man's logic and the brutality of the business she had entered sickened her. Looking toward where Saunders now stood, Darleen almost cried out. She had caught a glimpse of Sullivan nearing the doorway.

"Emmanuel, why do you have a gun?" she called out boldly.

Startled, Sullivan crouched, then crept forward cautiously.

"What?" Emmanuel said. "Enough of this absurdity." He pointed the gun again at Darleen. "At least I'll know that you died with me."

Suddenly Emmanuel's gun was whipped from his hand, and Sullivan smashed him in the face. Again and again, Sullivan hit him, and Emmanuel crumpled to the floor.

Swiftly, Sullivan turned him on his stomach and cuffed his hands behind his back. He yanked Saunders to his feet.

It was over in a few seconds.

Darleen found herself trembling uncontrollably, hot tears trickling down her face.

Sullivan shoved Saunders halfway across the room. "You're lucky I won't kill you!" he snarled. Turning to Darleen, he said, "Thank God you called out." He grabbed her hand and held it tightly. "At least we can get him for attempted murder."

Saunders gave a brief cold laugh.

Darleen pulled back. "No! He is going to stand trial for Mark's murder."

Saunders head snapped up. Both he and Sullivan stared at her.

"What do you mean?" Sullivan asked.

"Mark had a tape recorder in this room as well as the office. I got his complete confession."

"No!" Saunders screamed. "You're lying."

"I'm not," she said to him. "The world will soon see what you are like."

Sullivan held her again, shaking his head in wonder as Darleen clung to him tightly.

"I'm going to take him in. And this time Carter doesn't get near the tape."

He grabbed Saunders and pushed him toward the director's elevator. Then he turned sheepishly to Darleen.

"You'll have to open it. I left my key at home."

Shaking her head and laughing, Darleen unlocked the elevator door. "And I'm coming with you. I've been waiting for this moment for a long time."

A look of horror struck Emmanuel's face; the elevator doors closed, and he began his long descent.